I0460577

THE BONE-GOD'S LAIR

AND OTHER TALES OF THE FAMOUS AND THE INFAMOUS

THE BONE-GOD'S LAIR

AND OTHER TALES OF THE FAMOUS AND THE INFAMOUS

A.R. MORLAN

To
Petro Iamani

WILDSIDE PRESS

To
Petro Iamani
James B. Johnson
John S. Postovit

—long-time pen-pals, friends, co-writers and translator— While none of us has ever met, you're more like family to me than anyone with whom I accidentally happen to share some DNA.

Knowing all of you has enriched my life and my work. You are all special, and some of my best times have been the hours I've spent writing to each of you, and reading your letters to me.

While none of us might be considered famous, I like to think that we've done our part to make our time here worthwhile to ourselves, our loved ones, and our readers….

Copyright © 2016 by Wildside Press LLC.

"Taking Down the Book of the Rough Beast" appeared in *Space & Time*, #97, 2003. "The Sweet End of the Lollipop" first appeared in 1992. "Beyond Time and Face" appeared in *Astromancer's Quarterly*, Vol. 3, Aug. 1992. "At the Playgrounds by the Swings, with Big Chuck" appeared in *Supernova*, Issue #1, 1990. "Pillaging Poe" appeared in *Rod Serling's Twilight Zone Magazine*, February 1986. "Above the Capitans, South of Corona, Near Arroyo del Macho" appeared in *New Genre*, Issue #1, Spring 2000. "In a Fine and Verdant Place" was originally published in *Phantasm*, Issue No. 1, 1994. "The Redemption of Pop Gee" appeared in *Pulphouse; The Hardback Magazine*, Issue Seven (Horror), Spring, 1990. "The Gemütlichkeit Escape" was originally published in *Challenging Destiny*, No. 8, 2000. "Norm Littman's 15 Minutes" (with John S. Postovit) appeared in *Worlds of Fantasy & Horror*, # 1, Spring 1994. "He's Hot, He's Sexy, He's…" appeared in *Shock Rock II*, Jeff Geib, ed., Pocket Books, 1994. "Buddy Holly Night at the Bone-God's Lair" appeared in *Phantasm*, Vol. 1, #4, Whole Number 4, Spring/Summer 1997.

Published by Wildside Press LLC.
www.wildsidepress.com

CONTENTS

FOREWORD

"The two most important days in your life are the day you were born and the day you find out why."

—Mark Twain

This is probably one of the last pieces of non-fiction or fiction I'll ever write. I'll get to the why a bit later, but for now, suffice it to say that after roughly thirty years of writing, and often selling both fiction and the occasional work of non-fiction, I've decided it is time to stop.

Considering that this particular collection of stories deals with the famous and the infamous, both real and imaginary, I've come to realize that there is an inherent irony at work here—while these works of fiction (plus their accompanying non-fiction afterwords) all concern the lives of those worthy of note, and of historical and cultural significance, they were created by a complete non-entity.

Despite having had various things published on a moderately regular basis for about twenty years or so, followed by a more sporadic output (due in large part to being unable to use a computer or access the Internet), I have no illusions of personal worth, let alone anything which might come close to fame (with a lower-case "f"). I'm less than a footnote in the book of life; I don't even have a place in that book's index.

Not that I didn't try. At one point, prior to the publication of my first novel, close to a life-time ago, my agent made plans to introduce me to the writing community at a convention to be held at the Stanley Hotel in Colorado (aka the inspiration for The Overlook Hotel).

But my mother (unbeknownst to me at the time) had kidnapped me from my father after she'd lost custody of me. As a result, she lived a paranoid, frantic, apprehensive life of constantly taking peeks over her shoulder, lest someone arrest her for having committed a federal crime. And she had other ideas on the subject of me taking the next step in the writing world.

I was not allowed to attend the convention, and my agent eventually parted ways with me. My writing career was mortally wounded before it had been fully born.

I kept on writing, despite the massive setback…and I kept publishing. But I never became a household name—or any other sort of "name" writer. If I was in an anthology, my name usually didn't appear on the cover and, eventually, I ceased to be invited into anthologies anymore.

Then the editor who bought my first work of fiction told me that I was "too ugly" to have my picture featured on the back of my books. Hurt to the core, I agreed that it was probably best not to show my face to any of my readers, either on my book covers, or at any future conventions.

A recurring theme in many of these stories is the chance meeting of the famous and the never-to-be famous. My own closest brushes with that sort of thing include a phone conversation with Dean Koontz (when we were both members of the newly-formed Horror Writers of America), letters received from Robert Bloch and Gahan Wilson—and a personally-signed postcard from Stephen King. I also shook hands with Tommy Thompson, the former governor of Wisconsin…and there was another well-known writer who took me to task for "living in a stupid little hick town" and for not making the effort to attend conventions. This writer apparently never heard my editor's comment on how ugly I was!

There was one other contact of note—which is the basis for the first story in this collection—and the Afterword explains why I won't ever reveal who that person is.

But aside from that, I've pretty much managed to stay under the Meeting Important Public Figures radar. My father, with whom I've had some brief contact, since becoming an adult, once shook hands with former prize fighter, Jack Dempsey—which in his view, trumped my hand-pumping moment with Tommy Thompson!

My father also weighed in on my career, calling me a "Lost Cause" because, in addition to not achieving any other milestones of note (dating, marrying, having children, etc.), I had totally failed as a writer. He came to this conclusion after reading a story of mine which he did not understand. In his mind, if a writer wasn't a household name, they weren't a "real" writer.

He told me something else. My mother had insisted on having a baby (me) during their hurried-up courtship—and subsequent hurry-up wedding. Which brings me to the "why" behind my decision to stop writing.

Following the departure of my mother from my life—and the fact that my father and his family finally decided to look for me after half a century had passed—I began to hear stories from various family members. These little bits of information they'd been reluctant to pass on while my mother was still in the picture, formed puzzle-pieces of all that had happened prior to my birth. And I finally figured out why I was born.

My mother's mother was a secret pedophile. As a result she had been denied access to a young female relative with whom she was obsessed. And my mother, who had always been her mother's en-abler, managed to produce a "replacement" for that lost object of affection. Me.

She stayed with my father only briefly after I was born before asking for a divorce. Only she didn't bargain on his lawyer enforcing visitation rights. And that is the reason she and her mother took me out of state and kept me hidden from my father and his family for so many years.

The only reason I exist is because a mentally-ill pedophile convinced her daughter to produce a replacement sex toy for her. When I finally figured that out, I knew it was time to give up writing—or any dreams I may have had for becoming "somebody."

Sex toys are not human. And only humans can write fiction.

—A.R. Morlan
July 2014

TAKING DOWN THE BOOK
OF THE ROUGH BEAST

I.

*Long, long after the near end-of-the world has come and gone,
I have still kept their letters.* His *next to the verse which so nearly
caused his triumph,* hers *next to the lines Yeats might have written
about her, had he nearly known her—much as I almost did. Thus,
together but duly separate, their frozen words rest, enfolded in arms
of voice-stilled verse.*

*But, often—especially on evenings like this one, when the fir-
mament is awash with the eons-old brilliance of the stars (some no
doubt dead and dark in the distance beyond their long-shed light,
perhaps as far-off as* his *desired destination, others no doubt still
brilliant and viable, much as* she *still is)—I find myself taking down
that volume of Yeats' verse, and resting* The Collected Poems *on my
desk before me. Almost magically, the book opens itself, the pages
parting next to the letters I have hidden in the volume itself.*

*But I do not open any of the brittle envelopes; I know their con-
tents far too well. It is enough for me to merely see them resting there,
neither read nor ridiculed, just simply* unknown *by others. Satisfied
that they are still there, I slide my hands under the covers of the book
and slowly shut it, bringing my hands together in a semblance of
prayerful rest, separated only by the leather-covered pages between
them. Once the book and its non-poetic contents are closed, I often
find myself gazing out my window, at those live, dead or dying stars,
ignorant of the fate of any of those individual points of light even as I
press my old, old face into their more ancient faint glow, as if I could
ever presume to hide from myself, or from my thoughts:*

Does the light from one star ever cross paths with that of another
star? Would such an intersection affect the stars, or the resulting light?
And what if each of us on this oh-so-insignificant earth was like unto

a star, with each human's achievement being so much like the light of a star, only originating at a set time and place, but still retaining the ability to shine long after the human in question is years dead? *Then* might the crossing of paths be of more consequence? And if so, what of the *duration* of that crossing? Would the brevity be a detriment… or an eventual blessing?

And, as the darkness above me grows deeper, more depthless, more infinite, with the promise of much beyond *the ends of that endless starry expanse, the questions become deeper, and more to the point:*

If she *had* answered me, would it have changed my ill-disposition toward *him*? And what of the consequences *then*…if indeed there would have been a world left in which to wonder at all?

Yet, even though her response might have initiated so much damage, would it really have affected things so drastically? Was I *really* the only hope he had of succeeding, or could someone *else's* path have crossed with his in an even more potentially disastrous manner?

But the stars hold no answers for me; they only offer a moment's sanctuary, before I finally turn my head away from them. No one can hide forever, even in the biggest crowd of stars. Not as long as one's memories—especially the most tangible ones—go into hiding with one. And nearly independent of my governing thoughts, my hands seek out the hidden secrets in the book before me, gently acknowledging the existence of each letter with a single touch, before closing the volume one last time.

Rising with a lamentation of ancient bones, I again find myself placing the old book upon the shelf, even as the last of the questions unfolds in my mind, like an exotic evening blossom:

But what if she *had* replied again? Would it have been worth the whole world?

I'd never thought I'd ever grow so old that I'd need to postulate any sort of answer to that last question…but then again, I wasn't such an old, old *man in those days….*

II.

I first made the literary acquaintance of Mr. W. Whately in the fall of 1924, back when I was head librarian in Providence, Rhode Island. To this day, I'm not sure if the gentleman from Dunwich singled me out because of my position, or because of that scholarly effort of mine, *The Darkness Drops Again*, which had been published the year before by an obscure (even in those days!) university publishing house in my native state of Massachusetts. As I was to later learn from several sources, Dr. Armitage among them, Mr. Whately's access to more recent works in the annals of dark and forbidden literature was less than favorable (due in large part to his living in such a backwards region of north central Massachusetts where few, if any, modern books were readily available), but at the time his correspondence was so particular, and so undeniably *pointed*, that I had difficulty ascertaining whether or not my individual contribution to the field of ancient (as well as more modern) prophetic literature had indeed compelled Mr. Whately to initially write to me—and keep on bombarding me with letters, right up to his untimely demise.

(Dr. Armitage assured me by both letter and phone that I was by no means the only correspondent Mr. Whately had contacted during his short and rather curious life, but I dared not ask how *often* Mr. Whately wrote to the other scholars and librarians of his limited acquaintance, for fear of unknowingly singling myself out for undue ridicule and speculation on the part of the other scholars in the literary arsenal.)

Regardless of his motives at the time, Mr. Wilbur Whately *did* find my address (or, more rightly, that of the library where I was employed), and taking pen in somewhat unearthly hand (if the account of Dr. Armitage is to be believed without question or reservation), began the letter which ultimately came into my possession on September 17, 1924. A Wednesday, "…child of woe," and all that superstitious twaddle—or so I initially thought:

Dear Dr. ___ (Whatley's letter began),

I would like to ask you if I can borrow any books from your library by mail. If so, I am most interested in books published in ancient times dealing with what is now known as "forbidden lore" of the "ancients."

I am looking forward to your reply. You need not worry about the books. I will take good care of them.

Sincerely,
Mr. Wilbur Whately
Whately Farm

Dunwich, Mass.

There was nothing *overtly* wrong with the letter (aside from the faint redolence which I noticed on my fingers when I happened to brush them under my itching nose) or its contents, but the name niggled at my memory....Whately, *Whately*—

I found my answer in the musty-scented stacks of *The Boston Globe*. That series of articles in the Sunday pages, published in 1917, recounting the bizarre growth of a four-and-a-half-year-old lad living in the most awful sections of my home state. Not to mention the fœtid environment in which the precocious lad lived, or his vile relatives. It was reported that young Wilbur resembled a youth in his early teens...a strange child-man who poured over the shelves of ancient rotting volumes in a fulsome rickety farmhouse—

Never mind his over-active glands, and his uncleanly surroundings—the words "rotting volumes" were enough for me. Even as I performed the simple calculations which informed me that my erstwhile would-be borrower was only twelve-years-old (which in itself meant nothing—I knew of many very trustworthy ten-year-olds who regularly borrowed books from my library), I had already made up my mind *Mr.* Whately—despite his no doubt sincere promises to the contrary—simply couldn't be trusted with any volumes (ancient or not) from my library. But, as I began my letter to him, I couldn't help but feel a ripple of empathy toward him—after all, he certainly hadn't *asked* to be born into such a *squalid* environment, nor did he personally request whatever physical problem was responsible for his over-zealous rate of personal maturation...just as I certainly didn't wish prior to my own birth to be part of a family headed by a drunken father, nor did I long to be blessed with weak, myopic eyes and prematurely thinning hair—so instead of harshly scolding Mr. Whately for even presuming that he would be granted permission to borrow books from my library, I found myself writing:

My Dear Mr. Whately,
        I am deeply sorry but it is impossible for you to borrow books by post from this library, due to the possibility of said books being lost in the mail. You are, however, welcome to personally browse through the stacks in the even that you should find yourself in the Providence area.

Until then, I wish you the best of luck with your studies.

Your Humble Servant,

Dr. James _____

Once the letter was posted, I put away the back issues of *The Boston Globe* and forced myself to forget about *Mr.* Wilbur Whately, of Whately Farm. I certainly had no reason to believe that he'd pursue the matter any further. Quite obviously he'd wanted to borrow those more curious books in the library, and once he'd found out that that was impossible, he'd naturally turn his attention elsewhere.

I suppose now, looking back on the whole thing, that I should have read over the *Globe* articles more carefully before consigning them to the stacks of other back issues. Perhaps it would have given me more of an *inkling....*

III.

Over the many, many years which have gone by since that heady, horrible time in the mid-twenties, I've found occasion to ask myself: Was it a coincidence or something deeper, more tangential, which made me go to that movie house, and watch that particular motion picture so soon after I received that first missive from Mr. Whately? Did he make me more willing to ultimately reach out to her through his desperation, or did he merely awaken that subtle need for connection, for purely platonic reaffirmation of myself and my humanity, due to his ultimately inhuman agenda?

Can a star care when its beam of light intersects that of another star? Does the difference it makes affect the original star?

And are human lives really *any* different than the random stars they so metaphorically resemble?

If not...why does such random intersection *hurt* so deeply, once it does occur?

IV.

Being the head librarian gave me certain privileges not necessarily associated with the volumes entrusted to my daily care; namely, I had the right to grant myself an occasional day of liberty from my cloth, leather, and paper charges. I chose to do so a couple of days after receiving Mr. Whately's letter—*why*, I am not sure. It certainly wasn't an especially lovely day outside, nor was there anything special going on in either Providence or the surrounding area which might have warranted my sudden need to be free of the confines of the library surroundings—whatever it was that permeated Whately's letter didn't come off my fingers until I'd washed my hands six times with good strong soap—which made me want to keep away from the library. Or perhaps it was the even more deliberately vague memories of my own childhood surroundings. Regardless of the motivation, on Friday, September 19 1924, I found myself wandering the streets of my adopted home town, until the realization sunk in: I had no idea what to do with myself, nor did I have the slightest inkling why I shouldn't simply curl up on the downtown bench and go to sleep.

Since the option of sleeping in public was no viable option at all, I decided to do the most acceptable thing, given my state of boredom-induced drowsiness—I went to the nearest movie house and bought a ticket. If I chose my seat carefully, and didn't allow myself to snore or likewise give away my somnolent state, I felt that no one would bother me.

Given my initial mission, namely to take a mid-afternoon nap, it does not surprise me that, to this day, I cannot clearly recall the name of the movie I saw that afternoon, even though I did see the title in the 1920's; silent (as were all the films I'd seen up to that point), very jerky, and ill-lit. Even the exact plot escapes me. But a few minutes into the movie, during the otherwise incomprehensible action, I began to notice one of the actresses up on that screen. She wasn't *the* lead, but her role was clearly more than a supporting one, given the amount of time she was featured on camera.

Memory also dims when it comes to the plot of the film, or the actress's ultimate part in said plot. Let it suffice, though, that it was one gesture, one fraction of a second, which brought her to my undivided attention. The young woman was (I surmised) in the process of dismissing someone from her sight, from her presence, but it was the *way* in which she did it which captured my admiration.

The "acting" in early motion pictures often brings ridicule upon its practitioners when those films are shown today; much of that derision was undoubtedly called for, since he histrionics of those silent screen stars were often beyond the understanding of even the most ardent audience previously accustomed to live theatre and the stage.

Despite not being able to call upon actual dialogue, some of the actors and actresses of the time went much too far in attempting to telegraph their motivations, emotions, and the like, to the point of appearing ludicrous.

But this young woman (how young it was impossible to guess, although, given her costume, I surmised that she was supposed to be a very young girl, despite a certain level of maturity in her bearing) transcended the inherent limitations of the silent movie; her movements and gestures (despite the unintentional jerkiness of the film stock as it wound through the projector) were inherently natural and correct—so much so that it was quite easy to understand her motivations without any undue or overt over-acting on her part.

And when she made that one gesture, a subtle movement of her right hand, as if she were whisking away something invisible, yet no less offensive, I was in awe of her. Not that I was enamored of her; to her credit, she did not project such a base emotional state, and, accordingly, I did not respond to her in that way. But to feel such admiration for the talent of another…that, in and of itself, was the intoxicating thing.

My desire to sleep unobserved left me as I watched the remainder of the movie; true, I paid little attention to the goings-on when she was off-camera. But when she *was* before the lens, I was enthralled.

In my particular field, research and criticism, there is little opportunity for one to be actively captivated by the work of another literary scholar. No matter how heartfelt another's words might be, no matter how artfully they are phrased, they are still just that—dry words on ultimately brittle paper. The reader often supplies whatever emotional fire is present in those words; it is impossible to know for certain if the writer fully intended the ultimate effects of his or her own words, or whether the reader is actually filling in the missing spark. And when you begin to dissect the words of another, they eventually die in the manner of all vivisected or dissected things. All you are left with is separated words and ultimately meaningless phrases, divorced from their original sentences and paragraphs.

But there was no way anyone could distill or dissect that gesture of hers. It was so complete a thought, so honest an observation on her part, that it was incapable of violation by professional critics or scholars like me. And her entire performance had a similar completeness, apart from the frantic arm-waving and grimacing of her fellow performers. I wished I knew her name; unfortunately, I wasn't sure what her character's name was, so I was unable to identify her in the closing credits. All I knew was *what* she was, up there on that screen. I knew nothing of her background, her age, her training. But it really didn't matter, either; she had created something complete, in and of itself, something which actually needed no further amplification or elaboration.

Nonetheless, as I left the movie theatre later that afternoon, I would have given almost anything to at least know her name. And it wasn't until several years passed that I ultimately learned the price I almost did pay to find out only that scant amount of information about her, and little more than that.

Yet there are times when I wonder if the cost might not have been worth it, regardless of the brevity of the resulting satisfaction

V.

My next letter from Mr. Whately arrived late in December of that same year, 1924; since it was delivered to the library during one of my legitimate days off, I am not exactly sure when it was sent (Mr. Whately neglected to include a date on the letter itself, and I was loathe to closely examine the muddy postmark on the envelope), but obviously my letter to *him* had arrived in Dunwich in a timely fashion, for he wrote:

Dear Dr. _____

I am sorry not to get back to you sooner. It is all right about the books. I might be in your area in the future anyhow. I still mean what I said about taking good care of your books and would do so if I should need to take them out of the library in person. Certain obligations are keeping me at home now, but I may need to go afield soon.

If I do travel your way, I will need to see a certain book, so I would like to know if there is any possibility of red tape holding me back from checking it out of your library. The book I need is called *Necronomicon* by Abdul Alhazred, in—

(and here Mr. Whateley became very specific, underling his text)

—Olaus Wormius' Latin translation, which was, I think, printed in Spain in the 1600's. At least , this is what I have been told I need. The book *must* be in a complete state.

This is real important to me, so I would appreciate it if you could please tell me if I can borrow it should there be a need. I will try elsewhere for it (closer to home) but you may be my last hope. Thank you.

Sincerely,
Wilbur Whately

There was something desperate behind Whately's polite words; setting his letter down on my desk (careful not to actually let it touch the blotter, lest the odor permeate its soft surface), I looked at those neatly penned lines for a long time, as if I could force Whately's hidden meanings out from hiding behind each word. His language was somewhat irregular, but not obviously so; Whately was supposedly home-educated and, considering his lifetime home, I couldn't really expect him to be a completely well-rounded scholar. He could spell well enough, and his syntax and grammar were passable...but still, I sensed there was *something* amiss.

What did he actually want the *Necronomicon* for, for heaven's sake? I'd dipped only sparingly into the horrid volume myself, purely for the sake of research while writing my book, *The Darkness...* (which was an attempt to codify the various themes of the Second Coming in religious works and popular literature through the ages), but I *had* listed it in the bibliography of my work, so perhaps—if he did actually read my book—Whately had some notion that I was an expert on that mad Arab's grotesque ramblings. But that still didn't answer my question about his *need* for the book. Clearly he wasn't in the process of writing his *own* tome on the theme of the Second Coming—I doubted he could write more than a coherent *letter*, let alone a scholarly work of non-fiction. And who would buy it once he wrote it? I'd had great difficulty getting *my* book published (and never mind actually selling copies).

Vaguely worried, I went back to the stacks, in search of the *Globe* articles about him. Nothing concrete there, although I did find the references to his grandfather's Black Magic somewhat disturbing. But those backwards types are often associated with such vile doings (I'd often wondered if the lack of movie houses and up-to-date libraries had something to do with the rural fascination with ancient and pagan practices); such a reference in the *Globe* didn't necessarily mean for *certain* that Wilbur Whately was anything more than a mature-for-his-age youth with a great deal of albeit morbid curiosity.

Although it *was* unusual for someone from that region of the state to have the ability to read Latin, be it for research or recreational purposes. And then there was the business about "obligations"—whatever *that* meant.

Nevertheless, I felt no real reason not to respond to Mr. Whately's latest letter; after all, I was head librarian, and should I deem Mr. Whately somehow unsuitable upon meeting him in person (if the occasion were to come about), I could merely say that the book was currently unavailable. It was, after all, my job to supply the curious with information; without that mission, my job was ultimately meaningless.

> My Dear Mr. Whately,
>
> In answer to your latest letter, yes, this library does have a copy of the book you requested, but no, it is not a complete version of the text. Since I do not know whether or not this library's particular version of the *Necronomicon* might not be complete enough for your purposes (whatever they may be), you are still quite welcome to come here personally and determine for yourself whether or not our copy of this work might fulfill your purposes, despite its slightly incomplete condition.
>
> I am sorry to hear that you cannot travel freely at this time; I do hope that this situation will be rectified in the near future.
>
> > Very Cordially Your,
> > Dr. James _____

Having discharged my duties so promptly, I decided to treat myself to another for-no-reason half day off.

But none of the movies I saw that afternoon featured that young actress; I couldn't believe that those out in Hollywood could so blithely ignore genuine talent....

VI.

Between the beginning of 1925 and continuing through early August of 1928, I received no fewer than ten letters from Mr. Whately, at intervals ranging from a week to twenty weeks (the latter in 1927, when he wrote to tell me that he'd been busy 'moving my library to more secure quarters' before offering his apologies for taking so long between decidedly unlooked-for letters from him).

And what did Mr. Whately write to me in those ten letters? Considering the revelations of his ultimate plans (as related primarily by Dr. Armitage and his associates, all of whom were present in Dunwich a little later in 1928), Whately's letters were almost prosaic in their studied blandness:

> Dear Dr. ___,
>
> Been hard at work with my studies, but I do think that I might accept your offer to at least look at your copy of—

> Dear Dr. ___,
>
> I hope all is well with you. Not being able to get a look at the complete version of the *Necronomicon* has made my studies more difficult—

> Dear James,
>
> Thank you for your offer to send me the list of pages contained in your copy of—

> Dear James,
>
> Looks like I might have to travel down your was after all, unless—

I don't know what made him begin to address me so informally; gradually his letters (while remaining politely distant) did begin to resemble something akin to correspondence between old acquaintances rather than a purely scholarly exchange of letters, perhaps due to a lack of similar response on behalf of my fellow librarians and scholars in Mr. Whately's circle of correspondents. I was only being polite when I answered so quickly and directly to him; there was no real desire on my part to continue the exchange of letters (especially since all his correspondence was a variation on his first query—he wanted the dread book, and I was to somehow circumvent library rules and let him have it on his terms), but for a reason I cannot now fully rationalize, I did continue to respond to Wilbur's letters— even after Dr. Armitage sent that note of warning to me and all the other librarians whose libraries boasted a copy of that insane Arab's despicable volume of archaic lore. Dr. Armitage's letter was as to-the-point as any of Whately's missives to me during the past four years; under no circumstances should Wilbur Whately be allowed to so much as look at any copy of the *Necronomicon*, let alone take it out of the sight of the librarian in charge of said volume. And, to underscore the urgency of his appeal, Dr. Armitage briefly described Whately's current appearance:

> ...is now fully *eight-feet-tall* (Armitage's italics) and sports a goatish dark beard over a rather weak chin. His voice is deep, almost unholy, and his manner, while polite, is also cunning. Do not heed any of his appeals! Do not allow him to so much as copy any passage of—

Dr. Armitage's letter went on, of course, although he did keep his most disquieting speculations mostly to himself. As I refolded his letter, prior to replacing it in its envelope, I was tempted to try calling Dr. Armitage on the telephone, to tell him of the persistent nature of Whately's letters to me, but something stopped me from doing so. Perhaps it was Wilbur's sudden use of my Christian name in his latest appeals. Maybe it was his occasional concern for my well-being. It could have been his unfailing politeness, despite Armitage's warning that that display of manners was merely a disguise for Whately's ulterior goals.

But...as I try to recapture my state of mind in those glorious, pre-depression days, when I had little on my mind save for academia and those infrequent jaunts to the movie theatres in the area (a part of me still thundered silently at the failure of all those movie producers to utilize that actress' talents in their recent productions), the only viable rationale I can come up with for failing to inform Dr. Armitage of my prolonged contact with Wilbur Whately came down to a couple of simple words.

"Thank you."

Wilbur Whately always found a way to thank me for responding to him; despite the mild annoyance I eventually felt upon receipt of

one of his letters, that inclusion of thanks for my previous correspondence always managed to negate my feelings of ill-will toward my
albeit unwanted correspondent. Perhaps it was a cunning politeness,
perhaps it was genuine. But it was consistent.

So I put the letter from Armitage into my file of letters from various scholarly acquaintances (Whately excluded; his letters—despite
everything from exposure to sunlight and stints in the fresh air—
continued to *reek* ever so slightly, so much so that I was forced to
keep them in a used biscuit tin under my desk), and settled down to
reading the latest issue of *The Globe*, prior to putting it out for the
public. Actually, I was an issue behind, since it was a Monday, and I
was reading the Sunday edition.

Given that slight time delay, I skimmed over the mundane news
articles, and paid more attention to the non-news features. I was
about to turn a page when a small photo caught my eye—that young
actress, she of the careful gestures and impeccable mannerisms, was
the subject of a feature article in that portion of the *Globe* catering to
lovers of the theatre.

And it was then that I learned that this woman had been spending
her time in the live theatre, both in this country and abroad—never
mind those buffoons in Hollywoodland. She was back in Boston pro-
moting a new play, in which she was co-starring. Furthermore, the
article stated, she was a native of the Boston area, being born (as I
was to later figure out, using an atlas) a scant fifteen miles or so from
my in-Boston birthplace. And she was not only a talented actress, but
an erudite individual, having studied her craft in college years earlier,
prior to making that otherwise forgettable film of hers.

Judging from her transcribed responses to the *Globe* reporter's
questions, her ability to communicate wasn't limited to her capacity
to act; she was quite lucid, logical and humane in her replies, with
an underlying wit and intelligence which I found both appealing and
forthright. And when she mentioned a quotation from Yeats, well—
needless to say, once I noticed that the interview was not something
from the wire services, but an original piece from Boston, I began
to think and think hard, to come up with a way to contact this accomplished young lady.

I knew some people in the Boston area, mostly literary types, and
others with distant connections to the theatre—surely one of them

might know her? Perhaps they could ask her for an autograph, for a friend of theirs?

Then it came to me—*Silly, why not write to her* yourself, *in care of that fellow who conducted the interview?* Actually going to *see* her in Boston was somewhat out of the question; I'd already granted myself too many small vacations from work to justify a much longer stay from my desk. But what would be more natural for a man of letters than to write someone a letter? Even if she thought me somewhat forward for doing so?

Ah, that was the problem. Here I was, already somewhat past my youth, clearly approaching middle age; a sheltered academic man, with little of the easy social graces associated with other youngish men of my age (these were the Roaring Twenties, after all), yet I was seriously considering writing a fan letter to someone who had most certainly never heard of me before, and would probably laugh at me once she finished reading the letter.

Not that I was a stranger to the art of correspondence; I'd even written to Yeats himself, while writing *The Darkness Drops Again*. But that was strictly a fellow-to-fellow communication; he knew what I was about, and likewise I was (in a sense) on a par with him in that we were both men of letters. Being near-equals, there was no need for feelings of vulnerability, of constantly wondering, *Will this person think me a fool?*

Yet, she had mentioned Yeats—

No matter how long I shall live, I will never forget—or divulge—the contents of the letter I wrote that late morning. It was only a page and a quarter long, achingly polite, and specific enough to allow the lady no false impression that I was some swooning schoolboy feigning responsible adulthood. I was careful to mention the name of the book I'd written, in case she wished to verify my status *as* a trustworthy adult. I felt like a complete yet fulfilled idiot as I signed my name; my doing this would accomplish nothing in all likelihood, yet I simply could not pass up the opportunity to merely *thank* this woman for the pleasure I'd felt as I'd watched her in that movie house in 1924, as if she needed to learn of one insignificant viewer's gratitude for her efforts.

Perhaps it was only an echo of *my* need to be appreciated, a need to pass on the display of gratitude that Whately fellow included in his letters to me (however self-serving his motives were). At any rate, I stamped and partially addressed an envelope for my letter, which I folded around the letter for her; after writing a short, polite cover letter to the author of the article. I put both letters and the stamped envelope inside a second envelope, which I likewise stamped and addressed to *The Boston Globe.*

Once the letter slid from view into the mailbox near the library that late winter afternoon, I felt like a complete ass, but the matter was out of my hands now. It was all up to the *Globe* reporter who had interviewed the young woman; *I'd* said what I wished to say, to the person I'd chosen to read my words.

Much like a star which sends out a ray of light, not even being sure that there will be eyes to see the light in the distance, I'd gone against my better judgment and actually initiated real contact with someone whose reality (for me) was confined to a flickering, star-bright image on a screen in an almost empty movie theatre. Even after I'd read her own words in print, that still didn't make her quite as real as I knew myself to be; always, there is that *distancing* effect to consider, be it through the intervention of a movie camera and film stock, or the printing press and fragile newsprint.

Yet, be she really *real* or not, I'd gone and written to her. Rather a huge leap of faith, when a person thinks about it.

(As if I'd expected her to somehow *be* as real as I was, human frailties, imperfections, and all....)

During the walk home that chilly afternoon, it never occurred to me that any of my correspondents (Whately included) might share my view on the subject; I suppose all of us humans are cursed with the limitations of our own reality. *I* am the only human observing this life, therefore only *I* am sure of my *own* reality—and the reality of this world. We all live, but just one life at a time, in one body, and in one reality. Even as we tacitly acknowledge the reality of other people daily, we can't share *their* reality; it is forever distant from *our* reality, and with that distancing it thus becomes a little less ur-gent, and subsequently a little less...*real*.

We all share this earth, this life, yet we are all so blasted *sepa-rate*, in all the most important, essential ways; ways which cannot be bridged through the touch of a hand or through a shared gaze into an-other's eyes. All we truly have to break down that isolation is words, or whatever passes for deeper communication for those who cannot use language *per se*. Yet, even then, words still have no meaning if they cannot be acknowledged….

VII.

I will never forget what that Armitage fellow told me over the phone later that year, in 1928. How Whately was little more than sur-face-human—or perhaps merely humanoid—*and furthermore, how he'd been planning a fate for the entire world which was so hideous, so unthinkable, that it could only have been an act of Providence which allowed mankind to escape relatively unscathed—*

—but even as that august gentleman's voice whispered in my re-ceiver-cupped ear, I longed to tell him, No, kind sir, not Providence… only bruised pride, and the slightest possible lapse in etiquette.

* * * *

I spent the week after writing that letter to the young actress in a slightly giddy haze; I found myself wondering if the reporter had been able to resist unfolding her letter and reading it, or if the gentle-man was about to forward it at all (plays do have a way of closing early, or moving on to other cities), or if the actress ever bothered to read mail from strangers. Such speculation was senseless, of course, whether or not she'd ever see my letter meant virtually nothing in itself. Most certainly, it wasn't as important as the hastily-penned notes I received from a couple of my fellow librarians in Cambridge and New Haven; it seems that early spring was a busy time for Mr. Whately, since he'd been tromping about the region in search of his elusive *complete* version of the *Necronomicon*, if those staid gentle-men in Cambridge and New Haven were to be believed.

Apparently, Wilbur had grown much taller, approaching a full nine feet or so, which lent him a most imposing, threatening demean-or, even though my distant colleagues both hinted that Mr. Whately himself did seem to be *terrified*, as well as bullishly determined and desperate. But they followed Dr. Armitage's advice to the letter, and convinced Whately to seek out his evil text elsewhere.

Since I'd assured Wilbur long ago that *my* version of that evil tome was incomplete, I felt no fear of being paid a visit by the hulk-ing, bearded giant, so I simply filed the latest letters next to the ones from Dr. Armitage—after making a mental note to gently chide Wilbur for his ungentlemanly conduct around my brother librarians. Backwater upbringing or not, such behavior simply wouldn't *do*. Certainly not in my library....

Although I had made up my mind that evening prior to falling asleep that, whether or not I heard from Whately first, I'd have to (politely) take him to task for his rude deportment in New Haven and Cambridge, by the time I had a chance to look through the next morning's mail, my firm resolve in regard to Mr. Whately dissolved in an effervescent moment of reality-skewing delight when I saw a certain letter mixed in with my usual assortment of library-related journals and publications.

Written in a flowing, yet neat, hand was my name and the address of the library on an envelope which bore the first initial and last name of that actress in the upper left-hand corner.

All of my speculations evaporated as I slip open the envelope with my dagger-shaped letter opener (nearly ripping apart the skin on the hand holding the envelope because I was shaking so), and then shook out her note. She'd only written a few lines, but they quite clearly indicated that she'd not only read my letter, but enjoyed the contents. And—with words which temporarily shattered that otherwise unbridgeable distance between one isolated human being and another—she actually mentioned the title of *my* book in her reply. Now I was on nearly equal footing with her; she knew I existed, and that I had created something in my own right—not quite the same thing as the film she'd been in, or the plays she'd turned to after her stint in motion pictures, but still, she was now aware of my accomplishment.

But what she'd actually written (words which I shall not repeat; first because they *were* meant for me, and second, because the lady is still living, and thus might be in a position to be embarrassed should she ever read *these* words) temporarily paled when I noticed that she'd included, perhaps as an afterthought—not that I'll ever know—perhaps out of polite habit, a return address in what I presumed was her new home state. No request for a reply *per se*, but still—

Tapping the note against my left palm, I asked myself why such an individual would take pains to write down a return address...and then it became clear. She'd mentioned Yeats in her original interview, and she'd referred to my book (about Yeats, among others); ergo, she wanted a copy of *my* book, but was too polite to simply *ask* for a copy.

The rest of my mail went unsorted and unread that day; since *The Darkness Drops Again* had been by no means a best-*seller*, I still had copies of it in my possession. And, better yet, I had a few of them on hand, in the library itself (aside from the volume I'd put on the shelves, as a donation to the library).

My assistants must have thought me quite mad; I spent the morning scurrying about the library, seeking out just the right box, the softest lining paper, and the sturdiest string with which to bind up the packaged book. Inside the volume itself, I'd penned my most sincere best wishes; sentiments I included in the short note I slipped inside the tome itself. Just as she had been too shy (or so I imagined) to ask for my book, I was also too diffident to request her thoughts on *my* creation, or any sort of acknowledgement of its receipt. Perhaps I was too confident, perhaps I was plainly too obtuse to foresee the obvious.

But…obtuse or not, I tucked the painstakingly-prepared package under my arm prior to quitting my post that afternoon, before confidently carrying the box to the post office. Where I insured the package, just to make certain that she would receive her gift in perfect condition. That part mattered to me the most, at the time.

For the life of me, I cannot figure out *why*, now.

I doubt it would have made the outcome any different….

VIII.

After a time, once the embarrassment and the mental kicking of one's own posterior subsides, it isn't too difficult to look back upon such an episode born of over-confidence and misplaced trust in the assumed propriety of others and tell oneself, All of this was partly my fault, too—

Especially when I allowed myself to get so carried away….

The next few weeks, and then months, were much like the mental viewing of a ping-pong game; first I'd be surreptitiously sifting my daily mail, in search of anything addressed in that familiar handwriting, then I'd be scanning the theatre columns in *The Boston Globe*, trying to figure out where her new play might be staged next, then

I'd be hunting through the other area periodicals, still searching for notice of that play, then I'd gently shake out the day's mail, just in case a note of thanks somehow found its way inside the pages of some dry academic journal, then I'd—

My only breaks from this slowly maddening routine came in the form of more-frequent letters from Whately Farm in Dunwich. During the first few weeks of waiting, I was still in a jolly mood, buoyed from within by the miracle of actually forming a complete connection with another, of getting a genuine response to my no doubt clumsily-phrased words of praise for another. And while I was thus elated, I was in a position to take Wilbur's repeated requests almost to heart; the dire warnings and panicked pleas from Dr. Armitage and the others all but faded from my memory as I read:

> James—
>
> Most important that I find out the full extent of the ommissions [*sic*] in your copy of the *Necro*. If not too glaring, your book might be of use. Cannot find other full versions and time is growing short for (this part was too poorly scribed to be legible) in the Fall.
>
> Would be most grateful if you could please send me list of pages contained in your version. Please reply at your earliest convenience.
>
> Urgently,
>
> W. Whately

Given Wilbur's past reception at the previous libraries he'd visited, I had my doubts that he'd actually try to show up in my library, regardless of whether or not my incomplete copy of that strange Arab's ramblings might really be of serious use to him, yet, as I am most loathe to admit now, I was still basking in the good humor imparted by that young woman's response to my own letter.

She had been kind enough to respond to a stranger, a man no less unknown and unimaginable to her than poor Wilbur Whately was to me—and I had the advantage, no less. I knew much more about *him* than she could ever know about *me*, regardless of whatever personal insights into my way of thinking one might glean from a reading of my scholarly text. So, armed with that knowledge of Mr. Whately, I felt highly confident that my responding to the query would surely cause no serious harm to either myself or Whately:

My Dear Wilbur,

I would be happy to send you a listing of both the individual pages and the chapter headings of the book in question—time *permitting*. Since this volume (as you may well know) is under lock and key here, I must take time away from my duties in order to peruse the copy of the *Necronomicon* in my care; thus, whenever I am not occupied with more pressing duties, I will be happy to compile the listing mentioned above.

Please let me know if you wish to receive the entire listing at once, or whether installments of the same will be more suitable for your purposes.

Your servant,
James___, PhD

True, I did feel a slight twinge of guilt upon sending that letter to Massachusetts, but it was assuaged by the memory of my state of mind on the day I'd posted the letter to that young actress. Hadn't that situation worked out far better than I could have imagined?

At any rate, I hadn't given Whately any set time-table for the receipt of the entire annotation of that book's dire contents....

IX.

After these many, many years, I cannot clearly recall the exact sequence of my growing realization that somehow, in what exact manner I could not begin to comprehend, I had either been duped, or (far worse), I had somehow duped myself.

The weeks had indeed turned to months, and that young woman's play had long since moved on to the same city she had listed as part of her return address, but no note of thank you appeared in my daily packet of mail. No matter how many times I rifled through each day's mail; no matter how many times I tried to tell myself, You must have misaddressed the package, or You must have forgotten to place your return address on the front (for I was certain beyond *certain* that I'd properly addressed the boxed book—not to mention the insurance!); no matter how many times I reasoned that wading through a scholarly text isn't like breezing through a popular novel or the script of a play; no, the simple truth did take its time, before finally catching up with me—she simply chose not to acknowledge my gift to her. No mention of Yeats, no curiosity over my insights into the literature of the Second Coming, no…Thank you, at the very least.

I do not wish to imply that I was solely spending my time during those answerless months merely speculating on the ultimate date of arrival of her thank you note, far from it. During every spare moment, I crept into the dark room which housed that horrid, dank volume, and painstakingly wrote down not only the page numbers therein, but also jotted down the first and last word listed on each page, after Wilbur Whately had eagerly requested that I should do so. But, with the passing of those weeks, and then those months, I gradually lost my passion for my mission of academic mercy; my mind began to niggle me, asking, If she didn't feel compelled to bother with *you*, why in the dunce should *you* be so terribly worried about this Whately fellow, especially after he frightened the bejeebers out of someone as staid as Henry Armitage? You actually sent her something, and she didn't bother to do so much as *thank* you. After all, you've been warned not to let Whately so much as *see* this blasted book—now don't you think that that includes allowing him to know exactly how complete *this* copy of the text really is?

Oh, true. I never did try to have the post office trace the whereabouts of the package; I still felt enough respect and admiration for her not to want to bother her unduly, or impose on her any further. I did know that my printing on the label portion of the book was *quite* legible, so I seriously doubted that the package had strayed. And she *was* back in the area; I had the play reviews to prove it. So there were really no further excuses to be made….

And likewise, Whately's letters to me *had* begun to show a slight disregard for both the conventions of propriety as well as of grammar; perhaps it was his desperation, or perhaps his verbal slippage might be attributable to other mitigating factors, but, at any rate, I did begin to lose interest in my transcriptions from the *Necronomicon*.

To my advantage, I *had* informed Wilbur that it might take me a long while to finish my task; therefore, when late July arrived, I felt no compunction as I wrote to him:

Dear Mr. Whately,

Due to an unforeseen increase in my daily duties, I do not think that I will be able to complete the listing of extant pages in the copy of the *Necronomicon* currently owned by this library.

Enclosed is my work to date; I sincerely hope this will be of some use to you. Best wishes for the speedy completion of your scholarly pursuits.

Sincerely,
Dr. James ___

I didn't expect a reply to my admittedly curt missive but, just as my expectations about the young woman had ultimately proved themselves wrong, so was my assumption that Wilbur Whately would be offended by my note. For I received a reply from Dunwich the first week of August; a note which strongly bore a most distinct yet unclassifiable odor. Although the handwriting was far more deteriorated than it had been previously, I was still able to make out the message quite easily:

James,

Tahnks [*sic*] for the past help. Can see form [*sic*] what you sent is no good, will seek out full copy on [my] own. Must do this, will take precautions.

Wilbur W.

That maddening *politeness* stung; why in God's wide heavens and earth did *he* have to remain so *civil*, when such an erudite, cultivated person couldn't even—oh, I could go on, but the memory of the incident still pains me so.

Perhaps it was that very pain that served to insulate me when I heard the news about Whately's visit to the Miskatonic Library in Arkham; the horror of what Armitage, Rice and Morgan saw was and still remains indescribable. Whatever human graces Wilbur Whately had displayed during his correspondence with me must have been virtually the sum of all the real humanity within him. His designs for the entire world, perhaps our entire known universe, were utterly vile and incomprehensible—a true Second Coming, indeed! And through the devices of a being so *rough*, so beyond beyond-bestial, that I still shudder with the memory of Armitage's reciting of the barest facts over the telephone to me that September.

Yet, what is far worse, is the thought—no, the *knowledge*—that because of my temporary lack of judgment, that blithe insanity brought on by an act of reciprocal kindness between strangers, I was on the verge of allowing that evil to triumph.

All because of a few "Thank yous" in less than a dozen letters.... Although, more importantly—and poignantly—only the *lack* of those same two simple words saved the world. For how can I not be sure that, if I'd kept on with my listings of those *Necronomicon* pages, that I might not have finally brought even one important page to the attention of the being whose sole mission on earth was to demolish the world as I knew it?

Would that have been worth those two short words from her?

X.

Strange, how the passage of years can dull certain emotions while preserving the fire of others. After a time—a good long time, to be sure—I was able to re-read her only letter to me with the same degree of pleasure I felt the first time my eyes moved across her words. What she said was kind; what she wrote was proper. My misinterpretation of her motives was purely my mistake, nothing more. Perhaps my gravest error had been in not making a polite query about the whereabouts of the book after a decent interval, two weeks or so after sending off the book. Beyond that time, any further word from me surely would have been most rude, and unforgivable. So I went back into my shell of human isolation once more, lucky no doubt that the time spent outside of that shell had not injured me any more than was unavoidable.

And what of poor, wretched Whately? For him, staying in the confines of his all-too-fragmentary human shell was his only ticket to even minimal acceptance—and unholy success—in this isolated little world of ours. From what Armitage told me, Wilbur's sibling had even less humanity in him than Wilbur did, even as Armitage sought to discount that fragile vestige of Wilbur's human side, despite the unholy irony of the Whately brothers' conception, and how they'd been fathered by gods far, far older than any known to civilized mankind.

The same gods Wilbur had sought the knowledge of the Necronomicon *for in order to affect their return to this earth....*

Of course, while Henry Armitage still lived, and even for many years after his death, I dared not to disagree with his opinion as to what those unfortunate events in Dunwich, in 1928, meant. For he knew nothing of her and without that knowledge—which I could not, or would not divulge—Armitage's comprehension of the whole affair was just slightly lacking.

Oh, not that anyone ever knew. Even though the young actress is young no more, she is still what she always was, to me: a talented, erudite, gracious star, finally admired by far more people than she was in 1928, in the days when she was able to respond in person to a letter from a lone, strange fan of hers. Back in the days when I, too, wasn't loathe to communicate with a being far more alone, and undeniably strange *in the fullest possible sense, than anyone could have ever imagined. But, there's the irony of it all; aren't all of us strange (not to mention strangers) to one another at one time or an-other? And how are we to truly judge whether or not that individual strangeness will ever truly be gone from anyone we might meet?*

And so the length of the years since 1928 has given me more than enough time to think this all over…although the answers have been less numerous than the passing years:

I still do not know if the intersection of starlight does or doesn't change the resulting brightness, but I think I know that the duration of such an intersection really *isn't* important. That it *is* is duration enough, even as *is* becomes *was*, and long before it becomes a *might have been*. Contact is *contact*, be it good or bad or something indefinable, in a firmament filled with so *many* stars, *all* of them so isolated and distant, perhaps that brief contact *is* reason enough to keep shining light into the enveloping darkness, regardless of whether there be eyes waiting to take in that light. And regardless of whether or not those eyes belong to something unappreciative or uncomprehending of that radiance.

I only know that it is so, so lonely in the places *between* the stars, and that no matter how full the heavens may seem there is always that cursed room between, *waiting* for something.

Even if that something has motives which are unholy.

Even if that something is all too brief, and unrepeated.

For something, even if only for a short time, will displace *nothing*, and that in itself can make literally *anything* welcome.

Only, even if it did cost the world, I still wish she'd sent some word about the book. Even to say that she didn't like it.

For it is so lonely, here in the shell. In the places between.

* * * *

Inspired by H. P. Lovecraft's The Dunwich Horror, *and by the poetry of William Butler Yeats.*

AFTERWORD

This story requires a bit of backtracking…when I was in junior high school, one of my favorite horror stories was H. P. Lovecraft's *The Dunwich Horror*—I read and re-read that tale at least a dozen times. Absolutely adored that story. But I was taken with what amounted to a throw-away section in it, dealing with Wilbur Whateley's attempts to secure a certain dread volume from some regional librarians…and I wondered what might have happened if someone *had* sent him the material he requested. Just an errant thought, which I later tucked away in my mind, until the early 1990's, when I read an article in a regional newspaper about a performer who was originally from a town not too far from where I was born, who was currently in a major motion picture coming out at the time, but in addition to that, the person had also been in another genre film I'd admired—to condense things a bit, I wrote to the person in care of the reporter who had done the original article I read, and my letter was passed on. I got a reply, I sent copies of my just-published novels as a thank you, and then…nothing. At least for a while; come Christmas time I got a lovely card and a short note from the person. We exchanged cards for a few years, until around the time when that one dippy fan broke into Brad Pitt's house and among other things tried on his sweat-pants. I lost touch with the person after that (which I don't blame the person for—one cannot be too careful when working in the public eye—and I wish the performer all the best), but the short lag between my sending off that package and the ultimate reply did generate the idea for this story. While the outcome was totally fictional, I consider this story—and the brief once-a-year correspondence which inspired it—special to me. And no, I will never say who inspired it—that's private, and since I do not know exactly why it was broken off, it's totally off limits for any further speculation on my part. I will say one thing—fans of the horror genre would probably know immediately who this person is, if I were to mention a name. But I'm not going to. Ever.

THE SWEET END OF
THE LOLLIPOP

"I do not think that I have seen anyone so beautiful; I was enchanted by her manner and her wit, at once so unmasked, so ingenuous and so penetrating. But one felt a terrible unreality about her—as if talking to someone under water. Bobby (Kennedy) and I engaged in mock competition for her; she was most agreeable to him and pleasant to me—but then she receded into her own glittering mist."

—From the diary of Arthur Schlesinger

"Kinsey says a woman doesn't really begin to live before she's thirty. That's good news—and it's also positive."

—Marilyn Monroe
On the occasion of her thirtieth birthday

As expected, the Subject was nude; as further anticipated, she was engaged in the careful shaking-out of yellow capsules from a prescription bottle to her right palm—but neither Deng nor the Observer could have guessed her reaction to their presence (their sudden, out-of-their-*then*-into-the-*other*-then, silent, still *presence*)—in her locked-from-within bedroom. Save for a too-fast jerk of her body that resulted in her lower left back—just above the hip—making obviously hard and painful contact with the corner of her bedside table, her face retained a look of detached equanimity both beautiful and heart-wrenching to behold. Not one of the yellow-sheath capsules dropped from the cup of her hand; with her dominant left hand she picked up a small glass of water from the table, as she said with a touch of sultry defiance in her purring, child-woman voice, "Excuse me, at first I thought you were Mrs. Murray or Doctor Greenson, trying to stop me...but—" she bobbed her head of blonde curls to Deng and The Observer's direction, close by the locked door, and roughly six inches *above* the floor of the Brentwood bedroom "—I see that they won't be stopping me after all…will they?"

Deng closed his almond-shaped eyes in silent thanks. The Subject had asked *him* a question; under the rules of Historical travel, and according to the rules of The Observer (whose silicon features betrayed no errant spark of recognition), Deng was now free to speak to the Subject. Unconsciously smoothing the flat of each ivory palm along the legs of his jumpsuit, Deng slowly shook his head and replied, "No…I'm sorry, but our purpose is only to observe, to ask questions of the willing—"

Padding over to her bed, saffron capsules still resting in her palm, water-filled glass sloshing gently in the opposite hand, the Subject sat on her bed, rounded legs gracefully crossed at the knee. Lowering her thick lashes over her gray-blue eyes, she said, "I've taken the other pills already…the knockout pills. So…whatever you came for, from wherever you're from…you'd better hurry with the questions." Although her lids were dropping in a parody of vampish seduction, Deng knew otherwise. Still speaking softly, mindful of the non-Subject female elsewhere in the house, Deng pressed his palms together, fingers pointing downward, as he began, "I am a historian, from your—"

The pink lips parted, showing the white perfection of the teeth underneath. "Like Arthur, the man at Arthur Krim's party. On the President's birthday. An elephant…I rode an elephant. Wore my skin and beads, only Adlai said he couldn't see any beads!" Her laughter was soft, yet muffled, as if bubbling up from fathomless depths where the black waters moved sluggish and cold. Deng made a move closer to her, but The Observer put out a prod-tipped arm, and Deng reluctantly retreated. The time was 7:50, Pacific time, the day Saturday August fourth, the year 1962…and Deng and The Observer had but five minutes more, if that, before they had to leave. Before the phone call came from the brother-in-law of the Subject's clandestine "friend," the call which would end with the slurred words, "Say goodbye to Pat, say goodbye to the President. Say goodbye to yourself because you've been a good guy." Perhaps…Deng could have timed his visit for a later moment, scant minutes before the phone rang, so that he could have heard those last words of sorrowful politeness and last dignity, but some losses were already too much, merely because they were losses. Deng was not seeking the death rattle of the soul, but the reason for the path down that black, one-way road into death and forever.

And Deng sensed that the Subject had both guessed the outcome of this evening and his purpose in her locked bedroom, for she curled her legs up under her rounded buttocks and tongued a few of the capsules into her mouth, dry-swallowing them, then drinking the water as an afterthought, before smiling laboriously and saying, "This made me more famous, didn't it? Made people wonder…for a long time, right?" She cast a sidelong glance at The Observer, at its silicon and metallic features. Deng nodded ruefully, adding, "Many, many years…and more famous than you can imagine, Ma'am. But many have wondered—"

"About this?" She held out the palm full of shiny pills. Popping some more of them into her mouth, she gulped, then went on, "To-night wasn't the first time I'd thought of it…you're the history man, so you…know that. But I was talking with Joe Junior…my hus—my ex's son, and we were laughing, having such a good time…" the thick-lashed eyelids dropped lower, a low sweep of darkness against her ivory flesh, "…then it came to me about the lollipop—"

"Pardon?" Deng longed to go forward, to poke his finger down that moving throat—but the presence of The Observer kept his humanitarian instincts hidden.

Leaning back against the wall, blonde head lolling, she said distinctly, but softly, "The *lollipop*…come on, history man, *you* know the line. From that movie…one where I lost Arthur's baby. 'The fuzzy end of the lollipop,' the bad end…talking to Joe, it came to me. Which end *was* the fuzzy end of it." Her voice was faint, a gentle watery drone, trickling away from Deng. This time, The Observer allowed him to move forward a foot, still suspended above the floor, as the Subject continued, "Fox wouldn't give in with the movie…but something's gotta give, like that clapboard says…we were laughing so hard, and it just came, like that—" she tried to snap her fingers, and dropped the yellow capsules on her thighs. Deng knew that she would eventually pick them up, all of them….

"The fuzzy end. Not the end you'd think…it's the sweet end when all the sweetness is gone." She waved her right hand around, the veins on its surface becoming prominent. Deng knew that she used to stand with her hands elevated, to make the blood go back down her arm…Deng knew much about his Subject, save for what he was hearing now.

"And the more you try to suck the last…sweetness away, the fuzzier it gets. Just…paper in your mouth…and 'you're better off dead when all the sweetness is gone'—no, no, that wasn't it…they're right, I am no good at lines—"

Deng shook his head, murmuring, "That will not matter, not at all."

The Subject gave him a small smile, barely a movement of her lips, and asked him the one question The Observer would never let him answer—not because it would ruin the Time Stream (the visit with the subject named Hemingway had already proved that it would actually do surprisingly little harm)—but because it would hurt the *Subject* too much.

"You can take me out of here, can't you…let me live?" It was not a plea, but a statement of fact.

As images flooded his mind (the infamous drawing of the Subject at fifty, wrinkles surrounding the famous beauty mark, circling those lidded eyes; the line of shoes bearing her name and lip-print; the nauseating recreations of her air-blown skirt, her pink-gowned affirmation that a certain gem *was* the best friend of the female sex), Deng let his silence convey his negative answer. Picking pills off her soft skin, pushing them past her lips, she said, "Even if you could… I wouldn't. Because…if you stopped me, you'd have no reason to *come* here, right? People…they'd forget, wouldn't they? Just an old has-been sucking the fuzzy end of the lollipop…" Eyes closed, her head weaved, blonde curls picking up the room's soft lights, but she kept talking, kept remembering one last time, "You…you read about the orange. When I was little, and…the foster…family…they forgot to buy me…presents. Christmas, no presents…other kids…presents, and a…tree. One gave me…an orange. Never forgot the…orange. And the Strasbergs…chicken gizzard. Saved it for me in the pot. For *me*." Those blue-gray eyes opened, warm and—for the first time during Deng and the silent Observer's visit—*happy*. Gulping down the last of the water from the glass, she said, "I knew…I knew you wouldn't do that to me. Take away….this from me. Be…cruel to *stop* it, wouldn't it?"

The last of the pills were gone, down that lovely throat. Deng knew from his scholarly pursuits that the fellow-Asian who performed the autopsy in only a few scant hours would find 8.0 mg of choral hydrate in her blood, 130 mg of pentobarbital in her liver. Most of the rest of her insides would be tossed out by the time twenty-four hours had passed. Being a habitual pill-taker, the Subject's internal organs would baffle people for years to come; some could not understand how her system would be able to dump such a load of pills without causing more than some petechial hemorrhaging. Even when answers were supplied by a pathologist, people would still choose to Believe Otherwise…a form of caring, in their own fashion. The wondering, the unwillingness to let it all rest. To let *her* finally die with the resting of the doubts.

A child once gave her an orange. A couple saved her a chicken gizzard in a pot of homemade soup. Millions refused to believe it was intentional, that she didn't want to leave them…not understanding that she *had* to leave, in order to *never* leave their minds, their imaginations. Deng felt lubricating sweat form between his palms, and, realizing that the silence of the room—tonight not even a radio was on, to aurally cover her nudity—was soon to be broken with the sound of a telephone ringing, Deng said, hoping that his memory of Ancient Films was correct, "'Sometimes your brain amazes me," speaking the lines a Subject named Russell uttered hundreds of years before—and a scant nine years before this night. Tonight's Subject raised the empty glass in a mock salute, and after thinking hard, harder than she had ever thought about a line after over a dozen years of uttering them in her movies, finally said the last line—and said it perfectly.

"'I can be smart when it's important.'"

The Observer tapped Deng; the current was off, but Deng felt the tingle of anticipation. To be gone, from this time, this place. Not to hear the phone being replaced in the cradle one last time, not to hear the footsteps of the non-Subject female outside the door as she noted with satisfaction that the phone cord was under the door and the light was on—meaning that her charge was all right—not to hear the tinkle of broken glass as the fireplace poker wielded by her doctor shattered the window....Deng had heard what he'd come so far and so *long* to hear—and cursed himself for not having guessed the obvious, the *simple*.. Yet, he felt comfort in the fact the *his* presence had signified something important to his Subject...not a desire to escape *this* fate; he had given her a last gift of *rightness*, the satisfaction attained after a last decision was made by her...and carried through.

He *could* have given her life...but robbing her of her fame was too steep a price. She was half-asleep now, head freely lolling—but Deng could imagine it snapping erect under the loose covering of curls, as the phone jangled. Nodding at The Observer (who remained, as *always*, impassive, *observant*) Deng gave the signal to leave, just as the phone did ring—and in the split fraction of a nano-second before Deng and The Observer left this Time, Deng found the time to whisper softly, with the nostalgia of an unrequited boyhood infatuation, "G'by, Norma Jean...."

> "Beneath all her insouciance and wit, death was her companion, and it may well be that its unacknowledged presence was what lent her poignancy, dancing at the edge of oblivion as she was."
>
> —Arthur Miller, Timesends

> "I don't want to get old. I want to stay like I am. I still can't act, not really. Monty (Clift) had his looks, but when he lost them, he was still a great actor. I'm not. I won't fool myself anymore. When my face goes, my body goes, I'll be nothing...nothing...all over again."
>
> —Marilyn Monroe

AFTERWORD

When it comes to this story, I'm of two minds; on one hand, I basically like the story itself (I'm a firm believer that self-determination is far better an end than murder, or even accident), but I loathe the circumstances under which it came to be printed. About that, all I can say is, there is no specific market listed for this piece in the publishing credits section for a reason...said reason involves the actions of the editor and the publisher, and those actions are so despicable I can't go into them here. Suffice it to say, I was f'ed over, royally, to the point where it adversely affected me for years.

As for the story, I always suspected that Marilyn Monroe was a far brighter woman than anyone gave her credit for, and even though she may have been killed, or may have accidentally died, I prefer to think she chose to end her own life. It is a more dignified way to think of her passing. While I usually don't *like* to write about real people all that often sometimes it simply has to happen within the confines of a story; most typically, I refer to cultural icons and historic figures when I do so, and when it does happen (using a real person), I try to treat them with some dignity. Once, I read about a collection of short-short stories written from the point of view of people who had just been decapitated—now that, to me, is all sorts of wrong, bad, evil, whatever. But if I've offended any of Miss Monroe's fans, I am sorry....

THE "TIME-VACATION" TRILOGY
I: BEYOND TIME AND FACE

"When the Gods wish to punish us, they answer our prayers."

Oscar Wilde

I

A 'loboard next to US Superglide 17, just outside of the Twin Cities III (Chi-waukee) pierces the morning smog-haze with the day-glo words **TIME-VAC WE MAKE THE PAST ALIVE NOW BACK IN TIME, EVERY TIME.** The throbbing red 3-D letters are compelling, arresting, but when compared to the lithesome figure above them, they become mere finger-doodles in dry sand.

The twenty-meter 'logram woman is carefully segmented, head to foot, into five epochal parts. Dainty feet shod in the latest Nike/Puma Soya-Crepe sport shoes. Shapely calves and knees encased in synthosilk "b'loon pants" of her great-grandmother's day. Thighs and hips covered by skin-tight designer jeans. Arms and smooth chest swathed in Victorian brocades and lace. Above them, the Face…the new Eve.

Simply timeless.

The basic concept for the Time-Vac holoboard is (even to the yawning commuter who happens to glance away from the newscan channel on the in-dash screen) an old, tired one. Familiar in the remote days of live magicians and non-holo adverts.

But the woman's face…tired or old, no. Familiar, definitely. She *is* the advertisement; the costumes and the blurb serve only as a reminder of the product at hand being foisted upon the gullible this month. Her face alone is endorsement enough, providing ample reason for anyone to want to own the product…as if it were a chance to own a tiny fragment of *Her*; to share a moment of her Being.

Further down SG-17, evenly spaced between the overhead solar arc lights and night-glo mileage indicators (*6 Km to Chiwaukee*) are more 'loboards, more of Her: saucily peering out from under a gigantic sesame-kelp bun perched on a steaming Klings SoyaPattie; gliding Ravaged Burgundy Banton's SupraGloss SoyaCote III over her incredibly smooth lips; seductively draped across the hood of an electric blue 2362 Takei glidecar. And when the commuter clicks off the autodrive at the city limits, s/he will again see, and see again, *the* Face—in window displays, on the sides of speedbusses, or just by turning his/her head in *any* direction.

Suzy Parker, Jean Shrimpton. "Hold the head higher, thatta girl, lick those lips, and smiiiile—" Paper icons ready-rolled in tubes; unrolled for bedroom worship. The chosen few—copied, remembered, forgotten. Twiggy, Varuschka, Cindy Crawford...Daria James... "smile." *The* Girl—Sakinia. BerNae Ayn—

—stands on the Time-Vacation, Inc. (Midwest Branch) Time-Pad™. This particular time pad, one of the twenty nation-wide, is located in the center of the large Departure/Arrival Room (affectionately called the *Aloha-Shalom* by Time-Vac workers), which is ringed on three sides with a dozen banks of the Time-Vac computer. The fourth wall is taken up by doors and dressing rooms, one of which contains BerNae Ayn's street clothes, IdentiCard, purse, and signed, notated will.

("Just a prelim, Ms. Ayn, everybody has to make one out, not that you'll actually, uhm, *need* it, but regulations....")

("Frig regulations....Get *on* with it, *will* you?")

BerNae clutches the black "patent leather" purse issued to her as part of the Native Temporal Epochal Garments pack (sterile, shrink-wrapped, contents guaranteed to withstand the rigors of even the most unsavory Time-Vac locale) which the Time-Vac computer/synthesizer coughed up, along with a date and a location for her vacation. Her free vacation, a tax-deductible part of her modeling fee for the Time-Vac 'loboard session. The popular "Surprise Day Getaway," for those with congested schedules.

BerNae is not smiling. So far, all BerNae knows all she *cares* to know, thank you) about her "day" is that it falls in the summer (hence the "cotton" dress) of the fifth decade of the twentieth century, during the Second World War, some place in old New England. Five centuries and hundreds of miles, to be bridged in seconds by the Time-Vac Computer/Synthesizer/White Magic Machine, which neither she (and few folks realize this) nor the Time-Vac people fully understand: all they are sure of is that after pushing the right buttons, twisting the proper dials, and (all ten fingers crossed now) tweaking the proper thingamajigs, the person standing on the oval Time Pad, under the Time-Vac Time-Field, will fade away to only the Computer knows where and then fade back into Now, when their vacation is over, and all the buttons, dials and thingamajigs are pushed, twisted and tweaked—in reverse order.

An Apple XXXIV-series 900 came up with the whole process after a bored comptech named Alexander D. Burgess Jr. programmed in the theories of Dirac, Schrödinger and Einstein, plus the first two chapters of a novel by a centuries-dead writer named Welles, as well as an article from a 1990's issue of *Discovery* magazine, then requested immediate correlation—while Burgess ate his lunch, still settled at his desk in the research department of the University of Illinois library, Science Division. Before Burgess had wiped the last crumb of soyarye and hamette from his lips, the Apple spit out a workable method for time-travel, complete with detailed instructions, diagrams, and a finance plan for weekend vacation packets. Burgess clocked out, sold his glidecar, furniture and house, using his credits to establish Time-Vac Inc. back in 2308. His indisputably wealthy (i.e. "filthydirtyrich") son hired top model BerNae Ayn for his new 'loboard campaign.

D. Burgess III doesn't understand Time-Vac either.)

As she watches the azure, amber and magenta lights flicker across the twelve "faces" of the Time-Vac Computer in a pattern beyond the comprehension of BerNae or the twenty Time-Vac men who are checking Date/Location/Pop Density read-outs, their watches, and mostly each other (the Computer really doesn't need checking, watching or monitoring during this stage, but consumer surveys proved that unattended Time-Vac Computers alienate Time-Vactioners), BerNae wraps thin arms around thinner model's body (cameras still add pounds) and thinks not about her trip, but about *them*. No particular person, or group, just the multi-faced, multi-voiced, single-expressioned *them*—

(you walk down the streets at night—can't go out during the day, too busy, too many eyes—and when you look in the plastiglass display windows you see your face under your reflection, a mirror facing a mirror, repeated into infinity; *you* looking back at *you*, only with a different expression, and in 3-D just like the holoboards that tower above you no matter where you go, or like the telescreens which are using you to hawk the frozen microwave holovision dinners you'll try to eat alone in your room tonight—like the dinners you eat alone *every* night—until you throw the opened box across the room because you can't stand thinking about eating something from a box with your face on it, so you go out again where they gawk and stop but don't talk except to say "Is that *her*?" and just keep staring when you grimace and stick out your tongue at them to force them to look away, only they *don't*, they just-keep-smiling-at-you—smiling like the pimply girl behind the counter at Kling's when she pushes back your ten cred note and hands you a CheezSoyaPattie: "No, take it please, from all of us, you bring in the customers, and the money," and the soyafoam carton *has your ever-smiling face on it*, and that ugly girl still smiles and *smiles*, even as you scream and—)

—even the Time-Vac Men are part of *them*, taking peeks at her (she bares her small teeth in a squared-off mouth) while supposedly adjusting the controls on the consoles…and *smiling*.

She has asked Time-Vac for a day, time and place which is ordinary; quiet, and very dull. No crowds of gawkers; surely beauty such as hers will transcend the centuries. Considering her past luck out in public, such an assumption is not to be considered a sign of vanity.

No…I'm not vain…just paranoid, she realizes, as she takes another look at her "dress"; BerNae remembers the paragraph from the Time-Vac Handbook—

(p. 78, rule 7: During Vacations in eras prior to 2206, natural vacationer camouflage is accorded to travelers by means of proper garments, due to the devolutioin in body size/maturity following WWIV [see Liliput Syndrome, appendix II—*World War Four and Us*, Martin Rusk, ed., Century Press, 2298] and subsequent physio-sexual regressions—)

—and comprehends that any attention to be paid her during her "Day" will differ greatly from that accorded her now; after all, how much notice will the typical Past adult take of a "child," no matter how lovely she is?

BerNae relaxes with that thought; her arms now dangle at her sides, her purse (which contains her TransTime locator/alarm) touches her starched blue "cotton" garment lightly.

(p. 32, Rule 3: ...function of this device is two-fold: 1) a homing signal, enabling Time-Vac to easily and unobtrusively locate Time-Vacationers. The Locator will not function unless the Time-Vacationer is isolated from the view of Time Natives. EXCEPTION TO ABOVE: If the Time-Vacationer is in danger, or in direct risk of Historical Interference, s/he is to press the red OVERRIDE button located on the underside of Locator/Alarm. 2) An alarm to be sounded when the Time-Vacation is nearly over, thus allowing the Time-Vacationer to seek an isolated or enclosed spot for retrieval. DO NOT LOSE OR MUTILATE THE LOC—)

BerNae toys with the thought of giving one of the Time-Vac men a slight smile when another Time-Vac Man and an alarm sound off at once: "Your vacation [beep] will begin [deep beep] now, Ms. Ayn [beep]." The Man grins; the alarm button glows tawny amber. The other Time-Vac men stare expectantly meaninglessly. (*What are those sops waiting for? Am I supposed to clap my hands, shout "goody-goody"...I wouldn't even be here if it wasn't for free*—) Again, BerNae wraps rigid arms around herself; she'll be damned if she'll smile, or wave or even acknowledge those staring, gawking Time-Vac assholes.

(*If you like what you see so much, go buy a Kling's SoyaPattie... with Cheeze.*)

II

Two seconds pass.

At first, nothing seems to be happening. Only when the Time-Vac men and the Time-Vac Computer lights become as insubstantial as reflections on wet plastiglass does BerNae start to relax; she is finally escaping *them*, even if only for a day. After ten years of wide eyes, pointing fingers and gasps, ten years of being the cynosure of the spending public (thought it was fun when I was sixteen, making all the geebs sigh and dream and *wish*…just as long as I had it over them, and not the other way around—) such a Day will be oxygen for empty lungs.

Six seconds.

Her surroundings shimmer, fade, and vanish into a cloudy, BerNae-surrounding wall. Which then, in reverse, shimmers and solidifies into distinct colors and forms and movements. BerNae has felt a greater sensation of stomach dropping while riding in an elevator.

Fifteen seconds.

Colors: Primary, sun-bright. Forms: Near-by trees, a far-off yellowish cloth edifice, farther-off buildings. Movement: People and animals, all huge, loud and slowly moving around.

Seventeen-point-four seconds.

A magenta light blinks on in wide-eyed wonder on the central Time-Vac Computer face.

Vacation Time.

* * * *

For the inhabitants of Hartford County (as well as a few from neighboring Litchfield, Middlesex and Toland Counties) this July has been (so far) a good one for children and fun-minded adults alike, despite the war and the rationing. The Fourth on Tuesday—

"Made too much slaw, be eating it till Thanksgiving at *least*—"

"Brucie burned his fingers on that sparkler, but boys will be—"

—and the circus today, two short days later—

"Too bad it ain't Friday. I'll never get Eddie up for his paper route tomorrow morning—"

"Hand me a clothespin. Thanks. I wish it was this weekend, Palmer's been dying to go, but the job comes first—"

—in a way, many of the seven-thousand-odd people milling around the circus grounds consider this day to be as good as, or maybe even better than, the Fourth; after all, what July Fourth parade could boast elephants, tigers and horses, plus floating balloons, cotton candy, long hot dogs, popcorn in striped boxes and Cracker Jacks, all in one place? Even those super-patriotic VFWers can't argue that one!

The crowd wandering about today, enjoying the second holiday of the week, includes tanned men in earth-toned gabardines, chinos and overalls, pale pastel shirts with clashing suspenders, and broad-brimmed hats; not-so-tanned women n cotton vionnet and rayon pastel dresses, open-toed wedgies or pumps, and sun hats; and boys and girls in smaller, simpler versions of their elders' clothes: notable among the children, but not too outstanding, is a little girl, blonde sausage curls caught up in two sky-blue taffeta ribbons (which echo her eyes), strawberry-cream-complexioned face framed by a white lace-trimmed collar which tops her smocked blue cotton dress. White anklets and new black patent Mary-Janes cover her tiny feet, and she swings a minute black patent leather purse from her left hand while holding a half-eaten foot-long hot dog in her right. She is a careful eater; not one crumb or drop of mustard can be seen on her face or dress.

The adults who look her way (a definite downward look; she is only three-and-a-half-feet tall) smile and murmur to each other or themselves. "Another Baby Peggy," or "Shirley Temple, eat 'cher heart out," then repeat themselves when the little carrot-top in green organdy struts by, or the towhead in pink dimity puts out her lower lip just so…with the blond girl in blue already forgotten.

BerNae doesn't hear the appreciative mutterings, or, rather, the sounds *do* reach her, but they do not register. Her initial shock over the massiveness of her surroundings (*people towering up higher than the Time-Vac ceiling, trees bigger than my whole apartment, and that undulating yellowish thing with the pointy flags, like at a used glidecar lot*—) turned to annoyance (*and I told them, no crowds, and nothing special going on…inept bastards*), which was in turn replaced by dazed acceptance when the white-jacketed hot dog man gave her a "dog" without a single prolonged stare or sigh; just took her large silver coin (thoughtfully included in her Time-Vac Package) and thrust the warm bun into her hand. No one had done…so *little* for at least eight years, certainly not after she signed that contract with Kling's SoyaPatties and became the SoyaPattie Girl!

While these people do see her, aside from the casual admiring glance, they hardly notice her. BerNae, in turn, sees, hears, smells and feels everything about her, but the input of this Past is too new, too varied and complex for her to take note of more than a few distinct stimuli.

Blue, blue sky, unfiltered by brackish smog. The hollow "pop" of a sucked-in pink bubble-gum bubble. An elephant's shriek. The frothy, yet rough-looking swirl of cotton candy that clings to a little boy's hands and face. Sour, ammonia-tinged scents near the big cat cages. "Maa-aah, he broke my balloon, hey, Maa-aah!" Hot sun on the part in her hair. Sweet-perfume of Jasmine and a too-hot dress. "Peeeanuts! Get 'cher peeeanuts!" Cigar smoke. Light, bouncy organ music. By her feet, a waxy-coated box of Cracker Jack, brown-sugared popcorn guts spewing out, ant-covered, onto the trampled grass. The grainy-smooth textures of chewed hot dog, bun and mustard on her tongue. A blister, forming on her left heel under the new hole in her guaranteed indestructible stocking.

BerNae finishes her hot dog (so that's meat…interesting, but I hope I don't get Time-Vac's revenge—), licks off her fingers cat-daintily, and notices that the crowd is moving to her left toward the gargantuan cloth structure, which they are slowly entering. The tempo of the music becomes fast, frantic. She looks up, up to see the banner proclaiming "Ringling Brothers and Barnum and Bailey Circus," half expecting to see her face incorporated into the swirling design.

Moving closer, she glimpses bleachers inside, with people already sitting on them, surrounding a huge empty space in the center. There are lights within, to offset the darkening sky outside.

Virtually ignored by now, she joins the throng of laughing, sweating, shuffling giants; before her is a family. Father sunburned, with peeling freckled forearms under rolled-up sleeves, sweat-stained buff-toned fedora pulled low over short, stubbly hair, and a cigar ashing into nothingness in his right hand. Mother likewise sunburned, neck, arms and lower legs (brown eyebrow-pencil seams painted crookedly down the backs of calves) flushed bright pink, green-flowered percale dress ringed with moisture under the arms, feet swelling out slightly over her pumps. Three daughters also well-done and peeling, pink, yellow and green gingham dresses limp around their thighs, white anklets drooping low around pudgy ankles. All five are fair-haired, like the fourth little girl who stands with them in the ticket line ("Momma, she came here *all by herself*, can she sit with us?"), politely munches the offered Cracker Jack ("Ma, Molly took the prize *again*!"), and slips unnoticed past the ticket-taker into the big tent.

* * * *

Six rows of bleachers up from the center ring, three little girls and one not-such-a-little-girl *oooh* and *ahhh* when the spangly-leotard-clad man and woman flip hand-over-hand-on swinging bars high, high above them, and giggle at the raggedy men with painted faces who never, never laugh at themselves, and cheer the grey, wrinkle-skinned elephants lumbering nose-to-tail 'round and 'round below them.

(*So this is what it feels like to be one of* **them**, *part of that slack-jawed nameless mass…they don't mean any harm at* **all**, *it's actually so* **easy**, *so* **comfortable** *to be one of* **them**, *to merge…oh God, I don't have to be so apart, so alone, maybe I* **can** *climb out of the fishbowl after all—*).

The *ooohs* and *ahhhs*, giggles and cheers of the little girls are echoed a hundred, a thousand, and seven thousand times and times around them; a fine, warm sound of shared delight (*—and be part of* **them** *back in my time, too…guess I can learn to live without having my face plastered on every—*) and awe, punctuated by the crunch of popcorn, the roar of lions, and the tissue-crinkle of flames—

The crowd-sound changes in double-time from a squeal of de-light to a twisted howl of fear. BerNae sees the flames lick up the canvas around her like vanilla soya-ice, and adds her screams to the towering wall of noise. Dropping her bag of peanuts, she starts to crawl head-first to the ground (*just get outside, then I can disappear from here, got to get—*), trying to dodge the legs of the giants around her. And feels someone's booted foot kick her in the neck and head. And smells the harsh smoke of panic and sweat. And hears a child scream once, faintly, as he falls and snaps his spine. And sees the purse fly off her arm as she is knocked off the bleachers…and then sees the horse stomp down on it, crushing the purse and its precious cargo into worthlessness…like a discarded Cracker Jack prize.

III

By Friday, July 7th, 1944, Hartford, Connecticut was no longer in a holiday mood; just the thought of those four hundred eight-seven injured, and one hundred sixty-eight dead—

"I know it can't bring him back, but here's a three-bean salad, you've got to—"

"If only it would've rained that day—"

—was enough to kill the holiday feeling clear into November, if not longer. The funeral directors, for once, prayed that the old, infirm and dying would wait, just please *wait*. Slowly, tears were choked back; the dead were claimed, mourned and buried. Except for a little girl, who looked to be maybe six-years-old or so, face still pretty and un-mauled, body in not-so-good shape, blue dress not at all crisp or clean; both shoes gone.

On Tuesday, May 18th, 2363, exactly three hours, ten minutes and seven-point-nine seconds after she shimmered off into a randomly selected "Day" in the Past, the Time-Vac Computer/Synthesizer/Not-*Really*-White-Magic Magic Machine gurgled, and BerNae Ayn's magenta light flickered like a candle in the summer breeze, then winked out forever on the Time-Vac Departure Board.

The Time-Vac Men checked their memories against those of the history books—no, nothing *seemed* altered or amiss. One of them muttered that it was almost as if BreNae Ayn had slid into a waiting niche in the Past, where she altered nothing, or, as yet another Time-Vac Man nervously joked, perhaps she filled a Time-*Vacuum*. It was a shame, they all agreed; *such* a beautiful woman. So famous, so adored....

They hoped it was a painless death.

No matter what had happened to her (they didn't *dare* go looking for the body, even if the Computer *had* retained the memory of where it sent her, which it didn't—utilizing the built-in fail-safe against further Past-tampering), there seemed to be no Time-Damage done, at least not in their continuum (if the good gentlemen Dirac and Schrödinger had been correct in their assumptions), so A. D. Burgess III and the rest of the Time-Vac stockholders could breathe easy.

Lloyd's of London came through, no questions asked.

BerNae's signed will was duly, *quietly*, executed.

Time-Vac unceremoniously dropped the "Back in time, every time" part of their slogan a week later, coinciding with the debut of the new Time-Vac Girl, fifteen-year-old Raina Tyne.

…coinciding with the debut of the new Kling's SoyaPattie Girl, fifteen-year-old Raina—

…coinciding with the debut of the new Takei, Ltd. Glidecar Girl, fifteen-year-old—

…coinciding with the—

* * * *

Months later in 1944, after the photograph of the unknown little girl's face made the rounds in Hartford, then in Connecticut, then in the rest of the nation, with no results—

"Shame, purty little thing like that, you'd think *someone*'d miss her—"

—she was buried in Hartford, in a donated grave.

Although many people thought that it was an inadequate and pathetic description, they called the unclaimed body "Little Miss Nobody," never realizing just how close they were to the truth.

In memory of Eleanor Emily Cook, who died in 1944, aged eight years.

THE "TIME-VACATION" TRILOGY II: AT THE PLAYGROUND BY THE SWINGS, WITH BIG CHUCK

I

It was just the way her brother said it would be, earlier that morning when he slipped the extra fifty credits into her hand over the breakfast table.

"The person behind the Time-Vac screening desk will say, with an authoritarian—mind, little sister, an *authoritarian*—shake of the head, 'A one week long Time-Vacation would *in*advisable,' and then will proceed to attempt to sell you one of those Surprise Day Get-Aways that amount to 'Slam-bam-back-home-again-and-please-give-us-your-first-born-son-as-payment, *thank you*!'"

The woman sitting behind the highly polished Lucite desk had given her an 'Aren't *we* the perfect little pigeon' smile and, with the predicted shake of her head—*authoritarian* shake, you're always right, big bro—said in a Nutra-Sweet drippy voice, "I'm terribly sorry, Ma'am, but one-week long Time-Vacations just aren't…how shall I put this…*advisable* for the novice Time-Vacationer. Too many problems can arise, considering how just anything can happen. Being tagged as a runaway child is a distinct possibility—we had one client spend most of his vacation in what the ancients called a 'Juvenile Detention Center'—being taken advantage of sexually is another, also finding lodging is difficult under—"

"—these circumstances, many public transportation systems won't accommodate solo 'children,' then there's the risk of exposure due to unfamiliarity with the various Time environments'…all that flak that they run by me every time I go Back Then for a week," her brother had continued over his scrambled soya-eggies at breakfast, "But just watch that iron reserve melt when you pull open your credit pouch and give the Time-Vac Screener a look at—"

"—twenty, thirty, forty…would fifty extra credits above and beyond the usual Time-Vac rates make any difference, *Ma'am*?" She gave the woman an "Aren't *we* the greedy, somewhat underpaid little Time-Vac toady?" smile, as she sealed her credit pouch…after leaving two neat piles of credits on the shiny counter between them. One for the Time-Vac, and the other one for…the *help* the woman could give her. She knew which pile would go into the Screener's credit pouch as soon as she was led into the Time-Vac Preparation Room.

Fifty, a hundred credits, no amount would be too much. Not for big brother to give little sister, anything to help her out with the completion of her collection. Which was an extension of *his* collection… with a few changes.

When they were young, his passion had been model glidecars, hers dolls. (Even after passage of the ERA last century, a full five centuries after it was first proposed to the U.S. government, little boys still naturally gravitated towards big machines that *went* places, while girls still naturally fancied little dolls that *went* all over. All that fighting over something like an ERA, and children found themselves in the same stereotypical pull.)

So being good little stereotypical kiddies, she and her brother amassed collections of toys that became the envy of their housplex playmates, and caused more than one friendship to wither in the green flames of jealousy.

And even though they, like all of the people of their time, didn't actually grow *up*, since three feet tall was the norm in 2542 A.B. (*Thank* you, Mr. A-Bomb for all the *lovely* changes thou hast wrought!), their intellectual tastes did mature. Glidecars were packed neatly in marked shoeboxes, dolls were nestled in soya-tissue and placed in the bottoms of dresser drawers, under the new soya-crepe lingerie.

With adulthood, big brother once again took the lead when it came to finding himself a new hobby, a new collection. Like most collectors, most *serious* collectors, early on he was content to form his collection with…*items* easily available in the Here and Now. Going Back Then had never occurred to him, mainly because bringing anything of a material nature back from Then after taking a Time-Vacation was a crime that invited one's imminent funeral, courtesy of the Government. Granted, it was done, but only bootleg recordings of readings by long-deceased authors like Shakespeare and Dickens, but only the truly Wealthy could afford—or even wanted—Past Masters recordings, but aside from the risks posed by sending bootleggers Back Then with tape recorders that *might* get left behind to interrupt the Past, what the Past Masters people did was nothing compared to smuggling back actual *things* from Then, things that just might be missed, or needed, or *something.* Even thinking such a thing was audacious.

And her brother *hadn't* thought of it, until the time when a friend of his invited him along on a Two-For Time-Vacation during the off season. They picked a day-long jaunt, in the 19th century. No Juvenile Detention Centers to worry about, just stay out of the way of the horses while crossing the street.

After the trip, that one day, the quality of the...*items* Back Then preyed on her sibling's mind. Thinking about his collection, how great it could be with certain "additions" soon progressed form a mere passion to an utter obsession, then...with a little Here and Now experimentation, a few dry runs, his dream became a practicality. A dangerous, life-threatening practicality, but at least his dreams, his *hopes*, might become tangible reality. The antique items could be *his.*

The only hitch was, he couldn't count on being able to get what he wanted in the one day Vacation Time-Vac usually sold. Being, in the eyes of the inhabitants of Back Then, a mere child, getting what he needed could be very, very difficult even under ideal circumstances. But in a week...certain things could be worked out, conquered....

But even after the outlay of extra credits, and the week spent Back Then, he didn't get much for his efforts during the first of his "Souvenir Runs"...except a fix of pure adventure, so she wasn't surprised when he announced that he was going on another run...then another, and another. By that time, she had begun to assemble her own collection, which was an extension of his own, with that typically feminine twist that no amount of equality-based legislation could eradicate. What with her job, and the time spent collection-hunting, she was often too busy to keep track of her brother's comings and goings in the Past.

He did keep her up to date whenever he got a new acquisition, first by viewphone, then, fearing a tap on his lines, he took to inviting her over to see the new additions firsthand. At that point, when she saw for herself the quality of the Past…*items*, she began to under-stand why he simply *had* to risk it all—the condo, the head position at Sinai, the three glidecars, not to mention his *life*—for the material from Back then. The antiques almost overshadowed the other things in the collection.

Hence, the satisfaction she would feel upon the acquisition of a new piece for her own collection began to wane, especially when she realized that the Past was simply *crawling* with…*items* which she could hunt down and bag as it were, on a "Souvenir Run" of her own. Being unattached, and parentless, she didn't have an awful lot to lose if she was caught red-handed with Time Contraband, and an…*item* from the endless supply just *waiting* for her Back Then would be priceless to a collector like herself….

"Miss, if you're ready, the Time-Vac Computer is all set to go—"

The voice of the Time-Vac Man coming through the door of the changing booth broke into her thoughts. Hastily, she crammed her contraband into the "purse" issued to her as a part of her Native Tem-poral Epochal Garments package, along with the rest of the clothing she presently wore. Looking herself over carefully in the wall mirror, she remembered her brother's parting words outside the Time-Vac Building, after he dropped her off on his way to work.

"Don't be afraid to show a little apprehension, sis. They're wary when a first-timer is too calm. Act too frosty and they'll be all over you with a magnifying glass in one second. Remember, they some-times do a strip search just for the hell of it, so you better have a good excuse for your paraphernalia if they find it," he warned, then reached into her credit pouch and extracted a small, longish object. Pulling her down to the glidecar, he whispered into her ear, "Better not chance *that* on your first trip. Be your luck to run into a Time-Vac Man who's into Rules as a Way of Life. They'll issue credits—*money*—you can buy what you need with that, once you get there….I know, I know, it's hard for a 'child' to buy one of *these*"—he fingered the object from her pouch—" But you'll see, the Past has lots of things that will do in a pinch. Now be a good girl, all right? Bring home a good one, something for the top of the wall," and before she could jump back into the glide with him—she didn't feel *ready*, not that she was *scared*—he shifted into autoglide and hummed away.

The woman—*little girl*, one must get into the right frame of mind—who looked back at her was an alien, a castaway from some twentieth-century playground who only wanted to go Back Then, back home…slinging her rigged purse, Trans-Time Locator/Alarm safely tucked inside, she gave the strange little girl in the mirror an apprehensive smile and a knowing wink, and left the booth.

II

One by one, the kids on the playground confided to Big Chuck the Monitor that the new girl sitting alone next to the swings—not on a swing seat, but on the ground next to the swings—was really weird.

"She don't know 'bout cooties, Big Chuck. We wiped them all on her and she went an' kept 'em," Lisa told him.

"I asked her if she saw *The Monkees* last night and *she* asked if the zoo was open after dark—what'd she mean by *that*?" asked Terry.

"Is she from *here*? She never says 'cool' or 'guy' or *anything* when she talks," complained Sharon.

By noon, fifteen of the neighborhood regulars had come to big Chuck, the college senior who helped watch over the playground each summer, with different tales of how "out" of it the new girl was; how she didn't know about *The Dating Game*, Nancy Drew, or what night *Star Trek* came on, even how to play *hopscotch*.

During the first couple of days she wandered around on the play-ground, no one had paid much attention to her, but by now the rest of the kids had glommed onto the fact that the little blonde girl wasn't a stranger…she was *strange*.

Big Chuck—dubbed that by the elementary-school-age children he supervised during the day because he stood six feet tall, and called the same name by his college-age female contemporaries for a some-what more personal reason—had noticed that the new blonde kid was odd long before the rest of the kids caught on.

It was the way she just sat, not running around spreading cooties, or twisting her long fine hair around her fingers, chewing bubble gum. But not the cowed sort of quiet exhibited by the browbeaten kids. Just content to lay back and take things in. Like life was a new experience for her. No parents ever came to the playground with her; that was something Big Chuck noticed by the second day she spent in the park-*cum*-playground on the outskirts of the city. He liked that. Parents who cut loose the apron strings early really got his vote. Best way to raise them. Just open the front door in the morning and let 'em go.

Not that the streets were a good place for kids to roam, but they could vent their energies in the playground, and the parents could rest easy because Big Chuck, clean-cut, short-haired, white-toothed Big Chuck—he wasn't one of those drugged-out hippie freaks, no siree!—was there all day, on the ready in case of any emergency. Of course he didn't breathe down the kids' necks…let the teachers do that come fall.

In the neighborhood's park-like playground, surrounded by and dotted with trees and clumps of bushes, as well as the usual tire-jungle, multiple swing sets, slides, monkey bars—funny, she didn't know about *The Monkees*—and painted-on hopscotch games, the kids were safe as long as Big Chuck was around.

Big Chuck had a big supply of band-aids, Bactine, and Vicks Cough Drops in his jacket pocket. Big Chuck had something in the other pocket of his jacket. Quarter. Lots of them.

Big Chuck didn't dispense his quarters the same way he gave out the bandages, antiseptic spray or cough drops, for just any "owie" or cough.

The kids had to earn a quarter from Big Chuck, and if a kid ever got one, he or she could never tell where he or she got it. That was part of the Big Secret between Big Chuck and them. Only some of the kids got those shiny new quarters from Big Chuck. Not the ones whose parents brought them to the playground, and picked them up later. And not the ones who'd usually wind up wearing pinned-on long black construction paper "Tattle Tails" on their sweaters and coats come school recess time.

Big Chuck was a very choosy guy. Only special kids could be his good friend. He chose only the quiet, *nice* little boys and girls to receive his special quarters. And they didn't even have to do much to earn those quarters, not like having to do dishes or make their beds at home. They didn't even have to lose a baby tooth, or anything like that. Big Chuck did it all, with his big hands.

(Sometimes the kids who got the quarters from Big Chuck wondered why their parents didn't pay them a quarter whenever they took off their underpants at home, or especially why the Doctor didn't pay them either, but they never asked their Mommy or Daddy or the Doctor about it. That would've been breaking the Big Secret, and if they did that, Big Chuck wouldn't take them aside to play the Game, and they'd *never* get another big shiny quarter. They wouldn't even giggle when the Game got tickly, for fear of ruining the game and not getting the quarter. Even if it tickled like a *million* feathers, none of the children would ever let on that it did.)

So it was natural that Big Chuck began to pay attention to the new little girl right away, and as he watched her today from over near the big tree next to the slides, his fingers rubbed and rubbed on the quarters in his left jacket pocket. For several weeks this summer he had paid out money, an awful lot of it, to most of the kids playing here today. He knew them better than their parents did. Even better than their doctors.

"Familiarity breeds contempt," …he had heard one of the profs at the college say once. Big Chuck had an improvement on that saying. Familiarity breeds boredom.

The coin between his forefinger and thumb was greasy from being rotated so much. He liked the quiet kids, but this one was special. For one thing, she never wore slacks or pedal pushers or shorts, but one of those cute little short-skirted sundresses, the kind that bunches up high on the thighs when a little girl sits cross-legged in the grass. Like she was doing now. The kind of dress that shows off a small white patch of exposed panty, peeking out between small crossed legs.

The fingers stopped rubbing the coin. She was *looking* at him. The sun-warmed skin under his flat-top began to tingle. She smiled a sunny little smile that showed off a full set of tiny teeth. He wondered what baby teeth like that would feel like, *there*. Now she was patting the ground next to her, on the side away from the swings. The side close to the tall bushes. Opening her plastic purse, she extracted a shiny, odd-looking bauble, studied it, put it back and took out a yellow pocket comb. After running it through her straight blonde locks, she dropped it back into the purse. He could hear the decisive *click* as she snapped it shut.

Hanging the pink purse on her arm—in the past six days she'd come to the playground, she had always had the purse within arm's reach—she reached behind her and picked up an empty eight-ounce soda bottle. She began to blow across the top of it, creating a low, moaning sound.

She never took her eyes off of his. Rubbing the coin frantically between his fingers, Big Chuck ambled over to the little girl sitting by the swings, big smile on his tanned face. The kids playing nearby who saw him approach the girl knew enough to play elsewhere. They understood the rules of the Game. No peeking, no nosing around. And no making any trouble while Big Chuck was busy elsewhere. Soon, the area around the swings was deserted.

"Hi." Big Chuck squatted down in front of the girl. She smiled shyly in return then resumed blowing across the top of the bottle.

"That fun?" A nod of her head.

"Can I try?" Coy shake of the head, and another smile.

He liked that in a kid. Not a big mouth. But fey. Something like that book he'd read in Modern Novels 355, the one he really dug. *Lolita*.

"O.K. Can you talk?"

Laughter. "Sure," she said in a husky but small voice. "'bout what?" She rested the base of the bottle on the ground, but didn't let go of it.

Sitting down cross-legged in front of her, Big Chuck asked, "Some of those kids been giving you a hard time?"

"I dunno." Downcast, but a trace of a smile on her pale lips.

"They can be mean, when they don't understand. Just because you don't waste your time passing cooties or watching *The Monkees*, they peg you as a weirdo…but *I* don't think you're weird."

"No?" She stroked the empty bottle.

"Why should I? Guy, I think you're a nice kid. And I sure like your dress." He looked down at her skirt, and beneath it. Suddenly, she straightened out one leg, to scratch an itch under her knee, and the panties moved aside ever so slightly. But *enough*. She smiled.

"I know a rhyme," Big Chuck began, then let his voice trail off, waiting until she looked quizzically at him, before chanting, "I see Paris, I see France, I see…a little girl's *under*pants!"

Giggles. "Know any more?" She didn't re-cross her legs.

"Sorry. Hey, you know what? All the days you've been coming to the playground, I've never seen you buy yourself an ice-cream bar. No money?"

"Nope," she said. She picked up the bottle and began to tootle across the top, a mournful hoot.

"Like some? You would? Wanna know where to get some?"

"Yeah." She looked at him expectantly.

Big Chuck jingled his pocket full of quarters, filling the air with a merry sound, one that the other kids knew very well. The girl cocked her head at the sound.

"Know what this is?"

"Money?"

"Yep. Guess who for?"

"I dunno," but her eyes did know.

Big Chuck smiled down at her, and her soft pinkish skin. Standing up, he dusted off his pants bottoms then helped the girl to her feet. As he did so, somehow she broke the bottle against the nearest leg of the swing. Big Chuck expected her to drop it, but she held on tight to the neck and the remaining three or four inches of broken bottle. Whisking the bits of grass which clung to her behind off of her dress with his big hand, Big Chuck suggested that she throw the bottle in the Dumpster.

"Uh. Uh. I like blowing on it." Big Chuck had to laugh at that; some of these kids said the damnedest things. Like the little boy who said bird dentists fixed other birds' "peckers." He and the boy played "bird dentist" for a *week*.

"You really like blowing on it, huh?" he asked as he guided her to the nearby tall shrubs, and she looked up at him, pink purse in her one hand and broken bottle in the other, and chirped, "Yeah, blowing bottles is *fun*," as she crawled into the space between the surrounding bushes. This one might be worth a couple quarters, he thought, keeping that neat row of pearly baby teeth in mind.

III

In her excitement, she almost forgot to press the button on her Trans-Time Locator/Alarm when the time for her to leave Back Then arrived, and since she wasn't able to fit it into her purse afterwards, she almost lost it in the bushes, and thus almost didn't make it back to Now at all.

She was glad that she had packed a *double*-ply soya-plast bag in her purse, although she wished that she had brought along the next largest size. She had to fold it in half. A bigger purse would have helped, but she had had no control over *that*. Maybe the next time she'd luck out and the Time-Vac Machine would issue her one of those "slumber-party-bags" that the girls on the Past playground used to talk about, only a few hours and centuries ago.

As she shimmered into Now on the oval Lucite Time-Pad in the Time-Vac Control Room, she hoped that her purse wouldn't start to *leak* before she made it back to her Changing Booth. And she had to remember to act as if the purse was *empty* and *light*. To avoid snoops.

She hadn't expected it to weigh so much, even though she'd hefted some of the antique...*items* her brother smuggled out of 19th century London. His English specimens, as he labeled them, the biggest and best parts of his collection. Once they were properly dressed out they were exceptional. And now her collection would have its antiques, although her collection would remain more specialized than her brother's. Whenever he was on a "Souvenir Run," he acted like a kid in a soyady shop, here a kidney, there an ovary, and the time when he brought back all those lovely, soft flaps of skin....Limited as it was, *her* collection would now be truly universal in size and scope. She was going to hang this one at the top of her collector's wall, a prize trophy in a special place of honor.

Materialization complete, she was pleased to note that there other Time-Vacationers waiting for her to vacate the Time Pad, which big brother told her was a good sign—the more rushed things were, the less time the Time-Vac Men had to scrutinize arrivals from Back Then. Quickly, she stepped down and unobtrusively made her way back to her changing booth. Once there, with the door locked behind her, it was out of the "sundress," torn "cotton panties," and other grass-stained Native Epochal Temporal Garments, all of them *whoosh* down the Incini-Chute, except for the contents of the pink plastic purse, which were neatly hidden in her credit pouch. The broken bottle she had left behind with the quarters. They had felt greasy anyway.

Walking out of the Time-Vac Building, she hugged her credit pouch against her small body. Smiling, she mumbled to herself, "Big Chuck, *indeed*," as she waited for brother Jack to pick her up.

THE "TIME-VACATION" TRILOGY III: PILLAGING POE

"Dim was its little disk," Poe, a slender man with lady-killer grey eyes and a neatly-mended tan waistcoat, paused, lowered his resonant voice to a conspiratorial hush, "and / Angel eyes alone could see the phantom in the skies / When first Al Aaraaf knew her course to be…"

Loftus, modern tape bootlegger, wished that a wind, any kind of a wind—be it from sea, land, or ceiling fan—would blow through this dingy lecture hall where she now sat; the combined fumes of greasy hair pomade, infrequently-washed skin, and tracked-in horse emissions reminded her of stale basement floors and glide truck station washrooms. Not that any of the Locations were a bed of soyablossoms, but Loftus especially dread doing her job (a.k.a. pirating) in enclosed spaces like this. Her last (only) really pleasant assignment had been getting Plato's Allegory of the Cave last month—summers in ancient Greece were all the better for the lack of smog and fallout. It was definitely worth the week she spent holed up in her dorm room with the Berlitz ancient Greek CDs.

Granted, those repeat trips she undertook before second semester fees were due—six of them in all, resulting in the complete five-compact-disc set of Dickens reading *Oliver Twist* had been brutal, and by the last day in the Past she was tempted to risk the mandatory prison term by breaking the "No Gifts/No Souvenirs" rule at good old Time-Vacations, Inc., and leaving behind a few paltry trinkets and baubles for the natives: Roll-on antiperspirant, a case of mouthwash, a can or two of foot powder.

But at least at the Dickens Locations, sometime in the late fall, the cold kept down some of the stink. As she sat on a hard fold-up chair in the front row of this dank lecture hall, Loftus wasn't certain if it was July, August, or perhaps early September. Nor was she sure of the city (Baltimore? Boston? Richmond?), but whenever or wherever she was, it was muggy. She could feel her stocking-encased legs sticking to the hard varnished hall chair through her circa 1840 "Native Epochal Temporal Garment," e.g., a yellow-checked long dress, a flimsy costume manufactured from the soyaprotein glop stored in the vat under the southeastern branch of Time-Vac.

Breathing through her mouth helped. A little. Yet Loftus really couldn't bitch about the conditions in this Location, not after she had begged Wagnall, the boss and master bootlegger at Past Masters Recordings to let her make this run, to let her secretly tape this Past Master reading his work. Part of her pleading involved her *supposed* major in college—American literature of the early nineteenth century…and her profound academic interest in the Past Master himself.

Not that she had had to grovel. Summer sessions—*indoor* summer sessions—weren't popular with any of the "employees" (read: Pirates, sound thieves, tape runners, mules, etc.) at Past Masters, and since reliably documented, *dated* events in the past couldn't be rescheduled during periods of nice weather. Wagnall usually had to beg for runners when it came to readings in closed, hot places. But sometimes her coworkers needed the overtime pay given on assignments like this one, so Loftus did some fast talking.

That night, Wagnall called up his graveyard-shift buddy at Time-Vac, some money passed under the hypothetical table, a specific date was punched in at one of the Time-Vac Computer Terminals, a modified item was added to the "Native Epochal Temporal Garments" package issued to Loftus, and seventeen seconds later Loftus found herself in a wet alley behind a brick meeting hall—a pretty good ruse for a Business and Econ major at Florida State, currently working on the theory of the Daisy Chain for her finals. Her micro-recorder was hidden in something Wagnall called a "reticule" (Loftus thought it looked more like a purse), which also contained a little plastic and metal "dealybob" called a "Trans-Time Locator/Alarm," her sole link with her own time.

"We paus'd before the heritage of men, / And thy star trembled—," Poe's voice poised on the verge of heartbreak and ecstasy, "as doth Beauty then!"

But this time, *this time*, Loftus wished to God—if She was listening—that she could chuck the Trans-Time Locator/Alarm, just pitch it in the nearest dustbin, and stay here, bad stinks, manure on the streets, and all. She may have been wearing the Epochal clothing of a child—since people of her time looked childlike due to genetic de-volution and a little friendly nuclear patty-cake—but Loftus's desire to stay was anything but childish.

Perhaps her reason for coming here was based on a desire so adolescent, so damned *girlish*, that thinking rationally about it made her face grow hot with amused shame. Perhaps she shouldn't have let a fancy so unrealistic lead her to this place, to this person. *I hurt, hurt bad*.

Suddenly she could see the wisdom in the Time-Vac Code: Do Not Disturb. Passive observation was the rule at Time-Vac; it *never* paid to try to make friends with people who were most likely dust beneath your feet back in your own time. Better to sit back and let the recorder do the work, let it impassively take back a little fragment of escaped life.

Having finished the poem, Poe lightly licked his thin lips, then softly began, "Kind solace in a dying hour / Such, father, is not—"

"Tamerlane." One of Loftus's favorites. Yet the pain she felt could not be lessened by the fact that her idol was now speaking the words she had often read silently to herself through self-indulgent tears in her childhood.

Once she had seen a show on Holovision in the basement of her dorm, an old 2-D documentary from the late 1980s called "Sing Blue Silver" about an English band with the echo-holic name of Duran Duran. While they played onstage, young girls began screaming, fainting, and had to be hauled off to the stadium infirmaries.

That night, sitting in a pneumatic lounger in the dorm basement, Loftus felt no kinship to the screeching little adolescents moving flatly across the screen before her. But here, on this rear-killing chair, surrounded by these huge, stinking beings, Loftus understood ex-actly how those girls at that music concert felt. Only *they*, if fate and backstage passes allowed, could talk to and touch and maybe—if they were sensitive enough not to slobber—exchange ideas, feelings, opinions with those improbably doll-like young musicians.

There may have been a thousand, ten thousand of them, and only five fellows to fight and cry over, but they had a *chance*. They didn't face a fine or a jail sentence for talking to them and possibly fouling up centuries of history, or eliminating countless lives, countless des-tinies. They never had to worry about certain execution if they gave one of those men a note saying they cared, that they were touched by the words, the music.

"O yearning heart! I did inherit / Thy withering portion with the fame, / The searing glory—"

When Poe first published this poem in 1827, Loftus thought bitterly, it sold for the grand sum of 12½¢ per copy. Just a hundred years later, *one* copy sold for $11,000 in New York City.

And when I finish taping this poem, this evening's performance, you poor, doomed creature, Wags will cut a master and sell the disks for over twenty-five thousand credits a copy. And he will press a million copies in the first run alone. As many as he can sell before the law hears about this one. Not that the law could help you much, my friend. You don't have any relatives left to pay royalties to. Nobody left to receive the money Time-Vac should pay you, but can't. (That's a law they won't break.) And you were poor, are poor, trapped as you are in this Time, your Now....

"The heritage of a kingly mind, / And a proud spirit which has striven / Triumphantly with human kind," the paper and paste scroll gently tapped against Poe's knees, as it gradually lowered to the floor. Not subtle, but dramatic. Must have gotten the flair from his actor parents; a move of the chin, that commanding presence.

The other Past Masters Loftus had dropped in on and clandestinely ripped off may have been better writers. Or more prolific. Or both. Dickens could do more with his voice; he had a greater range; a better gift of characterization. Shakespeare was fluency and grace combined. And Byron had a raw sexuality (maybe a bit too kinky for Loftus) and a voice to match. Loftus never regretted taping them and bringing back their work. She never hesitated to press that red button on the underbelly of her Locator/Alarm once she finished at a Location. The ethics of the situation, the cheating nature of the whole set-up, the money these people would never earn from their own efforts—Loftus didn't let herself think about things like that. Take the credits and run to the nearest Credi-Stor, fatten up her account by a few hundred credits per run. Most of the people she had taped had had the attention, the adulations, and the bucks in their own lifetimes. She had never been upset before.

But she was upset now. Here she was, sitting almost within touching distance of a man who probably never saw more than $1,000 all at once, who only received a modicum of critical and popular support, and who wound up saying, shortly before the DTs got the better of him in the Washington College Hospital, that the kindest thing someone could do to him would be to blow out his brains.

The *kindest* thing....

"It was but man, I thought, who shed / Laurels upon me; and the rush—"

Sure, Loftus thought, *after you were dead a few years, the French turned you into an icon, and eventually someone scraped up enough money to buy you a real tombstone. Sure, you're the unofficial poet laureate of the middle school crowd, the place where* I *discovered you. You got your face put on a postage stamp, and some guy wrote an opera about your life. Would it make you happy to know that you got elected to the Hall of Fame of Great Americans? Would it pay the bills and ease the demons and make your wife well again? She's gonna die, you know—TB. The cure for it was invented only a couple of hundred years too late to help Virginia, but what the hell, that's progress. Your trusted literary executor is waiting to screw you royally and trash your name and reputation. He's just aching to turn you into a synonym for "degenerate."*

Just this afternoon Wagnall had said, "You still interested in this lecture date for that booze-hound, Poe?" Know what was really wrong with you? A little screw-up in the genes. Something called "congenital alcohol dehydrogenase deficiency syndrome." Last year a Dutch scientist developed an in utero *test for it. Last year in 2367. Just in time for your dust to disintegrate. A man named Roger Corman made a frigging mint turning your stories into schlock-art films.*

"I was ambitious, have you known / The passion, father? You have not—" that tireless, silken voice, as beautiful as Loftus had often imagined it. Looking up at the one person she had often prayed to see alive, she kept thinking, *You're going to die—and die so badly! You're going to pass out near a place called Ryan's Saloon on Lombard Street in Baltimore after wandering around God knows where on a five-day toot, and then you'll get the DTs worse than ever before, until you're talking to the things crawling on the blank walls, and then...after a quiet rest, you will turn your head and say "Lord, help my poor soul," and die without your aunt or fiancée knowing you're gone...a man you knew slightly named Charles Dickens will give* *your aunt $1,000 after he finds out you've kicked the old bucket…but you'll still be dead. Even as I hear you. Even as I see you.*

"Firmly do believe— / I know—for Death who comes for me / From regions of the blest afar—" his scroll was almost touching his insteps now, as the crisp river of words ran on….

Despite her romantic fantasies about Poe, Loftus realized that he had played a big part in building up the walls of his own hell. No one twisted his arm and forced him to womanize, to drink even when he knew it knocked him on his ass, to flaunt rules and waste time mooning over his rotten luck. Poe had the brains, the looks, the charm and the connections to live a decent life, a respectable life.

But am I any better? Loftus asked herself. *Does Wags have to ask twice when it comes to Location runs? As if I didn't know that this set-up wasn't quite kosher. Like I didn't know about the fines he pays after the release of each disc, about the scams and violations of the law….*

Loftus was almost certain that she had made eye contact with Poe, just for a second. He probably thought she was just a little girl. (Funny, how she *always* liked tall men.) To hell with the credits waiting for her back in the parking lot at Time-Vac—Wagnall kept petty cash in the trunk of his glidecar—this uncertain, wonderful moment was payment enough for Loftus. Something that she had read long ago came to her, a passage from an interview with a twentieth-century woman of music and poetry named Patti Smith. This woman wore around her right wrist a bracelet engraved with the name *Rimbaud.* The fellow was a French poet, a fan (like Loftus) of Poe and this Smith woman honored Rimbaud because he and she might have been close…if only they could have met.

Smith never would have hurt Rimbaud, never would have ripped him off. She felt for him, cared for him, knew they could have been together—yet couldn't prove it. At least I am able to look at him, spend a moment in a broken fragment of time with him. I have my one chance, at least. Even though this time is forever barred to me again (damn Time-Vac and its screwing Codes). I have it.

And it was then that the idea came to her. And with it the absolution which allowed Loftus to dare something almost unthinkable— stepping up to a wooden platform in a silly costume and suddenly finding herself face-to-face with…what she had only wished before.

The reading was over. The poet rolled up his scroll of poems, bowed, and then stood graciously acknowledging the applause with regal nods of his broad-browed head.

Loftus clapped with the best of them, shouting "Bravo!" But she didn't leave with the rest of the audience a few minutes later.

* * * *

First a dim shimmer, then solid, Loftus appeared on the oval Time-Pad. Wagnall yanked her off the platform when she fully materialized.

"You get caught in the rain or something, Anabell? Where the fuck *were* you? One hour more and Mortan's replacement would've shown up and we'd all be behind bars....Are you *listening*, Loftus?

She could see the bleeding spots on Wags' lips where he'd been chewing. Not caring what Mortan the technician thought, she began shucking off the Epochal Garment right in the middle of the computer-filled room. Wagnall grabbed her now bare arm and repeated, "Just where were you for seven hours? Nobody talks for that long."

"Some people do." She wriggled into her own soyaknit shift, not bothering to brush it off, dropping the reticule before picking up her own purse and starting for the door. Mortan threw everything but the reticule into the wall incinerator hole before returning to his console. Hurriedly, he erased the record of this Time-Vacation. Wagnall shoved the little bag into his roomy jerkin pocket before following Loftus down the curving hall. He didn't notice that it was lighter than usual...lighter by the weight of a micro-recorder, to be precise. Wagnall had to run to catch up with her.

"Anabell. I'm sorry, I—"

"S'okay, Wags. I was late. Let's drop it now." She kept walking past Wagnall's glidecar to the slowly crawling sidewalk.

"Fine with me....Loftus, don't you want your fee? Anabell? Hold it." He covered the distance between them quickly. "Don't tell me it was so good you don't want your *credits*." He gave her an ear-of-corn smile, yellow and rather soft.

Anabell Loftus pretended to think it over before replying, "I guess you really had to be there."

Then she turned and walked away.

AFTERWORDS: THE "TIME-VACATION" TRILOGY

I: "BEYOND TIME AND FACE":

When I was a young child, living near Los Angeles in the early to late 1960s, my mother and her mother loved to tell me the same stories over and over again—tales of their family tree, including a spate of cousins, great-aunts and great-uncles, as well as great-grandparents, all of whom I didn't know and never did meet; plotlines from their favorite books and movies and TV shows; run-downs of all the Chicago-style Bohemian funerals they'd attended, and, in among all those oft-repeated stories, was the account of Little Girl Lost, a child who had been found after the great and terrible Hartford, Connecticut circus fire, dead, but only slightly burned, yet she remained unclaimed...as if she'd somehow made it to the circus alone that terrible day, even though she was only a very young child, and in the 1940's, children that young were unlikely to buy their own way into a circus, especially without someone missing her wherever she came from that day. Over the years, I kept thinking about that unclaimed little girl, the one who was buried under a tombstone supposedly marked "Little Miss Nobody" (or so my family claimed), and one day in the early 1980s I came up with a fantasy rationale for her solo status at that circus. At the time, I'd just graduated from college with what amounted to a rather useless degree in English and Liberal Arts, and I was beginning to try my hand at sending out fiction to magazines when I saw an ad for the "Jade Ring Contest" sponsored by a Wisconsin-based writing organization which shall remain nameless due to the anecdote which follows: The contest was open to all writers living in-state, and only required a one-year membership fee to enter (all entrants would receive their newsletter for a year)—the first prize was some cash amount I no longer recall, plus a solid jade ring. I actually already had my own jade ring, bought during a forensics trip down to Madison during my junior year, so I wasn't interested in that, but a chance to get the story printed in their newsletter did sound interesting. Well, I sent in my smallish fee plus the story "Beyond Time and Face" and needless to say, it didn't win, but one of the comments written on the manuscript was a hoot: In regard to the line "So far, all BerNae knows (all she *cares* to know, thank you) about her "day" is that it falls in the summer (hence the "cotton" dress) of the fifth decade of the twentieth century…" whoever had judged my paper wrote in the margin "Just say 1950s, okay?" Well, I hate to tell whoever was judging my effort that the 1940s *were* the fifth decade of the twentieth century. I guess s/he forgot about the '00s in there….

As it was, I was soon appalled by what these folks considered writing credits—they felt that if one got a letter to the editor published anywhere, in even the smallest hometown newspaper, that said letter was to be considered a formal writing credit, to be added to one's total of credits when submitting a story. Oh yeah? If that were the case, I could've listed *Movieline*, *The Chicago Tribune* and *Premiere* among my supposed writing credits…not that I never would've dreamed of doing that. Needless to say, I didn't re-up with those folks.

But getting back to the story, a few years later, a national magazine printed a story about the unknown little girl, revealing that she did have a name, and a background—her family had also been in the fire, and when they saw her body, no one wanted to admit it was her, perhaps trying to keep hope that she might be alive, somewhere, intact. Mystery solved at long last. But I had written two other stories in the Time-Vacation series by that time, both of which had already been published, so I still wanted to get this little tale into print, just because I still liked it, and thought it was a nicely done little bit of sf-fantasy...two years after the second-written and second-published story came out in a now defunct small press zine, I found an editor who published a digest-sized mixed-genre prose/fiction magazine who was interested in putting out something new from me, so I gave him this orphan tale. It came out in 1992, over eleven or so years after I wrote it. (And the third tale, which was written last, came out first. Go figger!)

II: "AT THE PLAYGROUND BY THE SWINGS, WITH BIG CHUCK":

Yet another historical mystery, "solved"…this one all but wrote itself; I've always been interested in Jack the Ripper (personally, I think that mentally ill Polish fellow probably did it), and I have an absolute loathing for pedophiles and perpetrators of incest, so consider this one a blend of historical soap box and wish fulfillment. This premise was so near to my heart that I even rewrote it as a non-fantasy piece, called "At Funlands by the Swings, with Big Chuck," which I published years later in a very small zine called *Red Eft*, about which I know next to nothing, save for the fact that the editor contacted Cecilia Tan over at Circlet Press, asked her for my address, and asked me if I'd like to contribute a for-copies piece of fiction to her new magazine. I sent that version in, and received my contributor's copy, and that was it. (The non-fantasy version of this tale also appears in my collection, *Homely in the Cradle, and Other Bedtime Stories*, Wildside Press, 2015).

III: "PILLAGING POE":

This story was designed to be the culmination of the Time-Vacation triad, but instead it proved to be the most mainstream sf/f/h-oriented, in that virtually all sf/f/h fans know who the heck Edgar Allan Poe was, and—I now suppose in retrospect—the plot-line was far more reader-friendly than a beautiful model being trampled and burned, or a playground perv getting his 'nads severed with a broken soda bottle. Rereading it now, it doesn't make a hell of a lot of sense as a solo story, i.e., without the other two stories to better explain the whole Time-Vacation/small child-like people situations, but hey, I was paid well for it, and it appeared in a publication inspired by my favorite series from my childhood, *The Twilight Zone Magazine*. What is not to like about that?

As far as the subject matter goes, Poe has always been one of my biggest literary influences; his life both fascinated and saddened me and, what perhaps most awed/appalled me was the fact that he didn't make much of anything during most of his admittedly self-destructive career, yet millions have been made off reprints of his short story collections, and from movies and whatnot inspired by his work. But even though he's been dead for over 160 years, he's still as current culturally as virtually any modern writer working today. Not bad for a man who lived hard and poor, and who managed to alienate the majority of his contemporaries. Personally, I just wish his life had been better…especially for a fellow cat-lover. One last thing…in February of 2014, I legally changed my first name to Ana.

As in Anabell….

ABOVE THE CAPITANS, SOUTH OF CORONA, NEAR ARROYO DEL MACHO

Windblown grass has always reminded me of hair, smoothed down with the sweeping motion of a vast, invisible hand; it has this way of rippling, like water coursing over and through the strands, so that some lie flat, while others shift and sway.

That the color of the grass was so similar to the shade of Eduard Addison's hair was a poignant reminder of him. Under these circumstances, as I sat cross-legged on the still-warm hood, letting my own hair glide over my face and shield my eyes from the past-noon glare of the sun, I wasn't surprised that these grasslands would invoke memories of the man who'd once visited them. Perhaps the same circumstances which had brought me here had also lured Eduard to pause and reflect upon the almost immeasurable vastness of this patch of protected ground—maybe even after a short time of labor here.

But, of course, I couldn't ask him if my musings about this place, about the way the wind-blown grass looked, or about so many, many other things were in any way close to what he must have been thinking on that afternoon when he came this way, all those years and years ago—

Even after the passing of more than a decade, the gay rights and UFO people were still sending sign-carriers to stand quietly before the front gates of the Federal Correctional institute in Seagorville; sweating, SPF-85 slathered and facial pierced, the trio of young men held neatly-lettered placards which read: **FREE PROFESSOR ADDISON! LIFE TERM = DEATH SENTENCE!** And **IMPRISONED FOR A CRIME OR FOR SEXUAL MISADVENTURE?**

While the duo of earnest-faced, sun-weathered women in flip-flops and sunglasses sported sandwich boards emblazoned front and back: **HOW IS WHAT HE DID DIFFERENT FROM THE AREA 51 COVER UP? And WAS WHAT ADDISON DID ANY WORSE THAN ROSWELL?**

During the years I'd spent in Europe, then in Malta and Gaza, I'd kept up with the Addison protestors, thanks to CNN's overseas coverage; while the days of the vociferous, gesticulating picketers were long past (around the time even Amnesty International lost interest in Addison's albeit self-inflicted cause), I still felt a pang of weary nostalgia as I watched the five people and their mute vigil. Pulling my rental car up close to the gate, I kept thinking of those early days, when Eduard Addison was first brought to this place, shackled and handcuffed, in that bus whose passage was all but blocked by the crush of yelling, screaming people who tried to prevent his incarceration by brute force.

That protest was cut short with a few tear gas bombs and swarms of National Guard troops armed with stun guns...but the presence of those five people, with their carefully-lettered signs and their stoical indifference to the hard-baking Texas sun, made me realize with an almost savage intensity that my former colleague's impulsive act on the equally-hot August afternoon in New Mexico twelve years ago still resonated within the American psyche, though somewhat selectively, somewhat less-stridently.

* * * *

By the time I was escorted to the small, bright room where my meeting with Addison was to take place, I'd been subjected to a pat-down search, a few indiscreet passes of a hand-held metal detector, and two different guards had examined the tape recorder I'd been given not long after I received Eduard's invitation to come visit him—and was finally granted permission to actually do so, under certain conditions. Said conditions consisted of the tape recorder and ninety-minutes-to-a-side double-length tape which I had hidden in my canvas carry-all bag. Not an outright gift—the people who "requested" that I carry it made it quite clear that it was the property of the United States Government and as such I was merely obligated to turn it on prior to my meeting with Eduard and leave it running while we spoke.

For a firm ninety minutes, Eduard and I were to have no more relatively unsupervised time together—the guard who waited outside the glass-paned steel door would make certain of that.

And under no circumstances was I to let Eduard know about the contents of my oversized purse, nor was I to rewind or even touch the cassette player—unless I wished to remain stranded in the United States for good, my passport invalidated, my ability to pursue my career as a forensic anthropologist forever hobbled.

(Not that I didn't sputter initial protests of my own; but...with those undergraduate drug charges on my record, not to mention those ostensibly-dropped resisting arrest and obstructing a police officer charges which, "might reappear on your records—you know how computer glitches can be," I realized that Eduard's innocent invitation for me to speak to him could and would affect my entire life, let alone my career.)

While I was being searched, I began to sweat, despite the double layer of antiperspirant I'd rolled under each arm; the stifling heat in the prison had been reason enough not to put a wire on me, lest it possibly short out. Trying to take my mind off what I was about to do—or what the individuals who'd contacted me days ago hoped I would be able to do—I tried to imagine what Eduard was going through, prior to his admission to our harsh-lit, table-and-two-chairs meeting-place. I doubted the passage of more than a decade could lessen the indignity of body cavity searches—regardless of Eduard's sexual orientation. I'd known him long enough to remember his acute need for privacy, both in his personal life and in his work.

How he'd managed to keep his secret *secret* in the face of such an on-going and ceaseless lack of privacy was beyond my comprehension. The Eduard Addison I'd known never would have stood for such repeated assaults on his dignity—

But, I reminded myself, *the Eduard I knew would never have purposely tainted the results of a dig...let alone stolen the artifacts themselves.*

"Wait here."

The guard steered me through the doorway of the visiting cubicle, not waiting for me to even turn around before slamming the door shut behind me.

"Eduard, what in the hell did you get yourself into?" I whispered into the windowless room. Gently, I placed the canvas bag with the tape recorder in it on the table, making sure that the microphone side was close to where Eduard would be sitting. Behind me, I heard the muffled shuffle-clink! of someone in shackles being escorted down the bare hallway, and—as I snaked one hand inside the bag to press the Record button—I asked myself, *Never mind Eduard...what the hell did I let myself fall into?*

The metal-on-metal rasp of the door opening behind me made me start; never, ever, would I be able to get used to such a sound.

"You have exactly an hour-and-a-half to spend with the visitor—after that the door is opening and you'll come with us." The guard's voice was close to mechanical. Then: "Thank you...I'll be ready to leave by then."

It was and it wasn't a voice I'd heard so many times before, back when we were both members of the West Texas State University archeology/anthropology departments...the near-lack of a Texas accent was the same, as was the precise, yet somehow casual diction, but yet, there was a resigned, almost tired undercurrent of acquiescence in those few words which made hot tears pool under my closed eyelids.

The same shuffle-clank! I'd heard through the door was now close, unfiltered by the slab of steel, as that same known/unknown voice said—just as I imagined the clear strip of the cassette tape winding past the recording heads—"It's been too long, doll...*too damned long*—"

The warmth in that voice forced me to blink back the unshed tears and turn around in my chair.

Fluorescent lighting never makes anyone truly look good under even the best circumstances...but as I let my gaze travel upward, past the rumpled, faded prison-issue pants and cotton shirt Eduard wore, up, up, toward his face, I realized the most tender incandescent lighting would not have softened the visage before me. Or masked the obvious. The cinched-in waistband of his pants was a tacit warning, but as my eyes met Eduard's, I silently prayed that he wouldn't be able to see the shock which shot through my body like a snapped whip.

Professor Eduard Addison was dying.

The last time I saw him, before that foray of his into the New Mexico hinterlands, and the trial which quickly followed, he'd been a large man, not fat, but muscular over big bones, with straight thick hair the color of long-ripened grass, a golden tan, and slightly narrow, crinkling hazel eyes. The face which hovered above my own surely couldn't have belonged to the Professor Addison I'd known.

Under the greenish-white glare of the overhead lights, his skin shone with a greasy slickness, which only accentuated the furrows in his brow and long the crescent-shaped juncture between his cheeks and his lips. Beneath his partly-unbuttoned shirt front, I could see the chest hairs there stood far away from the dark-mottled flesh below, the irregular splotches of purplish-maroon vivid against the surrounding waxy beige.

He no longer looked like the forty-one-year-old man he was; his disease had not only robbed him of his looks, but it had stolen something far less tangible…not so much his youth, but his confidence, his *élan.*

"Eduard," I finally whispered, as I half-rose to greet him. After glancing through the small square of double (triple?) pane glass in the door, and not seeing the guard's head, I leaned into Eduard's chest as he bent down to embrace me, while hugging him tight against me with arms that still shook from the remembered violation of that pat-down search I'd endured minutes earlier.

I could feel his aorta beat through his chest, a hard, steady thump-thump that reverberated through me. He smelled like soap and… something piquantly medicinal.

"When was it that we last saw each other, humm? You had to leave for that damned dig in Bosnia…I was already in custody, wasn't I?"

Eduard's large, flat hands were gently patting my back, then moved over to rest on my shoulders, as he stepped back and smiled down at me, while I sniffed and said, "I think it was that jail in Corona—some damned place. Before they transferred you to Texas, I do remember that. I tried to write, but you hadn't included me on your list of visitors and correspondents…I couldn't find anyone at the University who was on the list." Eduard let his hands slide gently, asexually, down my shoulders and finally to my hands. Grasping them, he moved over to the chair opposite mine, still squeezing my fingers as he sat down across from me.

I think he did that so I wouldn't notice the leg irons clanking against the tile floor with each step.

Giving me a wan smile which revealed his still fairly-white teeth, Eduard said, "They weren't on there because I didn't want them to go through any of *this*—" he let go of one hand to wave his own nonchalantly at the surrounding cell. "—or to see me in this state. I thought it best…to let them go on with their lives—"

"But everyone wanted to talk to you, to help," I insisted. I reached over to cover his free hand with my own. "Everyone I called while I was overseas was worried sick. And your lawyer wasn't much help—"

"Nor was I to him, I'm afraid." He smiled. "After all, there wasn't much he *could* do for me, given the circumstances of everything that happened out there that day—"

("He'll probably want to get his off his chest," the man from the government had told me in my hotel room the day before. "You're the first person he's asked to see, and considering his health, our profilers figure that this is something he needs to share with a trusted colleague before—"

"Before he drops dead in his cell, right?" I'd snapped.

"Something on that order," came the benign reply.)

"—and my admitting to enough of it to get me a room in this establishment," Eduard finished, with an unsettlingly merry wink in my direction.

Reflexively, I glanced at my wristwatch; he'd been in the room with me about four or five minutes. A lot of very tightly-coiled tape was waiting to unwind in the cassette player before him.

Harsh sunlight, golden white in color, beat down on my unprotected skin; its heat reflected against my crossed thighs and buttocks by the hood of the four-by-four, but the increased warmth did little to displace the lingering chill I carried within me, for so many miles, after my last visit to Eduard. That sterile brittle coldness of the prison, despite the ostensible warmth of the room itself.

Out here, with wind-caressed grass rippling all about me, there was precious little that didn't seem to speak of openness, of unlimited, unending warmth and sunshine, of the potential for never-ending summer and growth, and the eventual ripening of all that lived and thrived. All those natural things Eduard used to live for.

All those things he deliberately turned his back on, after that one extended jaunt to the countryside.

I pulled my upper lip between my teeth for a moment before moving my hand off Eduard's and gently patting the table top with the flat of my palm. Releasing my lip, I swallowed and said, "That's something none of us at the University could really understand—your saying as much as you did about all of this. God, Ed, your state-of-mind wasn't the most…stable. And from what we heard on TV and in the papers, you *were* legally drunk when you came back from… where you'd been that day. I mean, all the while I was working in Bosnia, trying to identify those war crime victims the peacekeeping troops found in the ravine, your case was all my team could talk about. It was macabre, really…brushing the dirt off skeletons while discussing what you'd dug up—speculating on what all of it really was and why you were being so severely punished for…doing whatever it was you *did* with it—"

Eduard rested his hand over my reflexively moving one; with that outlet stilled, the tension coursing through my body moved up to my eyelids, making them blink convulsively, but not so rapidly that he couldn't see which direction my eyes kept looking in…or figure out why. Taking his other hand off my still-curled fingers, he made a forefinger-up ssshhhing motion before his dry lips, then reached over to lift up the free end of the canvas bag, exposing the end of the cassette player. Then, just as quietly and as gently, he let the fabric drop, before saying in a voice unaffected by what he'd just verified, "I suppose the gag order on the trial made things worse, no? I heard that even the transcripts are still considered Top Secret—although one of the other prisoners here told me that a reporter for *The Advocate* was working on obtaining them through the Freedom of Information Act."

Eduard leaned back in his chair.

"What all was in the papers about me? After my arrest, I didn't get to read much, or see too many TV broadcasts—my lawyer and the government types were constantly questioning me, grilling me, what have you. Did you realize they tried sodium pentothal on me? With my tacit permission, of *course*."

"No. I trust it didn't work." I smiled thinly.

"I guess not. There was a good part of a twelve-pack in the back of my truck. Left over from the construction crew who'd been putting up that fence behind my place. I think most of them were illegals, but damned if they didn't do a good job. The foreman wanted cash, after all…but I got the better of the deal." Here he leaned toward me, his eyes mischievous. "His truck broke down and I lent him mine for the last day of the job—he forgot a post-hole digger in the back. It must have slid under one of my tarps. Along with the remains of the beer. I guess he figured the loss of the stuff was worthy my silence about the illegals. I still hadn't heard from him a week after the job was done, the day I got the call from Hathaway—"

I doubted that the people who would listen to the cassette later on would have any trouble figuring out who Hathaway was. Dr. Brian Hathaway had testified at Eduard's trial, after all. Not that he was the one who found the artifacts in the first place, out in the middle of nowhere above the Capitans, south of Corona, near Arroyo del Macho. One of Hathaway's students, some beer-swilling dirt-biking nonentity with no regard for the ecosystem, happened upon the buried items when he'd gone back to try and find his girlfriend's sorority ring. He'd been wearing it on a neck chain that had broken somewhere out there. The girl had discovered the missing chain before he did, so he hadn't the time to simply go have a duplicate of the ring made. Instead, she rented him a metal detector and insisted he go find the thing. Or else.

Thanks to it being the August dry season, the kid was able to find his tracks easily, and proceeded to scan the area for the lost ring. Probably had visions of getting laid by his grateful sorority sweetie when he heard the detector ping—

"—all excited because one of his students had called him with the news of some really 'strange' stuff buried out in the hinterlands of New Mexico. I suppose it was Hathaway's enthusiasm that made me throw my equipment in the back of my truck without really thinking this thing through—I've never told anyone this, besides my lawyer of course...for that defense of his which didn't work anyhow...but when Hathaway's call beeped through on my Call Waiting, I was on the line with one of those places where you send off your little number-coded blood samples to...the same place I'd called dozens of times over the years, my fingertips still stinging from where I'd pricked them to get the blood samples for those test cards...only, that day, the person on the other end didn't tell me I was fine, have a nice day, blah-blah...I should've known, right after I gave her my latest code number, just from the *sound* of her voice as she said, 'Let me see...number 54-42-41-84-25 slash 85...I'm—' and she didn't have to get to the 'sorry' for me to know.

"It's the response they never show on those commercials...oh, I had the possibility in the back of my mind ever since I began testing myself, but always, you keep thinking, if you're careful enough to test yourself every time, what can go wrong in between? And if you're just plain careful, or think you're being careful....

"Anyhow, she managed to get out the rest, you know, 'sorry, but your test indicated you're HIV positive; we suggest that you go to your doctor—' and all the rest of that happy horseshit, but by then, I heard the Call Waiting sound and just thanked the woman and switched over to the other call.

"I barely had time to say 'hello' before Hathaway began rambling on and on about something a student of his located, out in the middle of just about *no*where in south-eastern New Mexico. About twenty or so crow-flies miles from Roswell. I remember, when he mentioned Roswell, I was staring out my living room window, out at my truck parked near the mailbox, and for some reason, I imagined trussed-up little aliens stored under my tarp, all lined up in the truck bed. Just waiting there, all mummified and grayish, under that big paint-splattered tarp....

"God knows why I'd think *that*...I suppose it was just having learned that I'd soon be in a similar condition, I mean...the aliens and Roswell part I could understand, it's virtually Pavlovian by now, but somehow, I couldn't top picturing dead little bodies, stacked like cordwood in my truck. Even after Hathaway made it clear that his boy found something metallic, buried underground. Not bodies.

Artifacts. Something…strange enough for the kid to have had the good sense to rebury after brushing the top layer of soil off of it."

Eduard paused to run one palm over his left cheek, the sound of his slight stubble too loud in the close, still room. Lowering his gaze to the tabletop, and the canvas bag, he finally went on, "Remember when that farmer in England found that cache of Roman treasure? When he was looking for a hammer or screwdriver or whatnot out in his field? Can you imagine how he must've felt, after hauling out the first few handfuls of coins and jewelry? Besides the rush of touching all that gold and silver, can you really put yourself in his place? Just think, knowing that no one has seen you find any of this, that it's just you and the money and the baubles—

"England has that law, remember, about reporting all buried treasure? I'm sure that was foremost in his mind—"

Eduard let out a dry, almost hacking bark of a laugh, before waving both hands in my face and saying, "Places like *this* wouldn't exist if everyone paid heed to the laws of the land…oh, you're right, of *course*, he knew the law, and obeyed it…but *think*. He stashed enough of it in his trunk to almost fill the damned thing—I saw the footage of his vehicle. Now, knowing what he did, that all of this rightfully belonged to the Crown, why do you suppose he started to take so much out of that hole? When there was no one around to see him take it out in the first place? What really would've stopped him from going to the black market? Or just hoarding it?

"Don't you think—" he leaned closer to me, eyes growing larger, "that the farmer was swept up in the sheer euphoria of his find? That was a pretty deep hole full of loot…and it *had* to be old. Can you just *imagine* it, doll? For those minutes he spent pawing through the dirt, pulling out handful after handful of precious metals, *he* was the sole owner. He *knew*, and he *had* it. Because it was so obvious that whoever had buried the things wasn't about to come back for them. Every coin, every spoon of it, every last ring and bracelet was *his* now.

"And can you imagine the let-down, when the realization sunk in? That it couldn't really be his after all…not unless he wanted to spend his whole life constantly waiting for that invisible tap on the shoulder, and the crisp order, 'Please come with us, Sir.' But that realization still couldn't negate the initial moment of discovery. Those minutes when it *was* all his."

He leaned back resting his head in the hammock of his inter-twined fingers, and closed his eyes. "Hathaway wanted me to come right away, which I then thought a blessing. Something to take my mind off other things. It was only about an hour's drive from my place near Farwell...only took me a matter of minutes to load my sifting screen, tools and work gloves into the truck then I was off down the highway.

"Once I was about twenty miles from my trailer, mental autopilot kicked in, and my mind began replaying all the Area 51 and alien au-topsy shows I'd ever seen on TV. For the life of me, I couldn't figure out how anything could've been overlooked by the government for over sixty-some years after the initial crash of the ship or balloon or crash dummies or whatever it was that landed. So I figured, whatever the dirt-biking little punk found *had* to be either more modern, like some air-crash debris or whatever, or more ancient, perhaps an ex-ample of early metal working. Or something the Spaniards lost, from the Conquest.

"Hathaway had told me to use my cellular phone once I passed the upper arm of the Arroyo del Macho, a few miles south of Ramon on Highway 285, because the exact spot wasn't on any map. He told me to take State Highway 42 west about twelve miles or so, then it was more or less get out of the truck and walk, which is what I did, phone in hand. Hathaway had done the same—his truck was parked not far from mine.

"I couldn't yet see either Hathaway or his student, but I knew I was sorry I hadn't taken the time to change out of my dress boots into something easier to walk in. Lots of desert willows, cottonwood, some mesquite, but still a lonely spot of land...undulating ground, but for some reason it wasn't soothing, like rolling hillocks sometimes can be. As I followed Hathaway's directions—south, then west past this or that rise—I started to feel this...sort of cold apathy toward the place. Like, I had no business here, which was insane; I'd spent virtually my whole life in the southwest, including some years in New Mexico while getting my BA...about the only extended period I'd been gone was when you and I and Hathaway joined that dig in the Russian Steppe region, remember, those ice tombs—"

I nodded my remembrance of the dig; neither of us were pre-pared for the remarkably cold summers in Siberia (Hathaway had been raised in Pennsylvania, so he was far less affected), nor were we emotionally ready for what we found in the sunken wooden tomb our group unearthed—it was a child's tomb. The boy couldn't have been more than eight-years-old when he died. I could still quite easily picture the small knife and wooden animal his people had placed near him in his tomb…small, bright objects, made shiny in the weak sunlight by the residual coating of ice which covered their surfaces. The same ice which made the boy's bones appear somewhat gelid, almost *soft*—

"—but that's close to how I felt that afternoon, despite the sunshine beating through my shirt and jeans…like I had back in Siberia. Knowing that that was *not* my place, even for the time I spent there. Feeling wholly alien in that land, not knowing the place or even wanting to…once I saw the two men waiting for me, I thought that sensation of not belonging would abate, but it didn't. Switching off my phone, I shoved it into my back pocket and put on that smiley-face I'd wear when facing my freshman archeology students each fall.

"Well, I could see right off that the lummox hadn't done much damage at all to the site; he'd started to dig down maybe two, three inches, until whatever he'd been using hit the surface of the artifact. Then he'd used his hands to fritter away the top dusting of soil over the upper region of the first item, just enough to reveal the lettering on it. He was a big kid, like a dressed-out side-of-beef, but I suppose not quite as addle-pated as he looked. Terrible haircut, though, half-scalped, with this fringe around the bottom. Anyhow, Mr. Hockey-Hair tells me, 'I didn't think that there was regular writing' or something equally erudite, before I hunkered down next to Hathaway to get a better look in the hole.

"The kid was right…it wasn't 'regular writing.' Not hieroglyphs, cuneiform, not Greco-Roman print…yet, it was so much like all of them to make the hairs stand at attention on my arms. I could tell from Hathaway's expression that he was thinking more or less what I was thinking…strange lettering, not quite Egyptian, but not unlike it either, silvery-bright metal, a smoothly-rounded shape—this thing was too much like the descriptions of the debris from the Roswell crash to be anything but *more* of it.

"Hathaway had the presence of mind to shoo the kid off; told him he'd done the right thing to show us this find, and that I was an expert in artifacts of 'this time period'…the kid had come out that way to find something else, so he decided to keep on looking for it, once Hathaway kept lying through his teeth and assured him that we'd be sure to put his name on the little card next to the artifact once it was safely on display in the Roswell Museum and Art Center.

"We puttered around the site for a while until the punk got back on his bike and roared off toward the Arroyo…neither of us wanted him watching the actual excavation. Or knowing how much more might be in there.

"Before unearthing anything else, we sifted through the soil that had already been disturbed, but the kid had been careful. No loose debris, nothing broken off…Hathaway staked out a small square around the hole, then divided the square into quadrants. I was in charge of mapping out the find, drawing the position of each piece as it was revealed. I'd finish each drawing while Hathaway sifted the dirt from each successive layer of soil…but the artifacts were quite intact. Judging from the actual crash site—which Hathaway reminded me had occurred somewhat closer to Corona than to Rowell *per se*, something *I* hadn't realized before—these items would be beyond degradation. I'd heard the witnesses who'd touched other artifacts say that the metal couldn't be burned or torn, despite it being so delicately thin it could be balled up in the palm of one hand.

"Whoever buried them had certainly chosen the perfect spot—no heavy traffic, no major flooding, just dry, arid soul. Something else occurred to both of us as we continued the excavation—whoever placed the items in the ground had been digging by hand. The ultimate depth of the hole was 10½ inches by 8¼ inches in circular width, the way you start digging in the soil from the middle outward, scratching deeper and deeper until you have an earthen bowl before you. Just enough of an indentation in the earth to hide a few small things.

No matter how brilliant the sunlight, its daily length, its seasonal accumulation, the earth below is ultimately cold. No matter where you go. Sometimes, you must dig deep to reach that frigid core…other times, the cold is close beneath each step one takes over ostensibly warm, sunlit ground.

The waving, rippling grassland before me suddenly belied that waiting chilliness; surely such expanses of pale gold could only speak the silent language of radiant plentitude, of living, light-feeding warmth. But men like Eduard, men and women who pry away the earth's turfed flesh from the underlying musculature of soil and sand and rocky bone... they know the truth of the earth.

After many an earthen autopsy, men like Eduard Addison have a certain feeling for what is normal, and to be expected...and what lies dormant, cancer-like, within the soil's tight-packed torso, that which is not of the body, and does not wholly belong---

"It took us only two hours or so to unearth all that was there...I wish I still had the drawings I made of the things, although I suspect they'll eventually be declassified. If that reporter from *The Advocate* lives a very long, long life, and," he added with a grin, "doesn't do something foolish, like I did.

"The uppermost artifact resembled a small pocket kerchief. Not much bigger when it was flattened than...oh, a cheap paper plate. But it could be crumpled...not that either of us did it on purpose, but when it was lifted off the things under it, it went somewhat limp. While I was brushing it off it draped around my other hand, and, reflexively, I wadded it up—remembering what one witness said about being able to ball up the material. I'll never forget how beautiful it was as it unfolded in the afternoon sunlight...the way the sun shone on the raised lettering, and the smooth places between. I copied what it said on there too, as best I could. The lettering was...not really *bas relief*, but appeared to be. Somewhat like holographic printing, but not that, either. It didn't actually change images or shapes so much as *recede*...which is why I'm not quite sure what I copied down was right or not. It was like spectacle blur, when you take out contact lenses and put on your glasses—things couldn't come into focus fast enough."

I noticed for the first time that Eduard wasn't wearing his glasses, nor did his eyes seem to be covered with contacts—perhaps there wasn't much he wanted to see all that clearly anymore.

"So...we set the round flat artifact aside and studied the next one. It seemed to be some sort of decoration, either personal or meant to hang from something else. The hole in the top was unmistakable—just think, whoever created the thing, no matter where he or she came from, solved the problem of how to hang something from a cord or a chain the same way we would, just make a hole in the top and slide the chain or whatever through it. The artifact was 2⅝ inches long, an inch and three sixteenth inches wide, and ⅛ plus a fraction thick. I was the one who did the measuring…it was cold when initially unearthed, but the more I handled it, the more tactile it became…not actually much warmer, but…I suppose I'd have to say flesh-like. The surface was burnished, a silvery grayish metal with fleeting hints of washed-out indigo, but there was such an appealing texture to it. Like running your fingers over the flesh of someone's inner arm, between the elbow and the wrist…just incredibly pleasant, almost sensual. I don't know which side of it was supposed to be the front… there was something scratched into both surfaces.

"Not imprinted, or carved, mind you, but literally scratched in and over it, very imperfect, very…hurried. As if whoever had done it was working quickly, or with unwieldy implements. The scratches were quite faint, nearly wrinkle-like against the surfaces of the item; they were so sloppy and imprecise that it was difficult to reproduce them. The…writing, if that's what you'd want to call it, was somewhat similar to the printed lettering on the round limp artifact, in the way that bad handwriting can be marginally linked to the typed or printed word of a given language. I copied a few of the groupings of symbols, but as I said, they were so shakily done…I never did take the time to polish those drawings.

"I suppose I began to actually think about these…belongings, as I was drawing the next one; the may've-been-solid sphere-like thing with the deep indentations running along its outermost circumference. It was a mottled bluish silver, like sterling silver that's been handled too much between cleanings…and I don't know if it was the pattern of the discoloration, or the smallness of the thing, how well it fit within my cupped palm, but a notion just struck me, out under that deepening gold sun, and wouldn't let my brain *be*; whoever or whatever had owned this thing had touched it. A lot. Had perhaps placed it close to its body, in a pocket or a pouch or perhaps even inside its garment. It just had that worn look, that extra level of softness around the indentations in the surface. And considering that it wasn't that heavy—according to the scale Hathaway brought, it was only thirty grams—I wondered if it might be hollow. And if something could be placed *inside* of it. Or had been sealed for good within.

"And the saddest thing was, there was no common point of human reference, of human need or want or understandable emotion by which I could even begin to guess the purpose, or the *significance*, of that small silvery sphere. With humans, even ancient humans, guessing the meaning of a heretofore unknown artifact can be done with a modicum of certainty—after all, a small figure of a human is a literal representation of a person. Be it a doll, or a fertility symbol, or a religious icon. You can at least start with the shape, the nature of the representation then move outward, to place it within a context—find it by a small skeleton, and it's a toy. Unearth it near a grain bin, a grinding stone, or farming implements, and it could be a fertility totem. Discover it close to an altar, perhaps near the bones of sacrifices, animals or people, and it becomes a holy relic.

"People, at least, haven't changed so radically that they have stopped sharing certain needs, certain modes of inbred behavior… perhaps we have to guess about certain human artifacts, but we can be reasonably sure that our guesses *might* be right, or might later be proved right. Pending other excavations, other discoveries which will link the first artifact to the second, and so on.

"But this…*thing*—it was a complete enigma. No way of ever *ever* knowing what it might represent. A sphere can be so many things, in so many different contexts…and we'd found it in a hole, dug quickly in the earth.

"The last of the artifacts was perhaps the saddest thing of all, to me at least. Hathaway was all but dancing about by then, sometimes hugging himself with glee, like the kid who finds the whole filled Easter basket during the egg hunt and doesn't want to tell anyone else. Anyway, that last…item…was resting in the very nadir of the pit. As if whoever put it there wanted it to stay hidden the longest. Or…just happened to throw it in first, although considering how neatly stacked everything was, perhaps it *was* meant to go on the bottom. Why? Who knows? The sides of the hole sloped down to a rather sharp point.…

"But for whatever reason it was at the bottom, the last artifact seemed incomplete…as if it was broken off of something else—there was a raw, semi-iridescent side to it. It was a many-pointed object, a bit like a burr, only with rounded tips. It could've been part of anything, I suppose...but that raw end bothered me. Had it been broken on purpose? By accident? It was heavy, almost as heavy as the sphere, despite being half again as small...so I assumed it was solid. In itself, it was virtually complete-looking, as far as small roundish things with multiple quarter-inch long protrusions can appear to be complete. But that flattish end niggled at me.

"The rest of whatever it was obviously wasn't in the hole...and if the kid's metal detector didn't pick it up during the many passes he made over this spot, chances were whatever it was wasn't here. So...either the being who buried these artifacts no longer had the rest of the thing, or he or she or it had removed it from the larger (or whatever-sized) item for some reason. Like taking a hood ornament off a vintage car, perhaps. Or copping off a piece of rock from a castle wall, as some archeologists are wont to do on the sly.

"It was just such a...sentient thing to do, holding on to a broken-off piece of something or other. And then putting it—hiding it really—in the ground, along with other unbroken things.

"While I was trying to sketch that last object, I remembered what that cache of treasure that farmer found in England looked like once it was all cleaned and polished and arranged by category in the museums...although it had been buried in a wooden chest, so it had probably been packed to some degree before being buries, I couldn't help but think about what sort of stuff was resting in the top layers of the chest, and what was below. The farmer found some money first then the personal items....I remembered how one bracelet had a woman's name on it. Latin for 'Julia.' Not that this Julia did the burying of it—could've been a servant, or someone who knew her, or of her, or...someone who just remembered her.

"I realize now that my state of mind was maudlin because of what I'd found out over the phone before Hathaway called...but at the time, memories of the English treasure, and the one item with a real person's name on it, just kept coming and coming in my mind. And another thought: What would you bury if you *had* to? What would be so sacred to you, so utterly important, that you couldn't consider letting anyone else see it, or have it, or just plain *know* about it? I didn't need to ask how I'd bury it—I'd use the same hands which had unearthed those once-hidden things.

"And as I sat with that smallest artifact balanced on my knee, while trying to draw it on a pad of paper balanced on my other knee, it hit me—Hathaway telling me how this place was fairly close to the Roswell crash site, oh not the exact spot, but considering that there was supposedly debris scattered for miles on that ranch, plus those little aliens if the more detailed accounts are to be believed, and some people claimed that at least one alien was walking around. How do we know that the being fell to Earth right where it was found? Or stayed in that exact spot after the crash? There was just no way *to* know really…that rancher came upon the site long after the actual crash itself. If at least *one* being was alive, right after the craft touched down, there's no way to know exactly what it did, or where it might've wandered…all I knew was that something had deliberately buried these artifacts. They weren't wedged in the ground as a result of blunt force impact. Hastily-executed, but still an action conducted with forethought. With intent. With…*reason*."

Eduard took a deep breath;

"For whatever reason it had, the being who buried these things did not want anyone or anything to see them…probably if it was captured or were to die. Everything was small enough to conceal even on a tiny body—that they were buried indicated that the being doing it had somehow decided that they would not be in its possession much longer. And none of them seemed to be overtly important—at least nothing, aside from maybe the little knobby thing, appeared to form a part of something mechanical, something like a weapon, or a means of transport or communication.

"Remember, darling, the kerchiefs those Japanese Kamikaze wore? The square of silk with messages from their loved ones written on them? I'm not saying that *that* was what we unearthed that day, but…how can anyone say it wasn't?

"Touching those items somehow made me feel like a grave robber, like someone who plunders for the sake of profit. Like despite my education and my expertise, my experience and all my care and concern for the artifacts I'd dug up in the past, I was simply doing something very, very wrong. These things could never have any true meaning, not in the sense any human artifact could in our modern eyes. There was no point of cultural reference, no…Rosetta Stone, if you will. Even if there *had* been spaceship debris collected back in '46, it wouldn't say enough about these beings to put these artifacts into any usable frame of reference…all these things would ever be were mere curiosities, something to stare at, speculate about, and all the while, their true meaning would *never* be fathomed. And what if that meaning was something sacred? Or something just too damn *personal* to be speculated about?

"And as Hathaway bounded about the dig, all silly grins and self-congratulatory jabbering, I felt myself grow sick and cold inside… this was a circus to him. He'd have his damned fifteen minutes of fame, his name splashed all over the TV and Internet and papers and…and mine would be there, too. Hathaway was going on and on about how 'we' would do this and say that once we brought this stuff to the attention of the world, and while he was rambling on, I heard this sound…it took a while to realize it was me. Crying.

"The soil we'd been digging through had some rocks in it, not big ones, but if you picked up a couple and placed them in a bandana, then wound the loose ends tight…Hathaway was heading for his truck, pulled-up stakes in hand, when I whomped him on the back of the head. Hard enough to draw blood, but by then, the sight of blood didn't bother me anymore, not like it had when I used to prick my finger for those HIV tests…I made sure he was breathing before I left him, and rolled him onto his side in case he vomited.

"I unwound the bandanna, dumped out the rocks, and scooped up the artifacts…I suppose I should've grabbed my sketch pad too, but like I said, my mind wasn't really right…and then I walked back to my truck. When I hit Highway 285, I could see some dark green vehicles driving cross-country toward the spot where we'd been digging…little hard shiny trucks, gleaming in the sunlight, like beetle backs. That's about the last thing I do clearly recall, aside from opening can after can of beer—I'd grabbed them from the back of the truck bed before heading out.…

"Supposedly, I didn't come back to the trailer until the next morning—not that I had the time to do much more than enter it and start to unbutton my shirt before the door was battered in by all those cops and military types. I vaguely recall the door slamming down flat, like *whoosh!*—then the place filling with people. I do recall that I had cuffs on me when they led me out of there. But I was too damned hung-over to really care at that point."

Eduard crossed his arms over his chest, and after glancing over at my hidden recorder, said, "Needless to add, Hathaway's cell phone conversation had been monitored all along…but it wasn't until that damned punk told some of his friends about what he'd found and they told *their* friends, and pretty soon the military heard of it, that everything hit the fan. They arrived on the scene in time to find Hathaway starting to come to…I'd high-tailed it away long before he was able to tell them that he'd had company. Apparently the kid neglected to mention *me* to his friends. Hathaway didn't know immediately what sort of truck I had…and my driver's license and registration wasn't much help since I'd bought the damned thing only a couple of weeks before, second-hand. Initially, they'd headed back to the border, to my trailer then realized that I'd driven to parts unknown. With the goodies."

Knowing that I'd be penalized if I didn't ask, even though I had no real desire to put Eduard through this yet again, I ventured, "And you can't remember what happened to the artifacts? Or where you… left them?

Eduard smiled at that, then leaned close and said in a loud stage whisper, "'*Left*' my ass, dear. I buried them. What else do you think happened? I couldn't very well burn them, or dismantle them, could I? The problem is, I have no idea where the hell I buried them. I logged over 500 miles on my odometer, and I know I was in the wilderness for about eight hours or more…who knows how fast or how far I went? But…does it really matter where they are? I couldn't have taken them, really…they were never mine to have."

Rhetorically, I blurted out, "But Eduard…so much might've been learned from them anyhow, their composition, their age—"

Smiling sadly, Eduard grasped both of my hands in his and as he gave them a gentle, affectionate squeeze, said, "Dear heart, all that was necessary to know about them was known. Their owner didn't want anyone to see them, to know of them. Their owner is dead. What more *is* there for anyone to know? If there was any meaning, any significance inherent in them, it had to have been too personal for anyone but the owner to comprehend."

"But Eduard…" I began, my voice faltering. All he did was lift up my hands, dry kiss them in turn, then say, "I suppose you're wondering why I finally did ask you to come. The doctors here tell me that this disease is spreading through me…the AZT and all that other crap can only work for so long. I've made out a will and you're my executor—"

"I don't think I want to hear this," I whispered.

"My family has more or less disowned me…not that I have much worth after Hathaway's lawsuit against me for wrongful assault and everything else. In the eyes of the government, I'm a traitor, a thief of government property…in society's view, I'm either that damned faggot who stole the might've-been-alien-artifacts, or I'm the ultimate poster boy for Gay Rights Oppression. But I still have a few things in storage, books and whatnot. Some of them might even be yours; you lent me some back before all this happened—"

"You mean Hathaway actually left you something after the civil suit? I heard he was able to retire off you," I tried to joke.

"Pretty much…but there were some things that even he didn't want, things no one had much use for. But they'll be yours. Okay? Don't cry, doll…it had nothing to do with you. It really had nothing to do with anything."

* * * *

That was the last time anyone from the University saw him alive. Three days later Eduard managed to procure a plastic bag from a fellow inmate. I suppose he didn't want to wait for the inevitable, the grossly-painful and ugly, to happen. Or…perhaps he didn't want to risk telling his story again, lest some small clue work its way into the narrative.

I handed over the tape to the men who came back to my motel room before I had a chance to check out that afternoon. They thanked me for my cooperation and for my service to my country.

If they found anything of value on the tape, it would surprise me,.

But…after Eduard's will was processed, and his meager belongings given to the pitifully few people actually named in the document (which included a couple of fellow inmates), I was left with a box of books, some of which were indeed mine. But the slip of paper left in the book about the Siberian Ice Tombs, the book which included

photographs of me, Hathaway and Eduard in the middle section…
that was never mine. I always loathed those little sticky notes, the
squares of yellow paper Eduard used to use by the gross when working, teaching, or driving. I'd ridden in enough jeeps and land rovers
with him to remember his habit of jotting down each road he went
down, just in case we were to get lost.

He'd shoved the folded over bit of paper deep inside the book,
far deeper than a regular bookmark might go. So deep it didn't fall
out when the book was paged through, or even shook open. As I'm
sure the Government must've done. How they missed the thing, I
don't know. Perhaps they did see it, and discounted it as a mere scrap
of paper. After all, he spent so little time alone that morning. The
penciled marks on it were quite faint, and seemingly random. Just a
series of numbers:

54

42

41

40 84

25/85

120 65

104 54

39 102

562 18

64/87

193 36

25/85

84 46

54 285

42

But I'd seen that first line—no, rather *heard* that first row of numbers, that day in the small room with Eduard. The number of his HIV
test…or so I had thought. But the slashed numbers made me think of
something else…not so much something to do with blood *per se*, but
instead with lines which often had reminded me of veins and arteries.

The red and blue lines on a highway map….

The route suggested by the numbers Eduard had jotted down that
day was a wild, twisting one, but with a definite, even searchable,

geographic region. I doubted that anyone had found the sheet before, or had understood it at all if they had seen it—not if they were still asking the help of civilians for clues about the artifacts.

Or maybe they didn't think he had the time to actually hide anything during the brief minutes Eduard was alone in his trailer, before the door—and his world—was bashed in. But he'd done it anyhow.

Whether or not he did or didn't remember doing it.

Stretching out for miles before me, the Kiowa National Grasslands are, perhaps, a far more fitting place for those alien remains than the site their owner chose out of necessity. At least Eduard had time, and a much better knowledge of the area, on his side…not to mention that post-hole digger which had been left in his truck.

True, I had no way of knowing for certain if this was, indeed, the place he'd chosen on his drunken flight, but it was a place he might have chosen, being a protected area, being something of a sacred place.

As I leaned back against the windshield of my four-by-four, I decided that it really didn't matter after all. The man who jotted down that yellow rectangle's worth of numbers was dead. The sheet was now buried in the soil of the grasslands before me, as deep as my fingers would allow.

That done, there was nothing more for anyone to know.

AFTERWORD

For me, this is a most delicate piece, perhaps a bit more lyrical than usual when it comes to my science fiction output. Being something of a pack rat myself, I do know the sentimental hold one's possessions can have on a person, and considering the inherent lack of space within any sort of space-going craft (be it a shuttle or the space station, et al.), I was struck by the notion that if aliens *did* come here, chances are they might have some sort of comfort objects in their possession, be they talismans, personal artifacts, or items to which we humans can place no known value. And if said aliens happened to crash, and knew that death was imminent, might they not wish to protect their possessions in whatever way might be available to them under such dire circumstances?

We are what we cherish; I know that for me, the thought of strangers pawing through my things—my books, my accumulated debris and cast-offs, my hundreds of photos of my house and my cats, even my clothes—is unbearable. No one will understand why I kept this or that, and unless whoever gets my things once I'm dead thinks they can eBay or donate them away, most of my life (as represented by what I have held onto over the years) will end up in a waste Management Dumpster, before getting ditched at the county dump. I find it heartbreaking…and no doubt any sort of non-human who is able to get from where they live to where we live might feel the same way about his/her stuff. So…if this being had the opportunity to hide it away from uncomprehending eyes, I suspect he/she would take it.

IN A FINE AND VERDANT PLACE

Diffuse sunlight streamed through the boughs of the Douglas firs, Ponderosa pines and Sitka spruce which surrounded Theodore and the tall, thin man who looked a little bit like Roy Rogers, as the pair of men walked across a gently-rolling field covered with brambles and damp weeds.

Not too long ago, Theodore wouldn't have dreamed that he'd wind up in a place as fine or verdant as this; after over a decade spent in the muggy confines of the place he'd just...*left*, with only an endless vista of bare walls and polished linoleum, interspersed with steel bars and steel doors to look at (not to mention the hot scrub lands *beyond* the gates), Theodore considered himself lucky, and blessed, to simply *be* here...regardless of what he'd done to both almost miss and finally gain this sanctuary.

The man who so reminded Theodore of his childhood idol Roy Rogers was speaking, telling Theodore that he *should* consider himself fortunate to be here:

"Yesssirrreee, this is one nice place to stomp around in, son... most folks like you only *dream* 'bout a spot as nice as this. Heard tell you had to *earn* this tract...was a real big thing you done, tellin' them lawmen what they wanted to know. Or most of it, anyhow," the tall man concluded without obvious rancor; as he tilted the brim of his blue mesh baseball cap slightly, against the glare of the mist-hazed sun, he gave Theodore a tobacco-stained smile which almost reached his crinkled eyes.

Theodore found himself nibbling on his left thumb-nail; quickly he jerked it out of his mouth and wiped off the thumb on the leg of his blue dungarees. While he'd felt slightly betrayed when he discovered that he'd made it *here* attired in his familiar apricot tee over a grey sweatshirt, as if he really *hadn't* been forgiven, redeemed, at least his hair was regrown, down to his double cowlick. And he was wearing a decent pair of hiking boots, not the slightly *déclassé* jogging shoes

or the green rubber thongs issued to him along with the rest of his…
uniform in that other place.

The other man kept walking along, past grape shrubs and over rotting logs, and Theodore did his best to follow him, loping along, head tilted slightly forward, blue eyes trained close to the ground, in case he tripped on anything. It was easy to do that, in a place like this; why, when Theodore had spent time in Washington, he'd almost sprawled forward many a time, especially when carrying—

Theodore stopped next to a brightly-flowering rhododendron, panting and reflexively patting his pockets for a cigarette. As if sensing that his charge was no longer tagging along after him, the man in the mesh cap stopped, turned around, and asked, "You winded, Ted—"

"Theodore," Theodore snapped before he remembered where he was, and how, up until a few weeks ago, he'd had little chance of getting here, and smiled apologetically.

"You winded, Theodore?" his tall guide asked again, still as friendly as ever.

"I'm just not used to all this…*space*, that's all. I-I haven't walked around like this in a long tuh-time," he finished, unconsciously chewing on a fingernail, angry with himself for stuttering again, for slipping back into his old nervous habit. All of those bad things about him were supposed to be gone, or so he'd thought, before he took that walk down to Old Sparky; his confessions were supposed to have *absolved* him, allowed him to seek forgiveness for what the *entity* within him had done to those girls.

It had taken so long for him to even *come* to that point; to feel the need to seek forgiveness, to finally admit remorse. Yet here he was, snapping at the man who looked like his hero, the cowboy star Theodore had once hoped would adopt him and give him a pony, back when Theodore was still Teddy…and before he became Ted.

But he was *Theodore* now, and forgiven, which was all that mattered. What was done was done, over, and today he was in this fine and verdant place, walking out *free* under the pale sun set in a hazy blue-grey sky, far away from Florida's harsh, unrelenting sunshine, and everything was lush and fertile under his feet, with deep rich smells and thousands of tiny, busy sounds to delight him. He'd almost believed toward the end that he would *never* come to this place, would never see another bird or another white-topped mountain.

But he was here. And according to the tall man who looked vaguely like Roy Rogers, this whole spread was Theodore's, to be in *forever*. One moment, he'd been strapped down in Old Sparky, his body jolted with a minute-long surge of power, and the next... he was cool, and walking, with this tall man in the mesh cap and the plaid hunting shirt keeping pace with him, telling Theodore that he'd *arrived*, that he'd *made* it.

Briefly, Theodore wondered if he'd started confessing *sooner*, owned up to what was *done* years before his time on the Row was obviously up, if he might not have earned himself an even *better* place, perhaps one with *people* in it. Someone to *talk* to, who used better English than his guide, most certainly—

He was doing it again, Being...*Ted*. Theodore paused, frowning, this time next to a maple, and leaned against the rough greyish-greenish mossed bark. As he waited for the mesh-capped man to notice his absence, Theodore inhaled deeply, taking in the mingled odors of dampness, mildew, the slightly-acidic soil, and the tangy smell of rotting vegetation...plus a faint undercurrent of something *else*, something fertile and *ripe* beyond mere foliage decomposition. Theodore's light blue eyes grew dark-flecked, turning to a deeper, more thunderous hue, as he tentatively sniffed again, his brows furrowing. He *knew* that odor...from an astonishing number of personal observations, in a place not unlike this one at all—

"Got to toughen you up son," his guide laughed, as he loped back to where Theodore stood. Reaching over to grab the other man's arm, Theodore asked, "Are there many animals here? Do they...k-kill things, leave them...."

Smiling broadly, the other man said, "Why *sure*...lots of critters 'round here. Bears, coyotes, rabbits, rodents of *all* kinds...you name 'em, we got 'em here. And they got to eat," the man reminded Theodore gently, before leading him forward once more, "They got to eat...."

Theodore nodded numbly, as he tried to keep pace with the older man, wondering if his companion had mentioned the bears first because of their sheer size, or because they were plentiful here. Not that anything could *happen* to Theodore, now, but still— "They don't attack, do they? The bears? They keep to themselves?"

The guide paused by a rotted log, a big grin spreading across his weathered face. "They're just a mighty fine disposal system, is all," the man replied, with a wink in Theodore's direction. *Déjà vu* washed over Theodore upon hearing those words, until he realized that they were his own, or close enough. Out of the corner of his eye, Theodore saw something shaggy and lean running off to what he supposed was the east, carrying a longish, branch-thick yellow-brown thing in its jaws. An object which had knobbed ends—

"Excuse me, but isn't there a place where I can...not to think that I don't *like* this place, but...I know it sounds self-centered, but is there a *house* anywhere on this land? A bed? A—" Theodore almost uttered the one word he thought he'd *never* repeat in a place such as this...a *cell*?

The older man laughed, until his head leaned back so far his mesh baseball cap almost slid off his thin darkish hair. "Oh you are a *caution*, boy? He finally said, wiping tears of mirth out of the corners of his crinkly eyes, before saying, "That would only *spoil* things...look around, just *look* at this place. Now what would you want a *house* for? It don't get dark here, and you don't need no more sleep, and you sure don't need food...that's all taken *care* of, son—"

For a reason he couldn't figure out, Theodore found himself thinking of the Benjamini ficus tree he'd once taken from a greenhouse; just lifted the eight-foot tree and carried it to his car, where he shoved it in through the sunroof, then drove off with five feet of unpaid-for Benjamini swaying gaily in the breeze...and he'd put the tree in his apartment, in the confines of its four walls—

Confines. A place where certain smells and certain small, gristle-crunching sounds did not penetrate. Theodore *did* love the outdoors, but mostly as seen from the confines of his VW...or for brief times when he came out to see how the animals were doing, how they were *disposing* of—

Theodore looked around him, at the gently rolling land covered with a riot of green, in all shapes and textures, and at the ring of mountains beyond...mountains he knew he could not cross, for hadn't the tall weathered man told him that this was *his* place, the spot where he was expected to *stay*? Running his thin, tapered fingers through his slightly curly hair, Theodore's eyes scanned the ground, the acidic loam covered so thickly with green, growing things, almost *too* thickly, as if someone had carefully spread fertilizer over—

Just at the outer limits of his peripheral vision in his left eye, Theodore thought he saw something long and snake-like resting in a moldy depression under a rhododendron; a trailing, jointed thing of tapering yellow-brown....

"—spread is *yours*, plenty of room for you to roam around in, with no guar—no man to tell you where to go or when to do it. Just you, and the trees, and the critters, forever—"

The faint breeze blew a wind-borne puff-topped seed past Theodore's face, and as it drifted past, Theodore caught a sun-enhanced glimpse of something adhering to the parachuted seed.

A long, single hair, reddish-brown in the weak sunlight.

"—'course, you almost missed out on all of this, but the Old Man upstairs, well, he *has* to forgive sinners when repentance is shown, and you showed it, son...so relax, enjoy yourself here. You've *earned* it, son—"

Theodore managed to stammer, "Buh-but I nuh-need a place to rest, to just sit *down*, and I don't see any—"

"Oh son, there's *plenty* of places to rest here," the older man said with an "aw shucks" sigh, as he pointed to a nearby fallen log, whose shadow almost concealed the dull gleam of something rounded and hollow-eyed at its base.

Theodore said nothing, but shook his head, thinking that he had been *forgiven*, that he'd *paid*, that he'd *confessed* (well, *almost* everything), so he shouldn't be *seeing* these...things. Not anymore, not after reaching *this* place.

"He can't do this to me....He can't," Theodore whined, but his guide only said, "'Course *He* can't...but that don't mean that you've been forgiven *entirely*—"

Theodore stopped, but he reached out and grabbed the tall man's arm before the latter could walk away from him again.

"Th-the families of the...the guh-guh-girls...the c-c-can't—"

The man who looked just a little bit like Roy Rogers shook his head, smiling at Theodore, before saying, "*No*, no...not to say that they all *have* forgiven you, but it ain't *that*. See, son, when you done what you did, you...well, someone *else* was a tad...*peeved* with you."

Theodore clutched the man's arm, thinking out loud, "Not my mother, she forgave me, I heard her…she said I was her—"

This time the man laughed in earnest, stained teeth glinting behind pulled-back lips. Gently shaking off Theodore's grasping hand, the man began to walk away, trotting fast now, as if not caring whether Theodore was left behind this time or not, but he said over his shoulder, "Son, ain't your *momma* you should've worried about offending, she loves you. But when you left them girls, out exposed and alone, or hid in the dirt, you got the *Mother* mad, and the earth's a lady who don't forgive too easily."

Theodore started to run after the man, protesting, "No, *no*…not *here…I can't* stay *here*—" until a sharp pain in his shoe made him stop short.

Sitting down on a large exposed boulder, Theodore quickly unlaced his right boot then shook out the foreign object which had been rubbing against his foot, all the while glancing up every couple of seconds, following the rapid progress of his plaid-shirted guide… until the man vanished from Theodore's view, as he walked forward and down, into a gully of some sort, and Theodore could see him no more, and realized that he was now *alone* here.

Only then did Theodore look down at the ground, to see what he had shaken out of his boot.

A single, pink-rooted, human tooth.

In memory of Ted Bundy's victims 1969-1978

Author's Note: The background information in the above story (including the Roy Rogers fantasy and the Benjamini ficus tree incident) was gleaned from Stephen O. Michaud and Hugh Aynesworth's 1983 book The Only Living Witness: A True Account of Homicidal Insanity, *as well as a January 23 1989 AP article about the impending execution and confessions of serial killer Theodore Robert Bundy (1946-1989).*

AFTERWORD

During the mid-to late-1970's, when Ted Bundy was killing his way across the country, I was in high school (until 1976) and also attended college (until 1980). Like many of his eventual victims, I had the admittedly bad habit of taking rides from strangers. I briefly wore my (always long) hair in a middle part, and I was roughly the same height and weight as several of his victims. As were many girls and young women I knew in high school and college—one college class-mate in particular could've been a twin to at least one of Bundy's victims.

So for a whole generation of young American woman, Ted Bun-dy was like a one-man Third Reich; what Hitler and his sycophants were to Jews, Gypsies and other minorities, Ted Bundy was to young women in the 1970's, and very early eighties. Once he'd finally been caught in Florida, and people began to put together the enormity of his crime spree, the realization that—but for geography alone—he very well may have killed virtually any young woman who remotely fit his chosen victim profile was a sobering one.

And if any killer deserved the death penalty, it was Bundy; when he was finally fried back in 1989, I celebrated. But prior to his death, I had read some of the books about his crime spree; one in particular, *The Only Living Witness*, detailed one of Bundy's childhood fanta-sies, including his desire to be adopted by Roy Rogers. For some reason, that image stuck with me, and after Bundy was executed, fol-lowing his macabre attempt to buy additional time by offering to tell the authorities more details about his crimes—as long as his execu-tion date was changed, I started to wonder what sort of Hell Bundy was sent to after his death. This story is the result of my musings on the subject. I thought the tooth in the shoe was a nice touch.

An awful lot of editors out there didn't agree with my vision of Bundy's final "reward"—this one took years to sell.

My only regret is, this version of hell might have been too good for him after all....

THE REDEMPTION OF POP GEE

When we hit Dodge County, Deaner decided to drive me crazy again. He'd run through his "This ain't happenin' in the *real* world, only like in a *'nuther* one" theory back in Ohio, but kept on bringing it up every hundred miles or so, because his only other option was to sit there and think about what was trying to flag down my car by just sort of stumbling into the front grille and chewing metal, and *that* was much, too much for Deaner. But after I told him about Pop Gee, adding right off that if he didn't like my plan he could go back to riding thumb, he just sat there quiet for a few counties, not saying anything, not spouting any new theories, until we reached Dodge County—and after he was lipping off for a quarter hour or so, I realized that ole Deaner didn't cotton to me wanting to drop by Pop Gee's place to pick him up. Pop Gee, not Deaner. I already had the latter fruit-loop sitting in my passenger seat, whining in that scream-cracked voice of his:

"It's like what my Ma had when she was carryin' me, she couldn't like stop eatin' coffee grounds, right outta the pot. Just scoop 'em out and cram 'em in her mouth, and they'd be shiftin' through her fingers into the sink and getting' all over her maternity dresses—seen the stains on 'em myself, I did, when she was carryin' my sister Doreen—and she'd just gulp 'em down w'out chewin' and Dad'd just about sick up on the spot. He called the doc the first time she done it and *he* tole Dad that it was something called 'pica,' and when Dad asked if it was catchin' the doc laughed and tole Dad that it wasn't *catchin'*…just *unnatural*. It was like a *cravin'*…'cause she was missin' somethin' from her body.

"S'pose that 'counts for why there was this big gap 'tween me and my next sister, Judy…*any*how, she only had this cravin' with me, not with none of my sisters. And later on, when Dad tole me about it, I gets to thinkin'—maybe me bein' a *boy* took somethin' different outta her that the girls didn't. And when this crap all hit the fan, I got to thinkin' again—maybe people ain't been getting' somethin' they need real bad on 'count of all them diet folks takin' this and that outta our diets. Like eggs, and all them fats that are s'posed to be bad for us...and all them actors and actresses on the TV, tellin' folks how *they* cut this and that outta their diets—"

"They had actors and actresses on the tube telling people they should eat beef," I reminded him, but that was when Deaner really socked her to me:

"You ever her 'bout how eatin' certain things takes stuff *away* from your body? Does. I read about it, don't know where, but I did. One vitamin robs another one from your body, checks and balances time, like.

"Heck, maybe it was eatin' all that beef that got us into this mess. Too much of one thing, not 'nuff of another...until the body got to *cravin'* you-know-what. Only this time, people didn't need no coffee grounds or soft clay, like the doc tole my Dad some women down South eat. Or starch...Dad said the doc tole him they eat that too. See, this 'pica' can mean a cravin' for *anything*...who knows, like maybe some folks had it all along, 'cause they wasn't eatin' the right foods...like maybe they lived alone, with no one to watch over 'em, tell 'em to eat right...and *maybe*, like if they was living *really* alone, with like no one likely to drop in anytime soon, they could satisfy this *cravin'* of theirs, with no one to know—"

I made a little throat-clearing noise even though there wasn't anything in my throat to clear out, but Deaner didn't take the hint.

"—and with no one watchin' they can chow down on *anything*, long as it satisfies this deep down *cravin'* they got...like Dad said, even watchin' Ma pack her mouth full of coffee grounds was pretty awful...'magine what someone chowin' down on...oh, like a *liver*, or maybe a raw *heart* that don't come from no butcher-shop must look like—"

I didn't care if Deaner was undergoing retro-shock over what he'd seen in that damn bait shop in Pittsburgh, I couldn't let him get by with a swipe at Pop Gee. "...or maybe a raw *heart* that don't come..." my gonads. I mean, Pop Gee told me himself that he was fixing to cook that thing just as soon as he got done in the shed. Deaner hadn't known Pop Gee. Hearing tales and seeing those Norman Bates movies didn't cut the mustard.

I stopped the car, parking slant-wise on the soft shoulder to put Deaner off balance. Physically, he'd already lost all the BB's in his upstairs ammo bag when I'd picked him up. Up ahead, there were lurching shadows coming toward us that weren't no deer getting high on fermented berries. Drunken deer don't wear clothes…and they usually don't hunger for meat. Fresh, juicy, Deaner-meat. On the hoof.

Deaner let out this little *waaaeeep* noise and tried to tunnel his butt into the bucket seat, but I wasn't buying it this time. I leaned over and opened his door, yelling, "Yo! Sushi-heads! Come an' *get it!*" Deaner grabbed my arm and shoved his face into mine, until I could almost see myself in the oily sheen of sweat greasing his nose. His breath was all Slim Jims and stale bile right in my face as he moaned, "You wouldn't *do* that, Glen…you *couldn't*…."

Slamming the door and settling back in my seat, I crossed my arms, asking, "Why friggin' not? My wagon. My Slim Jims you been eating. And you've been infuriating the living shit out of me since before Ohio. *So-why-not?*"

The first of the sushi-heads had reached my station wagon. Two long-haired ones and a bald one who still wore a mesh baseball cap advertising Jump River Rose's Deer Farm. Fellow who wore it had cheeks and a nose covered with blood that didn't come from no deer, but his teeth were clean, from the saliva sheeting over them in anticipation of getting dirty all over again, so to speak. Same thing went for the teeth in the long-haired sushis. One had tits, one didn't but out this way folks used to run to being plump, so trying to sex them wasn't any use.

Their palms left translucent greasy smears on the windows, the windshield, and Deaner *waaeeeped* again, slinking down in the seat some more. When the bald one butted his head against Deaner's door, it was kinda neat how his cap stayed on.

As Deaner keened beside me, I saw the rest of the pack shamble on down Highway 73, homing in on our smell. Had to be smell that attracted them to us 'cookers. 'Cause, aside from the blood on their faces, they sure didn't look any different than us, nor us from them.

"Gl-len, you—you are *sicko!* Worse'n that fisherman in the shop! Like…like…you're in *cahoots* with 'em. With them *sushi-heads*."

Mr. Jump River Rose baseball cap bent the radio antenna, getting the pointed wire stuck in his skin. In the failing light, I saw Karo-sluggish blood chug out in a snail-trail on his forearm, until the new arrivals—couple of kids no higher than the part of the car door where the window started, plus something in an Oktoberfest USA T-shirt—started snuffling around Mr. Mesh Cap, making sick dog sounds in the gathering twilight. Deaner was starting to stink worse than what was happening outside the car; either he'd pissed himself or was taking a shower in his own sweat. When the long-haired one with the boobies paused in the middle of a deep chomp on the bald guy's arm, and smashed its face up against the windshield, silly-putty beige skin flattening and spreading across the glass, Deaner gave up.

"Hokay, ho*kay*, no more 'bout your buddy…just start the car, 'kay, Glen? I give up…uncle, you putz, *uncle*—"

I think I rolled over the feet of a couple of the sushi-heads when I pulled away from the shoulder, spraying gravel high enough to hit the smeared windows. At any rate, only a couple of them tried to follow us, dragging chunks of the fat bald guy behind them.

* * * *

Deaner was a good little 'cooker until we reached Washburn County. Then, when he thought I'd forgotten what happened a few miles back, he began to ramble softly:

"Ever think 'bout how them scientists get to messin' with this or that virus, puttin' it into lab animals and the like, and once in a while them animal activists come in and take the animals, and like *maybe*, some cat or dog was carryin' a virus, and in *animals* it didn't cause no trouble, but in *humans*—you know, somethin' like how AIDS and the feline leukemia just sorta sprang up together, until a person gets to *wonderin'*…or it coulda been somethin' in like the *groundwater*, and you know yourself how some people don't take a sip of water even if their lives depended on it. Once, I had me this girlfriend, she believed she didn't have to drink no water, 'cause she took a lot of showers. Said it went into her through her pores. Or, like, maybe somethin' bad got put in the ground, like…oh, maybe was *buried*, like a dead person, and he—*it* was already infected, but nobody like *knew*. Or they knew but didn't like *know* what it really wa—"

I didn't wait to stop the car this time; with one hand on the wheel, I reached over and opened Deaner's door. The rush of cool air pouring into the wagon was soon tainted by the scare-sweat pouring off Deaner.

"Glen! *Noooo*—"

"No more picking on Pop Gee!" I bellowed over Deaner's whimpers, letting the car do crazy snakes and serpents all over the road. Highway 51 was empty anyhow, but Deaner got jostled up pretty good. To my left, the white-on-green sign said we had five more miles to go until we reached Pop Gee's place. Give or take. Good distance for a nice moonlight stroll…maybe if Deaner was lucky, he'd find himself some nice little sushi-head cutie. Stop for a bite along the soft shoulder.

"Glen, you are *whacked*! We're already in the shit up to our nuts, and you want for us to dive in head first!" My arm was starting to hurt from straining against the pull of his arm, as Deaner tried to shut the door. I went from seventy to fifty miles per, my arm still Heil Hitler rigid, holding out his door. Deaner was bawling, "—shoulda *seen* them fishermen, man they were sushi-chewin'-*crazy*. Like *you*. Hookin' lips and playin' *games* with what they was eatin'…I seen 'em use a *fish scaler* on a 'cooker. While he was yellin' and squirmin'—"

"And you were busy pickin' them off the fella, savin' his butt, huh?" I slowed down to forty, bumping along the shoulder.

"That ain't the point!" Deaner shrieked, finally chopping me in the elbow and slamming his door shut. Panting, he burbled, "It wouldn't have done no *good*, me comin' outta hidin' to help! Was just lucky they didn't nose me out…but what I hadda see was *worse* than dyin'…or tryin' to play hero. I just wanted some *bait*, that's all…wanted to catch me some fish. Then them fishermen barged in, thought they was 'cookers, till they—oh, they was *sick*! And all *I* wanted was some *bait*—"

The "bait" Deaner had been fishing for in that shop was flat and green and banded into thousand dollar-a-stack wads, and it was all fitted into my glove compartment. When I'd picked up Deaner, he would've let me fillet his mother if she'd been along, anything to escape those sushi-heads in the hip boots and fish hooks hats. He'd

insisted that I take his money…"all I wanted was some *bait*—"…
yeah, Deaner, when pigs fly. Or the sushi-heads pass up 'cookers.

One thing Deaner never did explain—since when does a man
need a Saturday night special just to buy some bait? But if he was
dumb enough to not put bullets in the thing, I suppose he deserved the
little floor show he got when them sushi-heads took over the store.

"—and it was just lucky I seen that fire door 'fore they did—'else
I'd be sushi-poop by now…like them lady friends of that *friend* of
yours. Like *you're* gonna be, once you—"

"Get real. Pop Gee's been dead couple-three years. 'Fore all this
shit hit the rotating blades. I *told* you that—hey, lay off the Slim Jims.
Mine."

"'*Mine*'…Cripes, I oughtta check in the back of this wagon, see
if you have some poles and hooks stashed—"

I braked to a head-snapping stop, and pointed to the back of the
wagon—which was loaded with whatever food I'd been able to lay
hands on, plus ammo from that sporting goods store in Sandusky—
yelling, "Chicken-shit inspect all you want, hero—and don't tell me
'nother one about '*bait*.' Not unless you was fixin' to use an awful
big hook."

Deaner was contrite after that, and kept his lip zipped until we hit
Plainfield a couple of minutes later. And when he opened his mouth
again, it wasn't to let in on his latest theory. In the darkness of the car,
Deaner's face took on an oily luminescence, like he'd been living
on whale blubber or something, and his voice was as hollow as the
moans of the sushi-heads we'd left in the last country as he asked,
"Glen…how come you wanna…pick up Pop Gee? Related to him
or something? I mean, whatever you got in mind, it's…like no *use*.
'Cause he's like kinda past *knowin'* anything—"

I shook the last Slim Jim out of the canister and tore the wrapper
open with my teeth, like a sushi-head peeling fingers. If I'd have gone
sushi, I could've inflicted a whole lot of hurtin' on Deaner. Turning
off toward the cemetery, I said around my half-chewed beef stick,
"Was just the way he kept saving his money, for that trip around the
world…like they'd spring him any day…."

* * * *

Pop Gee was already a fixture at the Central State Hospital in Waupan when I came to work there as a physical therapist in '75. He did carpentry work, a little masonry, even helped out as an attendant. The staff trusted the old guy. Hard-core nutsos weren't allowed to be attendants. ('Course, "hard-core nutso" wasn't an official term, any more than sushi-head is an official phrase for people who like their meat uncooked, and *moving*...but when you see a panhandler suddenly decide he don't exactly want the coin in someone's palm, just the palm, sushi-head is a whole lot better a term than plain old cannibal....Least the humor in the former name keeps a body's mind sharp.) Why, even Pop's lawyer liked him.

Anyhow, three years later Pop Gee was transferred down to the Mendota Mental Health Institute, down in Madison, the state capitol, on 'count of how he was starting to slip. Got weak, and addle-paddled. Not that he was a bean-brain to begin with, though.

That judge who tried him, old man Gollmar, he hit it right on the nose. Said Pop Gee was crazy...like a fox. Had to be, to have done what he did for so long. Oh, sure, he was crazy—anyone who shopped Hearse and Graveyard for his fine, handcrafted furnishings had to be off the beam—but Pop Gee wasn't dumb. Not at all.

Why, the year before I signed on at Waupan, Pop Gee read up on the law; found out that under Wisconsin law, those found insane at the time of a crime of their doing were not responsible—and therefore should be set free. But Judge Gollmar realized that Pop Gee was a simple soul at heart (ultimate Momma's boy, so to speak), and he declined to let the old guy out. Assuring Pop Gee that he'd find the outside world sorta frustrating, the judge said for the record, "people might not be very good to him." That was an *understatement* if I ever heard one.

After Pop Gee died, I read how his old neighbors had applauded when his house burned down, 'cause the fire department accidentally-on-purpose got to the fire real late. Like they couldn't find the place. I s'pose it was the talk of putting a museum in his farmhouse that set folks off. A third cousin of mine claimed that he and some drinking buddies had a beer party in the house when I was still in diapers, and he said no ghosts came over to nip them in the asses.

The law had already burned all of Pop Gee's skin masks, chairs, belts, and lampshades, so it wasn't like the house was a threat, or a continuing blasphemy. Them women was dead, blessed and buried (at least most of them were), and Pop Gee wasn't a hurting kind of man.

The Pop Gee I knew at Central State was a gentle old soul, all bleached out and stooped. Hard to believe he could be-head and gut out that lady, let alone hang her up by the heels in his shed. I saw the picture in the judge's book. I seen deer dressed out and hung more savagely than what Pop Gee did. I mean, there was no *fire* in what he done. No whiff of blood sport. And he believed with all his heart that he was doing God's work, and his Momma's will.

She was the planter of the sick seed; I don't feel that it's the fault of the poison fruit when another hand plants it. Wasn't his fault he loved his Momma, kept her room preserved like a shut-up shadow box stashed in a hall closet.

Like he told me once, he just hated to think of those women rotting quiet down in the earth, all the live parts of them turning to slush and worm-feed. Guess that's why he kept that box of pussies in his house, and I don't mean barn-kittens. Puzzled the hell out of the law when they saw how he'd painted one with gold paint, but Pop Gee was only being practical. Said that one was going bad, and he didn't want to lose it. For a psycho, Pop Gee was sensible.

Or the way he went "dear" hunting for the last time. Picked the opening day of the hunting season, deer of course. So no one noticed him toting a rifle around. And how he went about grave-robbing, going to three different counties so no one got suspicious. Didn't know what had gone down until they found the costumes and bone chairs in the house.

Sure, Pop Gee was nuts, a danger (maybe), and an all-around poor tourist attraction for the Dairy State, but…well, I liked the old geezer. He was so sincere about wanting to travel the world when he got out. You ask me, they've let out worse nuts than Pop Gee after they served so little time it was a slap in the victim's faces. Like that Singleton geek in California. To me, what Pop Gee did was *sick*, but not *cruel*…least not to the victims. The families, they hurt regardless if the dead person is tortured to death or just shot clean and fast like a big squirrel. S'pose it was Pop Gee's *creativity* that turned folks off…that and his dietary habits. Oh, Pop denied it to the law, but he didn't put that last woman's heart in the pot just 'cause it looked good there. And what he did with the supposed "deer liver" is already rural legend. Was a pity he went before whatever it was made people be sushi-heads came on the scene.

Trouble with Pop Gee was, he'd spent so much time with his Momma before she died slow from strokes, he just got used to company of her sort…but I've never met a man less down and out mean. He didn't kill for the fun of it, never. And when I read that Pop Gee died of respiratory failure in Mendota, I think I was the only person in the state to shed a tear. He'd wanted so much to go around the world….

* * * *

Once I got the car into the cemetery, driving over the fallen metal gate, I placated Deaner enough to make him unfreeze and climb out of the wagon, shovel in hand. I'd latched onto the fact that he'd seen all the *Psycho* films before that fateful day when one of the participants at the Iran-Contra hearings started saying, "Faaawn, *Faaawn*," and the world's first known sushi-head feast took place, on TV no less, which meant there was no *way* the government could hush the whole mess up, and with everything so flummoxed up in the world, they weren't exactly holding guided tours of the mock-up of the Bates house anymore—and Deaner couldn't resist the thought of "meeting" the guy whom Anthony Perkins had been playing, once I explained to him that he wasn't very likely to run into Tony Perkins. Anyhow, Pop Gee was the *real thing*. Even if he was dead.

Not that I was actually planning to open the coffin; I'd heard that Pop Gee wasn't autopsied, and I wasn't sure if they'd bothered to embalm him, either. Way it was, they planted him before dawn, between his Momma and his brother Henry. If they'd put up a stone, vandals might've carted it off, so there was nothing but sod between the other two stones. Not even so much as a flower. If I'd only come to visit, I'd have snatched a plastic-flowered cross off some grave, but if I was going to grant Pop Gee's last wish, the last thing he needed was anything, even a scuzzy funeral spray, over the coffin.

I'd left my headlights on high beam when we got out of the car (I prayed that no sushi-head could get it together enough to drive— but looking for fresh food seemed to preoccupy them to the point of oblivion), and there was a full moon out, so I figured we could see any sushi-heads coming, in case any of them were either dumb or desperate enough to stick around in a place where the meat was not only stale, but spoiled.

The fresh dirt had a sweet-stale smell in the cool autumn night; it made soft leather plopping sounds where it landed on the turf. Like bats beating their wings after getting caught between the wall-boards of an old house. Deaner's face was pure melted lard; his greasy hair flopped down on his forehead, the limp curls bobbing in time with his shoveling arms. I was hyper, ready to whack off the nearest sushi-head that lolled by, and as the shovel hit smooth pay-dirt below, I asked myself if maybe Deaner wasn't right. I mean, there we were, on the lam in a stolen station wagon, with hordes of sushi-head groupies following us, wanting nothing more than to just get a taste of their idols...and we were out in the open, exposed to the quivering nostrils of any passing sushi-head, digging up a *dead* guy, a seventy-seven-year-old corpse. And all because I'd nurtured this cockamamie idea of giving Pop Gee his trip around the world. Purely symbolic all the way, but I'd thought he would've appreciated it. And the irony of the world's current situation would've tickled him, I was sure. Maybe not, but after seeing those senators do some shredding of their own during those hearings, I sure as hell thought it was a knee-slapper. And the car I'd "found" had a luggage rack on top. Plenty big enough for a coffin.

At first I thought it was Dean's shovel that was making that funny *scratching* noise, but when he stopped to rest when I did, well...there was enough light for me to see the stick-stone-*scared* look in his eyes, just like I'm sure he saw it in mine. And there wasn't enough wind to make the brittle leaves on the surrounding trees rub against each other, either. But...if that corn-ball theory of Deaner's about something funny being in the groundwater was right, or maybe the virus one—

Since I'd known him, I jumped down into the fresh-dug hole with the limp fingers of worm bodies poking out into the air, and began to dig out more dirt on the side of the coffin...where the latches were. Up above me, Deaner was *waaaeeep*ing again, and believe you *me*, I'd just as soon have listened to another dozen of his theories, rather than listen to him making that noise.

Down close to the casket, I heard those scrabbling sounds coming from inside, *under* the lid, and then I had my hands on the latches… and suddenly *I* was the one with the stiffie-shakes. Deaner stopped making baby noises long enough to ask, "Well, you gonna spring him or not…he's *your friend*—"

And he was, at that; I may have been born and raised in Wisconsin, but I considered Pop Gee to be my friend, no matter what he did. I s'pose it was like admitting that Charlie Manson wasn't a half bad musician even after all that "Helter Skelter" and "dead-actress-with-the-live-baby-in-her-belly" mess. I mean…the bad may be a part of a person, but that doesn't have to mean that the person is through and through evil. Not everyone, not all the time. That's why I made this silly promise to myself after the sushi-head thing happened, after the world went nuts; I'd haul Pop Gee around the world, like he'd wanted. Didn't Sir Walter Raleigh's daughter blow smoke into his sliced-off head, 'cause he's liked his pipe? Sometimes, we living just have to do for our dead, because they were human, and some of us still are. Just because maybe four-fifths of the population has gone sushi-head, certain things like friendship and respect don't go away. Not unless we let them. And Pop Gee'd always been Pop Gee to me, at least in my heart…only I hadn't expected him to be waiting up for me.

There was plenty of moonlight coming into that hole to shine on Pop Gee when I got that lid open. Couple-three years down there and he still looked more or less the same, 'cept for the fine whitish lines, like webbing on his face. Sorta like when they open up a saint's coffin, or how they keep dead dictators in glass boxes. Still made my heart stop a beat, though. The lining on the lid was shredded; his nails had moved out of the skin a tad. But when Pop Gee saw me, he smiled, like it didn't matter that he'd been waiting a spell, like he'd just been sharpening his nails, for the heck of it. Didn't say much, though. Never did in life.

Topside, Deaner must've forgot all about the fishermen sushi-heads 'cause he was babbling something about this being "better'n Tony Perkins in a *dress*—" which meant I had to haul Pop Gee out of there by myself. He was small, and skinny, so it wasn't hard, but still Deaner could've offered a hand. Good thing neither of us had a pen or paper handy; the way Deaner was raving I was afraid he was going to ask for an autograph, or something dumb like that. Deaner wasn't scared shitless anymore, it was like his own grandpa had just woke up after a nap. But I can't criticize him; I was happy, too, happier than I'd ever been in my life—so happy, in fact, that I got careless....

I didn't know we were surrounded until I felt the hand grab my left arm, and even then Deaner was so out of it he didn't *waaaeeep* or anything. There were only three sushi-heads, but they smelled chow and we was *it*—and they stood between us and the car. And I'd left my shovel in the hole, in that vacated coffin. Grabbing Deaner's shovel, I did a melon-job on the head of the biggest one, forgetting that the little ones can grab for your kneecaps like that. Deaner's jeans went shiny dark and with that ammonia smell filling my nose, I kept swinging out in blind panic, sweat leaking into my eyes, blurring what little vision was available to me...until I realized I was swinging at empty space. Deaner quit *waaaeeep*ing, and in the quiet I heard a new sound. That of gnawing...and then I heard the muffled plod-plod-plod of something running away into the black-on-black darkness of the surrounding trees. With the headlights unblocked, I could see everything...and then I was the one smiling in the moonlight.

It was Pop Gee. He'd found the sushi-head I'd popped, and, well...he wasn't doing anything that millions of people hadn't already seen after that senator at the hearings went sushi-head, but he was the first resurrected sushi-head I'd ever seen, if you could rightly call him that. The guy Pop Gee was...working on was dead, which might've made Pop Gee one of us, a 'cooker, someone who ate it after it was dead, but the dead sushi-head wasn't exactly chipped beef on toast either—

I don't know if maybe Pop Gee had been one of the first people to be infected with this sushi-head virus, like Deaner had been speculating all along, or if he'd caught it in the groundwater like the rest of the 'heads, but whatever had went down, that old man was happy. And I didn't know if Pop Gee had been buried dead only to become infected later on, or if he gave the infection to the world, and was lying around waiting for his personal resurrection, but one thing was clear—according to Deaner, the other sushi-heads had taken off before Pop Gee noticed their buddy on the ground. Like they'd seen themselves in a mirror and didn't like what they'd seen. Or like they'd realized that they'd finally met *their* enemy, the grand-daddy of all sushi-heads....

Whatever the reason those sushi-heads took off at the sight of Pop Gee, it didn't concern me or Deaner...for Pop Gee ate no *fresh* meat, which meant a lot to a couple of slaughter bulls like me and Deaner....

* * * *

Pop Gee doesn't take up much room in the front seat; he fits real nice between me and Deaner. And he doesn't mind listening to Deaner's latest theories, either; Pop Gee never did talk much. But he doesn't have to. All he has to do is peer out the window at any approaching sushi-heads, and they take off running, 'cept for the ones I run over, 'cause Pop Gee has to eat too, or at least he seems to want to, and he doesn't care for Slim Jims.

I think I like Deaner's latest theory the best:

"Maybe this is like Pop Gee's time of redemption...like he's making up for what he did *then* by doin' what he's doin' *now*, for us 'cookers. To make up for what he done to them lady 'cookers. See, way I figger it, they ain't got much use up in heaven or down in the other place for a man of Pop's 'siderable *talent*, but what with things bein' the way they are with the sushi-heads, Pop Gee's finally paying his debt to society, ain't that right, Pop?"

And Pop Gee doesn't way much, but sometimes when Deaner isn't looking he gives me this little wink. I think Pop Gee's enjoying his time of redemption, even if we haven't been all the way around the world yet. Like I said before, we were friends. And if he doesn't tell Deaner that I wasn't exactly a physical therapist at Central State, I'll consider my favor to him repaid in full.

But I don't think I gotta worry 'bout that.

Pop Gee never did talk much anyway....

AUTHOR'S NOTE:

The biographical information about Ed Gein was gleaned from Judge Robert Gollmar's book Ed Gein: America's Most Bizarre Mass Murderer, *1981, and from newspaper articles printed at the time of Gein's death. One detail of his life behind hospital walls in the invention of the author; while his*

conversations with fellow prisoners are unknown, it is known
that Gein never admitted to being a cannibal while in captiv-
ity.

AFTERWORD

For those not in the know, the state of Wisconsin just loves to name things as the State This-or-That…we have official state muffins, dirt, birds, etc., et al. and so on-and-on-and-on. A legislative boondoggle, if you ask me, with a lot of tax payer money wasted on a lot of meaningless debate and voting on the latest State Whatever. But if Wisconsin was to ever get around to choosing an official State Serial Killer, it would have to be a close contest between Ed Gein and Jeffery Dahmer—but since old Ed has already inspired multiple horror-fiction and film characters like Norman Bates, Buffalo Bill (aka Jamie Gumb) and Leatherface, I think he'd win that legislative would-be debate. I actually saw photos of the body of his final victim, field dressed and headless like a deer, and as horrid as they were, they lacked the hideousness of the "work" of serial killers like BTK or just about any other sexual serial killer you can think of. They reminded me of the deer one of my down-the-street neighbors used to hang on a tree in their side yard come November. I think Gein's upbringing played such a major role in his eventual crimes, he has to be thought of somewhat differently than other killers. The guy was isolated, and lonely, and socially inept. What he did was evil, but he was so bland and so subtly vacuous, he's somehow easier to stomach, at least for me. The thought of making him an avenging zombie killer was just too irresistible for me not to write this….

THE GEMÜTLICHKEIT ESCAPE

"Bud, who are 'Adi' and 'Fuchsl'?" Maxine was holding Rolf's latest "Fröhliche Weihnachten" card between her pink-nailed thumb and forefinger, gingerly, as if she feared that the pair of deer pictured on the Christmas card might start nibbling her nail-polish. I took the card from her and slipped it back in the cardboard "tree" over the mantle, saying, "Friends of a friend. You wouldn't know them—"

"Naturally I don't 'know' about them, you won't tell me anything!" She glowered at me, hands on fleshy hips, while I settled down in my recliner and turned on the vibrating fingers. As I lit my pipe, my wife waddled back to the mantle, to scrutinize Rolf's card.

"What's '*Froo*-litchie Wee-*naken*' mean *anyway*?"

I had to chuckle at her wariness. Not long after Maxine and I were hitched, once Uncle Sam turned me loose in '46, she fell under Senator McCarthy's spell, seeing Communists and the Red Menace every place but the toilet, and I'm sure she looked twice before daring to flush. And what with all the talk of skinheads and Neo-Nazis on the television, it wasn't surprising that she viewed a simple German-made Christmas card as Nazi propaganda intended to poison my addled old brain.

"'Merry Christmas,' I think. 'Weihnachten' is Christmas, that much I know."

"Humph. Could use subtitles, at least," Maxine grumped, as she headed for the kitchen; in the doorway she paused, adding, "*I'd* want to put that bad business behind me, if I was you. It's not *healthy*, writing to an ex-*Nazi*—"

That did it. I shut off the magic fingers, and put down my pipe. Noticing my warning signs, Maxine leaned defensively against the doorjamb as I said, "Maxine, Rolf was *Wehrmacht*. Regular Army. You're thinking of the *Totenkopfverbände* we saw on *Shoah*. *They* were lumped in with the *Waffen SS* and ran the death camps. Rolf wasn't one of *them*. I spent two years with the man, dammit. He wasn't what you think he was, you didn't even know the man, so stop thinking whatever *small* thing you were thinking and get back to your baking. I think I smell cookies burning."

Maxine's lips fluttered, but she turned and went into the kitchen without further comment. Once I heard her open the oven, I got up and walked to the mantle, then took down Rolf's card. Inside, he had taped a recent photo of himself, a washed-out sunlit pose.

Tilting my head back to peer through my trifocals, I studied his smiling face. Rolf was wide and soft now, with dentures the color and size of Chicklets. His glasses had pale plastic frames, but the picture was too small for me to see if his lenses were bisected with tell-tale lines…like mine were. But he looked well, and happy. For that, I felt glad, as I glanced down at the gracefully scripted lines under the German-language greeting inside.

Rolf's English, good when I knew him, had improved. Considering the unusual nature of his schooling, Rolf was a good pupil. When the Allies liberated the camp, Rolf spoke English almost as fluently as the prisoners under his command.

Maxine was muttering in the kitchen, something about "not learning your lesson" tuning out her blather, I re-read Rolf's words, the ones which caused Maxine to worry so much.

> "Bud—Hope all is well with you and yours. As usual, I find myself thinking of Adi and Fuchsl, and of the Book (of course!). If only I'd had it when I knew them! Things might have turned out differently, no? Still I wonder if I had taken it to him in '45…but that is a futile thought, is it not? Well, Bud, we can always wish and wonder, right?
>
> To Gemütlichkeit, old friend
> Rolf

"…'we can always wish and wonder'…" Rolf knew me where I lived, all right. And the rub was, I could never explain any of it to Maxine, the kids, to *anyone*. For none of *us* had understood it when it happened; not me, not Rolf, not the rest of the guys in our camp. And I could only listen to Maxine's taunts, and see the silent accusation in her eyes, helpless and locked in by silence which I could not explain…*would* not explain.

Yet, there's a need in me to tell it all, even if it is only to a thick pad of yellow legal paper. Perhaps these words will go the way of the

Book, perhaps not. For the magic will never come again, as it did in Stalag 20-C somewhere in the middle of what is now East Germany. After all those days of riding in that stinking boxcar shortly after my capture, I didn't care where the camp was, as long as it was on solid ground. *Unmoving* ground.

And true, the ground didn't move. Nor did the double rows of wire fences around us, or the sixteen guard towers, or the twenty long low shed-like barracks into which we were herded. Blanket, bowl and spoon in hand, we were grouped by rank and nationality, our bodies lice-free and fresh-scalded in the white-tile delousing station, our clothes gassed and finally rid of crawling pests. Nothing moved much, not even the guards who kept the lines of incoming prisoners shuffling, shuffling forward, past the sergeant who wrote our names and serial numbers in a battered ledger, and past the other sergeant who handed us new dog-tags. Iron, with soda-cracker perforations down the middle. We put on our tags and shuffled along, past the already settled prisoners who cheered our arrival, into our barracks.

Nothing moved in there, either. The place was big, at least 350 feet long, bisected with a big wash room, and filled with rows of bunks two high, two wide and two long, intended for double occupancy per bed. No fire danced in the coal stove, and only weak grimy sunlight filtered through the barrack's few windows. Past those windows, beyond the nearby double fences, distant pines and firs stood silent and motionless.

At first, the rest of the lieutenants just sat, dazed, on their bunks, or on the few chairs around the plank table. I was pacing the room, looking into every dusty corner, feeling the interior of every rust-ringed sink (cold water only, that time of the day), peering out the windows, checking the flimsy wooden latch on the building's only door. After spending so much time crumpled in that boxcar, I needed to move around without feeling the floor move under me.

"Sit down, Berg, you're making me dizzy." That was Court, Lieutenant John Court, of the first bomber squadron to run a daylight raid on a German city, Wilhelmshaven, back in January. A few months later, still in 1943, he was part of another air raid, but this time things went wrong. His plane was downed and Lt. Court became P.O.W. Court. I suspected that that was the first time the good lieutenant was bested by anyone, at anything—and he wasn't about to let anyone forget it. Least of all the people who captured him, or the other prisoners unlucky enough to be stuck in the camp with him.

I stopped pacing, and faced Court. Six days of living with him in a reeking, chilly boxcar; six days of eating and sleeping and shitting in an old helmet with him already made me feel as if I'd known the son-of-a-bee for a lifetime. A long, miserable lifetime.

"Court, you were born dizzy. Fuck off, will you? I've had enough sitting to last me a—"

Court stood up, weaving slightly on his short bandy legs. The bastard was a turret gunner, the one spot on the bomber where being a weasel was an advantage. Court's fists were balled, and his brown eyes were locked on mine. The hate I saw there was enough to make my bladder taut and my legs quiver. Swallowing audibly, Court said, "When I'm done with you, sittin's all you'll—"

The knock on the wooden door startled both of us into silence. Two short raps, then a pause, then two more. We all waited for the guard to come barging in, but the door didn't open. The bottom of the door didn't come all the way down to the floor, I could see two dark patches against the light outside. Whoever stood outside was waiting to be *asked* in, or so I guessed.

Backing away from Court, I said, "Please, come in." The other fifteen men either stood or sat silent, glaring at me, as the door slowly opened; an officer in a field grey overcoat and decorated dress hat walked into the room and quietly shut the door behind him. No other guards followed him, although I guessed they stood outside the barracks, rifles out and at the ready.

The officer was middle-aged; of average height, but he had lost weight since his overcoat was issued. It hung on him in loose folds, as if his shoulders were no more substantial than a wooden hanger. Dull blonde hair framed a longish, craggy face. Steel-rimmed glasses obscured his light eyes, and his lips were sucked in under a wispy mustache. The man looked tired; his thin shoulders sagged.

The silence was a live thing in the dusty barracks. No one spoke; even Court held his forked tongue. I didn't notice the Kraut's 7.65 Walther pistol until he shoved it back into his coat pocket. Apparently we had passed some sort of test; the man didn't seem to feel he needed his weapon at the ready in our presence.

"I am *Oberstleutnant* von Kardorff, commandant of Stalag Twenty-Cee," he said in a low, yet piercing voice. When he spoke, I saw why he had held his lips puckered in. His teeth were awful, ringed in the front with thin bands of gold and steel, their dull ivory surfaces striated and stained with rot. Even though he was the enemy, I felt a stab of pity; teeth that rotten had to hurt continually. Especially in this chilly September weather.

Von Kardorff asked us whom we had chosen as barracks spokesman; when no one came forward, I said, "I am…I guess."

The commandant nodded in what I supposed was approval, and said, "After meal, we talk. To my office my guard will escort you." And without farewell he left the barracks. No sooner had the door shut behind him then Court mimicked, "'To my off-fush my guard vill es-cort you'—" until I walked up to him, standing with my knee poised close to his crotch, I said, "I didn't hear *you* volunteering for the job, Lieutenant,."

Court looked down where my knee was, and backed off, mumbling, "Who the fuck wants to be a Kraut-sucker anyway." The rest of the men laughed, and kept on laughing during the meal of millet soup and coarse bread the guards brought to us in a wooden cart. The bread tasted like wet wood in my mouth. I had to swallow half a dozen times before one bite went down.

True to von Kardorff's word, one of the guards escorted me past the numbingly same rows of barracks and endless criss-crossing strands of barbed wire, past tight groups of huddled soldiers, French, British and Belgian, all of whom looked at me with no more friendliness than the Germans did. The weak sunlight did little to warm me; I wondered if I'd make it out of the *Oberstleutnant*'s office alive.

After depositing me in von Kardorff's small, barren office, the guard left me alone with the colorless blonde man. There was a lone window in the west wall; the setting sun made von Kardorff's twin-pronged belt buckle gleam a dull orange-gold. I thought of the Black Hills gold ring I'd bought for my girl Maxine at home, and swallowed a lump in my throat.

"Lieutenant, you look…how you say, distressing?" My host leaned forward, shyly pushing a box of cigarettes toward me, indicating that I should take one. I did so; von Kardorff lit his and mine with the same match, before shaking it in the air to extinguish it. I filled my mouth and nose with harsh smoke, then expelled it, saying, "I think you mean 'distressed' but your English is quite good." I quickly added, "sir" but he shook his head, saying, "No need, no need, Lt. Berg. Out there"—he indicated the camp beyond the window with his cigarette—"*ja*, but not here."

I was about to relax, I was beginning to lean back in my hard wooden chair, in fact, when von Kardorff said, "An...alter-cation I heard inside your barracks, *ja*?"

Sheepishly, I nodded, eyes downcast. My cigarette was ashing, a long column of crinkly orange-black hung on the tip, but I was afraid to lean forward and use the ashtray close to von Kardorff's left arm. The ash fell to the bare wooden floor; as I ground it cold with my boot I replied, "It was Lt. Court, Sir...he and I, well, when we were on the train—"

"I understand. It is not to continue, but I understand what happened.' The German inched the ashtray closer to me; as I tapped my smoke into it I wondered, *What in the devil is this Kraut up to? Does he* want *something, or what?* The Germans I'd seen face-to-face ever since bailing out of my plane had ranged from aggressive to indifferent, but none of them had been so...*nice.*

And as much as I hated to admit it, the *Oberstleutnant* was doing his damnedest to make a good impression on me, one of his prisoners, and his efforts didn't seem phony. I'd seen enough prison movies back in the States to realize what his game was, the frigging Kraut was trying to soften me up, create a stoolie, a spy against my fellow countrymen. I'd seen the training films in basics; never trust a Nazi, and all that hoopla. I knew what the Nazis were up to, what they had in mind for the entire world. Before I'd shipped out, in August of '42, six Germans were executed for sabotage and spying after they'd landed on the East Coast in June in a trio of subs. Oh, I *knew* what old Hitler had in mind, all right.

Just like I was sure I knew what von Kardorff had in mind, despite his good English and kind-looking blue eyes behind the severe glasses. Taking a deep puff of my smoke (I remember thinking, *Some fucking* Nazi *made this thing*), I decided that come hell or high water, I wasn't playing von Kardorff's game.

"Sorry, but I'm not going along with it," I said flatly, while images of James Cagney and George Raft, tough to the end, flickered through my mind.

"Pardon?" The officer's mouth hung slightly open, and his pale eyes looked puzzled. Grinding out his cigarette, he went on, "I do not understand...'going along with' what?"

"Your game," I added, somewhat less confidently, as if Jimmy Stewart replaced James Cagney in my head. Across from me, von Kardorff leaned back in his leather desk chair (it squeaked as he shifted his weight backwards), arms crossed, his high brow furrowed. "'Game,'" he said wonderingly, until comprehension glowed in his eyes and he sat forward suddenly, a crooked grin light up his face.

"Oh, you think you are to be *spy*...oh my, funny that is," he said, lapsing into his native syntax. I grew uneasy as he began to laugh; I was afraid that one of the guards might come in. I didn't trust any of *them*.

Through his laughter, von Kardorff said, "If my title was *Ober-sturmbannführer*, then you would have cause to worry. *That* would mean I am Lieutenant-Colonel in the *Waffen SS*, not the simple *Wehrmacht*. I am only Army. Not SS." As if that was proof enough that he was just a regular guy, and could be trusted.

I merely nodded, as I finished my smoke; if von Kardorff didn't want to admit what he was doing, that was his business. He could offer me all the smokes in Germany and beyond, and I'd sit and listen to him laugh, but I wouldn't turn on my men. Even on that slime-ball Court.

The Lieutenant-Colonel lifted his glasses to wipe away tears of mirth, then said, "I haven't laughed in many months...years. *Ist* good for me. You come here, often, *ja*?"

So that's how it's to be, I thought, *the old fuck is going to jolly me up, brainwash me with laughter*. But the memory of Court's crazed brown eyes made even Nazi conversation seem less hideous. I didn't think the war would be ending any time soon, and the thought of being knee-to-crotch with that ball turret gunner wasn't a happy one. I knew I was supposed to be fighting for my countrymen, Court included, but that didn't stop him from being such an out-and-out *putz*. Nothing at all like the kind-eyed von Kardorff....

And even as I realized it that late afternoon, being half-Jewish and all, I was both pleased and deeply appalled that I'd found myself a new friend in the middle of mad Hitler's domain…and that man was one of Hitler's own.

As if to confirm what I'd just realized, von Kardorff said to me before I left his office, "You come back, to talk to me, *ja*? We are close to same age…we find things to speak of. Things apart from all of this." His hand indicated his office, the battered desk, the twin chairs, the flagpole with the red, white and black swastika flag, the framed portrait of Hitler near the door. The look on his face tore me apart; longing and pride and the most bitter thing of all, loneliness.

I stood by the door, uncertain. I'd enlisted at my relatively advanced age of thirty-seven with an eagerness to kill every damned Nazi on the planet, wipe them out for what they were doing to my ancestors on my father's side. I'd dropped bombs on their country with gleeful abandon, bombs painted with slogans like "Hi, Adolf," and "Good-by, Krauts." And all during the ride on the P.O.W. train with the orange-and-black banners festooning the engine and the last car—a warning to all planes that our train was off-limits—I had hoped I'd get the opportunity to personally choke the living shit out of some Nazi once the war ended. And yet…here I was, smoke from a Nazi—make that *Wehrmacht*—cigarette still in my lungs, facing a man who was asking me to spend some more time shooting the breeze with him. *Begging* me, judging by the look in his light eyes. It was so damned, damned *difficult*—

"*Juden*," I whispered then coughed into my balled fist. The Lieutenant-colonel just nodded his head slightly, and said, "I wasn't sure…but that does not matter. If you lived in Germany, you would understand our position concerning your people—"

"My father's people," I added quickly, wondering why I felt the need to go on. Somehow, it seemed important. "My mother was Gentile. I…was never *bar mitzvahed*."

"Oh…all right," he said with a nod and an uncomprehending half-smile,. "Either way, it does not matter to me. Makes *no* difference to me," he added quickly, as his eyes shifted away from the portrait of his *Führer*. In that moment, with that simple shift of his eyes, I sensed that *Oberstleutnant* von Kardorff had no grand designs on corrupting my patriotism, no desire to convert me into a "Heil

Hitler" automaton. But just what he did have in mind was still unknown to me.

Sensing that it was time I got back to my men, I said, "Thank you for the cigarette, sir—"

"Rolf," he said with a half-smile he quickly hid behind his cupped right hand, but his blue eyes were dancing as I replied, "Rolf, then. But only here, right?"

"Right. Otherwise, 'Lieutenant-Colonel' or "Commandant' will suffice…uhm, Lt. Berg, may I call—"

"Bud. It's better than Edwin," I quipped, before forcing the smile off my lips. Inside, I felt a strange glow, that glow which comes when you sense that a new relationship will indeed work out, and be lasting…but it chilled me when I glanced at the photograph of Hitler on my way out of the office.

Wehrmacht or not, von Kardorff was still fighting on *their* side.

* * * *

"Better check on Berg's breath," Court said as I walked into the barracks a few minutes later, "see if he has Kraut-crap on his—"

I was standing on his toes within seconds, my words echoed weirdly in the barracks as I said, "Remember that pistol the Commandant put in his pocket? One of the bullets has your name on it— he asked me to give you the message personally."

Backing off, Court ran his stubby fingers through his lank brown hair and said, "Third degree, huh? When we get out of this dump, the U.S. Army's High Command is hearing about *you*—"

In the back of the barracks, a voice rang out, "For Chrissakes, John, don't tell him—"

"Tell me what?" I crossed my arms and waited. Boots shuffling like a school bully caught in the act by the principal, Court said, "About the escape. Me and the others, you if you *want* to go. In the States, I was a well-digger. Water ones. I know dirt—"

"That's no lie!" Laughter bounced off the rough plank walls as Court went on softly, "Ground's not too hard, and we're awful close to the fence, between the guard towers. Take time, but we got that—"

"Do whatever you want," I said evenly, "and when they riddle your body with bullets and leave you hanging on the fence, I'll be sure to stay downwind of—"

"German dick better than American, Mr. Nazi-Suck-Up?" Court's eyes were glistening mud, slick and dangerous.

"Don't know how American ones taste…maybe you'd best make the comparison. Experience helps, doesn't it?" I walked away from him; a couple of Court's cronies held him back, as he said, "Yeah? You keep up with that Nazi, you'll need yourself a new asshole!"

"Pick one out for me from the Wish Book," I said from my bunk, referring to the annual Christmas catalogue back home, the one with what seemed like *everything* in it…everything but freedom, and an end to war, that is.

Court kept brisling, but I'd beaten him, and he knew it and the whole barracks knew it, so there wasn't much more trouble after that between him and me. For the time being.

* * * *

Months passed, a lot of them, one like the next, down to the Red Cross boxes each week, the trek to the latrine afterwards. The sixteen of us more or less stuck together, other prisoners had already formed *cliques*, and aside from occasional chats and exchanges of smokes or hoarded Red Cross candy bars (viewed with bored indifference by the strolling guards), my men had little to do with any of our fellow Allies.

Court began digging; a few boards were pried up in a corner of the barracks, and slowly he began to extract the dirt below, spoonful by spoonful. I let him; part of me hoped he'd get away with it and get out of my face, and part of me hoped he'd either be caught or killed. Gone was gone when it came to Court, no matter how it happened. And I didn't take the easy route, of telling Rolf what Court was doing, either.

As time went on, and I spent more and more hours in Rolf's company, hovering between trust and repulsion at what I was doing, and who I was doing it *with*, I had come to a decision: No matter how well Rolf and I got along, I was not about to turn traitor. It was strange, true; I like my enemy more than my countrymen, but I was still an American, and Rolf was a citizen of Nazi Germany, and that was that. I let court dig up German soil and sprinkle it on the recreation yard unimpeded; if the guards caught him, that was also that.

My men grew so used to my now daily treks to Rolf's office that even Court stopped commenting on them, aside from occasional jibes of "Still waiting for the Wish Book to arrive, Berg?" His words hurt, but not because of the long-ago argument about him buying me a new behind. It was not being able to *see* a real Wish Book that hurt; thousands of miles away, people were paging through catalogues, able to buy things that were denied to me and my men. Things we all missed: new gabardine suits, Ingersoll watches, Shirley Temple dolls, horsehide Cossack jackets with sliding fasteners on the cigarette pockets.

"—you know, Rolf, I even miss the crawl-lines on the bottoms of the pages…and they haven't had those in years," I said, taking a deep puff on my second cigarette of the afternoon.

Behnd his desk, Rolf blew a smoke ring, then another, before asking, "'Crawl-lines'?"

"On the bottom of each page. Used to say things like 'Order Blanks Are In Back of Catalogue' or "Do your Christmas Shopping from this catalogue.' They did away with them in the mid-thirties, I think. But I grew up with them, so it's like they're still…*real*, and happening now. Know what I mean?" I helped myself to another cigarette.

Rolf nodded. "Sometimes, things which are gone…*are* more real, because of the remembering—no, wait, that is not how to put it—because of *remembrance*," he finished triumphantly. It was important to Rolf to speak English well; he told me that he only knew a smattering of English when he was assigned to this stalag in 1941, but by listening in on the prisoners, he picked up a more current English than what was taught in school. That was how he'd heard the fight brewing between Court and myself; he'd been strolling between the barracks, ears perked for conversations.

"—if it got any worse, I was ready to burst in, pistol smoking, but when you said 'Please' after I knocked, I knew there was a sane man in there," Rolf had said to me months earlier, before we had come to the feet-up-on-his-desk phase of our relationship.

On this day, Rolf took his booted feet off his desk, then leaned forward in his chair, eyes glittering behind his polished lenses.

"Remembering something once it is gone is both poignant and happy, all at once…I remember, before the First World War, how I used to visit the local *Feinkostgeschäft*—fine food shop—and just *stand* there, smelling and looking, until I made up my mind what to buy. So much *gutes Essen*...good eating. *Sauerbraten*, with grated potato dumplings. *Königinpasteten*, with fish inside, *Schnitzel a la Holstein*—I'd eat the anchovy off the top first thing—and a good strong *Pichelsteiner Fleisch*. A stew of beef, veal, lamb and pork. And *die Gans*...in Berlin they have a saying, '*Eine jut jebratene Jans is eine jute Jabe Jottes,*' 'A well-roasted goose is a gift from God.' And it is true, is it not?"

I smiled and told him that roast chicken was more common in my house, to which he replied, "Right now, a roast chicken sounds wonderful...or some *Würzfleisch*, even. And spiced beef stew isn't even my favorite dish! I remember going into the *Konditorei*—pastry shop—before the war, and buying a *Mohnstritzel* and eating the whole thing by myself, right down to the last poppy-seed inside. That was near *der erste Wethnachtstag*—Christmas day. The Christmas before the war, as a matter of fact...afterwards I went to a *Gasthof*, an inn, and got stinking drunk on *Göttertrunk*. 'Drink of the Gods,' a wonderful punch made of port, brandy and strong black coffee. I passed out under the table like a *Bierletche*—a beer corpse at Oktoberfest in München (Munich). I was born there, in Munich," he added suddenly, as if it was something I should know then went on about that night so long before. "But someone aroused me, so I could partake of the *Dämmerschoppen*. The traditional drink at twilight. And the next morning—whew, what a hangover!"

Rolf took another smoke out of the box, tamped the tobacco down against the desk top, and said around the cigarette as he lit it, "I think my body knew that war and hard times were coming. We had food rationing during the war, and afterward, too. Right up until this war, as a matter of fact," he added without rancor, as he threw his match into the wastebasket, "And beyond. This is an expression we have, '*Wer Geld hat, mag Austern essen; wer keines hat muss Kartoffen fressen.*' 'He who has money may eat oysters; he who has none must feed on potatoes.' It is a bitter little rhyme, especially when you are the man dining on potatoes...or worse. You realize, don't you, what the bread you eat is...composed of?"

The gummy harsh taste of the bread in that prison never left my mouth, even after smoking half a dozen cigarettes. "Wood shavings, I'd wager...and peelings of some sort?"

"Yes...potato peelings. At home, my people are drinking tea made from apple peelings and crushed acorns. And they are thankful for *die Kartoffel*, even as they hate the sameness of it. I do not know if you are aware of this, Bud, but things have been brutal in this country for a good many years. Long before our *Führer* came to power...in many ways, he came to power *because* of the conditions. The terms of that treaty after the war, our loss of status, not enough to eat...that *does* things to a person. Makes the mind a little...strange. The belly does the thinking. And the mind merely goes along."

I blurted out, "And you're killing the Jews because you're sick of potatoes? *C'mon—*"

"No, no, it is not that simplistic...I am sorry. It is so complex, so long standing. I know it is difficult for you to believe, but anti-Semitic feelings have been a part of this country for so long...long enough to make me wonder why *die Juden* didn't leave long before all of *this* came to pass—"

I snubbed out my smoke and stood up, but Rolf waved me down with a frantic, "Please, Bud, I must—I must *tell* you. So you do not hate me, or my people...despite all this. It is engrained in all of us, this need for order, for...how you say, nationality—no, no, national pride. Before the First World War, there were rumblings, stirrings, among the people that had to deal with *Juden*. They were powerful people. They controlled the trade unions, the arts—in the war, many of them were clerks, while few were on the lines. Maybe it was luck on their parts. Maybe it was influence and money at work. I don't know. It was brewing for years....Bud, have you heard of the Passion Play at Öberammergau?"

All I could do was nod sullenly.

"Good. Well, for years, decades, it blamed the death of Jesus on the *Juden*. It's true. And people came from all over the world and heard this, and didn't *care* enough to protest! They merely *accepted* it. As if it was written as so in the Bible. And then there was *Ostara*. A magazine, very strange. It was occult, erotic and ant-Semitic, all at once. Printed well before the other war. I remember one headline, it went, 'Are you blonde? Then you are a culture-creator! Are you blonde? If so, dangers threaten you!' I am blonde, yet I felt no threat…but others of my people did, Bud. And the pictures inside… horrible. Huge hairy *Juden* mounting fair German women…and any-one—any *child*, even—could buy this trash! Each issue stirred fears of the *Juden* taking over the country, of ruining all that was here, all the new unity…a horrible prospect to my people. I never bought the *Ostara*, but it was always shoved in my face, the pages filled with one anti-*Juden* article after another.

"By the end of the other war, people were linking *Juden* and the Reds. A dual threat. And the Kurt Eisner insurrection that November didn't help things…he was a Red and a Jew. And he and his follow-ers, they were like the things in that magazine, like all the fears of the German people come to life. They made the madness *real*.

"We Germans are conservative…the Reds, the *Juden*, were not. Things were shaken up, the government in ruins…when Hitler changed the German Workers Party into a political organization in-stead of a mere debating society…people were ready for him, and it. Oh *Gott*, were we ready…." Rolf pushed up his glasses and used his handkerchief to daub at his eyes, then went on:

"Hitler hated Jews more than any of the rest…but when he wrote *Mein Kampf*, his choice of words fooled those of us who chose to believe that there had to be another way of dealing with the *Juden* situation. A bloodless way. When speaking of what should be done to them, he used the word '*Entfermng.*' It means either 'removal' or 'amputation' and I for one thought he meant that *Juden* should be removed from this country, and resettled elsewhere. When the book came out, the *Juden* should have left, for their own safety. It wasn't as if they were living in a vacuum. They *knew* it was obvious that they were hated, that things would get worse. And yet…they *stayed*. Even after *Kristallnacht*. I don't know if the love of country or the love of money kept them here, but in the end they will have neither. Which is sad…not all *Juden* are avaricious people. Just as not all of us Germans are good. And once they deprived the Jews of their property and privileges, on the false grounds that the *Juden* were not of this country…it was the beginning of the end. But…why didn't they *leave* sooner?"

Rolf's blue eyes glittered; he wanted to *know* so badly I myself felt sick for him. Fighting this was one thing…he was *living* it.

Without waiting for me to reply, Rolf went on. "And we gave them the chance to get out, or at least get their children out…yet so few took it. Why, I keep wondering, *why not*?"

"And now…the final solution is in motion…and we are killing *Juden*, radicals, undesirables faster than I can finish talking. Do you know what the *Totenkopfverbände* at the death camps are doing? Or what the *Einsatzgruppe* did? Liquidating *people*. Murder on a grand scale, hundreds of people no different than you or I, herded next to fresh-dug pits, or into shower rooms like our delousing station…only they do not come out. Not living. Then we pluck at their bodies like crows, taking gold fillings and hair and whatever else we can find. And we do find it, Bud. And we write down what we find, what we collect. Scribble, scribble, into our ledgers. This bundle of hair, that scrap of gold from a tooth. Wooden legs…oh Bud, I have heard stories, about rooms full of wooden legs with nowhere to walk to. Wooden limbs which remain while the body is in ashes.

"Do you want to know something, Bud? I feel sicker about it than you do. I see the paleness in your cheeks, the swallowing of your throat. But your people—your father's people—they are victims. When all is said and done, the victims come in for pity, because of what was done to them regardless of *whether or not some of them could've saved themselves*. And all the rest of us, the *Wehrmacht*, and the *Waffen* and even those swine the *Totenkopfverbände*, will be blamed equally, even though not all of us agree with this—"

I leaned forward, and pounded the desk with my balled fist until the skin stung. Mindful of the guards, I spoke softly but forcefully, "Rolf, you *are* to blame! Disobey your orders! Quit the Army! Surrender to us, or to the Brits—*something*! Go kill Hitler—"

"Some of us already tried that," Rolf said so softly I could barely believe I heard him right. Letting his breath out in a sad stale whistle, he leaned back until his head touched the wall behind him and said in a voice devoid of inflection or emotion, "It happened on the twentieth of July. Less than two months ago. In East Prussia. A bomb went off, right next to Hitler. He was only slightly injured. His *trousers* sustained more permanent damage than he did. Some of the officers plotted it along with politicians…before sunset those closest to the plot were dead. And more have been killed since then. Many of them were men I knew, men even you, yourself, would've liked, or at least understood. They meant it to be a more final solution, but I've heard that the *Führer* is more unstable than before…his paranoia, it has increased. Justifiably so, I imagine," he concluded mirthlessly.

The bombing incident was news to me, even with the makeshift crystal radio in the barracks, we'd heard nothing, or if it was reported, I'd missed it. But despite the hours we spent talking, I wondered if this all wasn't a trick, to test my reactions, see if I'd spill some Army beans.

As if sensing my wariness, Rolf said, "Your bombers have raided Berlin. In March. It is so close to being over, so close…yet the killing goes on. The *liquidation*," he spat out, before going on, "You know we've lost Paris, do you not?"

"Not much I do know anymore," I lied. Shrugging, Rolf added, "The general who was ordered to blow up the city didn't…Deidrich will be crucified for it once the war is over—he's already been court-martialed—but at least he didn't do it. You'd be proud of him for—"

"Of a *Nazi*? Never, Rolf. *Never*. I mean, you and me, we get on Ok, but that doesn't mean that—"

"We Germans are human?" A sad smile played on Rolf's lips as he ground out his smoke.

"No, not that…you Nazis. I mean, you've got the pictures on the wall, and wear the uniform, and give the salute—"

"There are some things men must do to survive. Long before the *Nationalsozialistiche Deutsche Areiter Partei* came to power, or *Gleichschaltung*—unification—began, I was an Army man. I served in the other war, and I stayed in uniform. This is my life. I love being alive, as do you. I want to stay that way."

"At the expense of others? Women, kids?" I pulled my smoke from my mouth and stubbed it out half-smoked, then stood up, saying, "Thank you for the cigarette, Lieutenant-Colonel. Good day."

"Bud, please, you don't—"

The slamming door shut out Rolf's words; the sound of that door rang in my ears all the way back to my barracks. It was a sad and ugly sound.

My ears were still ringing, in fact, as I walked into the barracks. So I didn't understand what Court said to me as I walked past the table in the middle of the room and headed for my bunk; being such a considerate gentleman, he repeated the question, loud enough for old Adolf himself to hear, whatever he was hiding:

"Hey Brown-nose, what'd ole Brown-shirt have to say today?"

Not bothering to correct Court's mistake about Rolf's affiliation I said flatly, "He said to tell you he thinks you're an asshole. Satisfied?"

In answer Court trotted over to my bunk and sat down on the edge, rubbing his short-fingered hands together. I groaned and covered my face with my forearm. I felt Court shift beside me. The rest of the guys were quiet, much too quiet. Anticipatory quiet, like kids waiting for the sound of Santa's reindeer dancing on the roof.

Curious, I took my arm off my face and propped myself up on one elbow to look at Court. The rest of the guys were all stationed close by in the drab ugly barracks; it struck me then that I'd been spending so much time with Rolf that the barracks were actually strange to me. It was a disorienting feeling. I let myself flop back on the bunk. Beside me, Court began talking.

"Hey, Bud, you know how you and me are always shootin' the breeze and tellin' each other to 'pick one out of the Wish Book'? Well, I don't know if you've noticed it or not, but there's a whole lot of nothin' to do around here, and me and the guys we already done about as much of it as we can stand, and—"

After listening to Rolf for close to a year, Court's syntax made me wince. And *he* was born in America.

"—got to thinkin' 'bout the Wish Books back home, and the more we thought, well, we got to thinkin' that it would make the time go faster—"

I turned over and stared up at Court's greasy face. "What's the matter, you got tired of digging? Or is there a toll booth in the tunnel—"

Panic filled Court's eyes. "Not so fuckin' *loud*, ok?" he whispered. "Yeah, that's still a goin' concern, but there's only so much dirt a man can carry outside in one day. Them Krauts, they got eyes in the back of their helmets. But not all of us can dig, and not all the time. And somebody went and checked out all the library books—"

Sarcasm didn't suit Court. He was too stupid to pull it off.

"Go ask the Brits. They have books. Go trade with them—"

"That's no good, Bud. Lissen, we all got to thinkin'…how 'bout we make our *own* Wish Book? Something we could pass from guy to guy. Something to *do* for cripes' sakes. We don't got no Kraut buddy to spend time with—"

"OK, what am I supposed to do about it? You want me to help, don't you?" I got up off the bunk, mainly to get away from Court, who proceeded to dog my footsteps as I made my way to the table.

"Well, yeah, Bud. But not to draw it. We can do that—"

"Thanks a lot—"

"That's not it, Bud." Court pulled up a chair and sat down next to me, saying, "We don't got anything to make the Wish Book *with*. We need paper, pens, ink…colored ink's best, but quinine tablets in water work ok, too. Them Brits want too much in trade for the stuff, and who speaks French, huh? I figure the soup's so gummy it'll work for glue, but we *need* the other stuff, Bud. And we figured since you're chummy with the—"

"Not really," I said succinctly, as I left the table. Court tagged behind me, whining, "But you know how it *is* here, Bud. We got so *damn* little. And them Russians they've been bringin' in across the fence, they got even less. When you're sittin' and gassin' with old Goldteeth, you ever notice them Russians? They ain't got *shit*, or the pot to crap it out in. Least you could do is get a little something for us. The supplies, Bud. Get us something to do besides go out of our minds, huh? C'mon, Bud, we can do it. You'll see, it'll be great. Lots of pictures—I did the Betty Grable on my plane, real professional lookin' and—"

"Will you shut up if I try?"

"Sure, Bud, you just get 'em, ok? Be a swell guy and do it. We got to have something to do or we'll pop before the you-know-what's dug." I turned around and looked at Court, and at my men beyond. Everyone's skin was waxy, skinned potato pale. And their eyes….In a little while we'd all start looking like those poor Russians over in the adjoining compound. The ones who stared through the fence as if they envied *us*. The ones Rolf chose not to speak of.

"It'll be done. Tomorrow." I went outside to visit the latrine, beyond it the Russians were watching me. A couple of them waved. I waved back before entering the latrine, and waved again after I left it. No, Rolf never mentioned the Russians, the ones who didn't rate so much as a monthly Red Cross supply box. With the *Juden* problem gnawing at his mind, I doubted that he thought much about the Russians, period.

I hadn't thought about them before that day myself.

* * * *

That afternoon sticks in my mind not only for what Rolf said to me, but also for the dream I had that night. An old memory, really, there was little imagination in it.

I was twelve again, and living in the big house on Ariel Street in that suburb on the outskirts of Milwaukee. The place where I spent part of the summer and most of the fall, on account of Dad's job. He sold air conditioners to theatres, and got transferred around a lot because he was so good at "company motivation and sales," as he liked to say.

Like I always did, I found myself a lot of friends, mostly Jewish kids like me. I guess I was good at motivation myself. Only, I never told any of my friends that my mom was a Gentile, and that meant, of course, that I'd never be *bar mitzvahed*. When you're Jewish, and twelve-going-on-thirteen, that's a big event; it was for my buddies , and I pretended it was for me.

Why not? My birthday wasn't until January. I'd be long gone before then. I pretended I'd go through the ceremony too, that my parents never bothered to joining a synagogue no matter where they moved made it easier for me to get away with the deception. I knew what the other kids *would* be doing to prepare, so I faked it out. Oh, I was a glib little shit. Full of motivation and fun, but deep inside, a deceptive child.

No matter where we moved, we'd gravitate toward the most Jewish part of town, and that little suburb was no exception. All my new buddies were Jewish, only full-blooded Jews, not half-*goyim* like me. But I was never around long enough for them to know, so.... They'd never see the little Christmas tree Mother'd put in the dining room, near the menorah. They didn't *need* to know.

It was late, late summer, when summer haircuts are all but grown out, and the shadows take on that odd blue-grey color when the clear, clear sunlight fades, and I was with my buddies, all of us growing tall and straight-limbed, nearing manhood second by second. We were invincible; weren't we all going to be Men soon? But a dark shadow fell over us, literally. A kid I didn't know tried to cross our path, just a regular kid with dark hair and light eyes, like most of my other buddies. I didn't recognize him, but Hermie Fischer did.

"Hey, *Goyim*, get out of our way!"

The boy, who was about our age, cringed as if Hermie had doused him with spit, or worse. He tried to walk off quietly, but Hermie and the others surrounded him. The kid looked at me, as if to say, "Hey, I'm not doing anything, leave me alone, please?" but I waited to see what Hermie and the others would do. Benjie Roth spit at the boy; the goober hung on his tee shirt like a slow raindrop, dribbling down. Hermie started the chant, and one by one all of us picked it up shouting at the boy as he ran across lawns, streets and finally the highway, bellowing with our voices in cheerful unison:

> *"Goyim, Goy,*
> *"Mamma's Little Boy!"*
> *"Couldn't find a Woman so*
> *"Daddy Married a Shikseh, oh!"*

I never found out the kid's name. I didn't need to, I already knew my own. And because I didn't want any of the others to know, to chase me and spit on me, I ran and shouted with them. Even as tears stung my eyes and phlegm collected in my nose. I ran and ran, but suddenly a man in dark grey clothes stepped in front of me, a thin man with dingy blonde hair and sad, sad blue eyes behind glasses that winked in the near-autumn sunlight.

"There are some things man must do to survive," he said, as he bent down to scoop me up, and I fought in his arms but he was lifting me higher, higher, and beyond his shoulder I saw the ovens—

I awoke to snores and flatulent stink in the darkness around me. Gasping, I left my bunk, and hurried to the nearest window, where a strange light glowed. Outside, some of the guards were burning trash, a small guttering fire that leapt from glowing scrap of wood to charred and smoking animal bones. Rolf was standing just beyond the fire, his glasses oval pools of red light. His head turned my way, and he gave a little wave, a tiny motion of his hand that culminated in him tipping his hat forward. As if he were afraid the guards might notice his gesture.

"There are some things…."
Oh yes, Rolf, indeed there are.

* * * *

I put Rolf's stinging words behind me, and sucked up to him the next day, asking for the pens and nibs and ink and plenty of paper. Rolf was enchanted with the idea; I'd suspected he would be. But Court wasn't thrilled when I told him what Rolf had requested in exchange for the supplies—

"The fucking Kraut wants to do *what*?" Court gasped as if I'd been grinding my boot-toe in his nuts for half an hour.

"He won't sit here all day. He just wants to see what's going on. Guy's never seen a Wish Book. Man's curious, that's all." I shrugged, but Court screeched, "It's a *trick*! He knows about you-know-what and wants to trap us! You told him, didn't you? He knows all about—"

"The commandant isn't above having me shot. He can have me draped on the fence afterwards. Quit with the heebie-jeebies, ok? Besides, he can come waltzing in here any damn time he chooses. And you know he always knocks fi—"

"After listening at the door for who knows how long?"

The little runt of a turret gunner had me there. Rolf had admitted to me that he often listened to the prisoners talking in their barracks…learning conversational English my fat fanny—or flat fanny, to be more accurate. And it would be like a Jerry to let us dig an entire tunnel and *then* burst in and fill the thing in on us. Rolf could give me that line about not being personally responsible for what was going on, and about all of us sharing the blame for what was happening to the Jews (to some of my distant kin, no doubt), but that didn't mean that he really *meant* it….

"Listen, Court, this is his ball game, on his playing field. We're lucky he's agreeing to get the supplies for your damn book at all. You realize that he has to requisition all this crap from his higher-ups. Maybe he has to give an accounting for it, too. You know how the Krauts have to write down every shitting thing—"

I had to do some more arguing, but eventually Court buckled and agreed to Rolf's request. Rolf was quick to fulfill his part of the bargain; by the end of the week we had our supplies, including a fresh, unopened package of typing paper. I never did learn how Rolf scored that coup, especially so late in the war, when supplies were low. But he came through; I figured he was desperate to get his skinny hide into our barracks.

Oh, he was desperate, all right, but in a way I never would have dreamed possible....

* * * *

"Lt. Court, you are forgetting the crawl-lines, are you not?" Rolf leaned across our rough plank table, peering at Court's latest page-in-progress, oblivious to Court's grimace of dismay. The ball turret gunner shot me a sour look, but I shrugged. It was Rolf's paper, Rolf's pens and ink. I sat down next to court, and said, "My fault, John. I was telling the Lieutenant-Colonel here about them, and how I missed 'em from before—"

"Yeah, yeah...I was gonna add 'em later on. Hey, Mitchell, you write down some of the stuff from the bottoms of the pages, the stuff 'bout order blanks bein' in the back and all. C'mon, chop-chop."

And that was why the 1944 Stalag 20-C Wish Book had crawl-lines at the bottoms of its pages. But the funny thing was, Rolf's wanting to see them there made the entire project more involving for *all* of us (even the guys who couldn't draw so much as my fabled new asshole), for all of my men had seen a Wish Book. By thinking hard about those past issues, we all took an unexpected furlough, when you have so little in the here and now, the past *does* become more real, more wonderful, and magical, than it was during the living of it.

Within an hour, we covered a precious scrap of paper with close to a dozen healing crawl-lines:

"We Pledge to Satisfy You and SAVE YOU MONEY"
"Do Your Christmas Shopping From This Catalogue"
"See complete INDEX in the BACK of this catalogue"
"PRICES in this Book are for MAIL ORDERS Only!"
"Order blanks are in the back of this catalogue"
"Be Sure to Include Sufficient POSTAGE with Your Order"
"Your Order Shipped Within 24 Hours"

And then there were the unanimous favorites:

"Please LEND This Book to Your NEIGHBORS"
"Stamps are CHEAPER than Gasoline—BUY BY MAIL"

Even Rolf had a good chuckle over that last line.

Eventually, Rolf screwed up the courage to *ask* Court if he could help do some of the lettering on the bottoms of the finished pages. Now Court hadn't been bullshitting when he bragged about being a good artist; his Shirley Temple dolls and Ingersoll Mickey Mouse watches were easily as good as in the real Wish Books, so he was reluctant to let anyone but himself do the fine work on the catalogue pages. Court sputtered, fussed and fumed—as much as he could without blowing his rights under the Geneva Convention—but then Rolf quieted him by taking a small notepad from his pocket (the same pocket where he kept his pistol), and, after borrowing Court's pen, writing a copy of one of the crawl-lines ruler straight. The crawl-line even went in a different direction from the thin lines on the paper itself.

From that day on, and for the months that followed, Rolf stopped by our barracks every afternoon and patiently inked crawl-lines and page numbers on the bottoms of Court's finished pages. As the two men worked, and while the rest of us did fill-in details like coloring in pages with quinine ink, or doing whatever cross-hatching Court didn't feel like doing, Rolf told us stories about the "other war."

"I was part of the 16th Regiment, only a Sergeant then, though. Things were so awful in the trenches, in the foxholes, that I sometimes wished I *would* get captured, just so long as I wouldn't have to live in a sea of bloody mud. The only thing that kept me and my fellow soldiers going was the thought that the next day, or the next after that, might bring us a package from home. A bundle of food, not the stale zwieback or fresh-killed roof rabbits we could find—"

"'Roof rabbits'?" Court paused in his work, pen hovering above the half-finished drawing of Loretta Young wearing one of her "Autographed Fashion Worn in Hollywood" gowns. Rolf didn't miss a letter in his crawl-line as he replied, "Cats. Before the war, I never thought I'd have to eat one of my favorite animals, but when there is nothing else unspoiled….

"Anyhow, we all lived for those packages of food from home. All of us but Adi. His family was broken apart by death, a bad thing for a young soldier with little to look forward to either in or out of battle. And it was so sad about Adi, abecause he was always the one ready to cheer the rest of us up. Always urging us on when there seemed no reason to keep on fighting. And brave. He received the Military Cross, with swords, the Iron Cross, *die Verwundtenabzetchen*—something like your Purple Heart—*die Regimentsdiplom* for bravery and *die Dienstauszeichnung*. A Service Medal. Plus others, I think.

"When I knew him, I figured Adi to be a model soldier, but he had other ideas...I know he loved to draw. That was something he did to cheer us up, he took post cards and drew cartoons and little pictures on them. To boost morale. I still have a few of the ones he did for me. He wasn't as good a draftsman as your Lt. Court, but he did the cards so quickly, to help out immediately....

"It was so strange with Adi, he did so much, he gave of himself so freely, yet he refused to accept any food from us, from home. He said that if he couldn't give food in return, he couldn't accept it. 'That's silly, Adi, you have already given so much to us, we need no more payment,' I'd tell him, but he was too proud to listen. Sad, really, how he valued himself so little. While being so proud of himself at the same time.

"Poor Adi, he was full of pride and hunger, too. He had to buy or barter food from the cook and mess workers. Always hungry, always eating himself up from within. *Vielfrass*, we called him. 'Glutton.' But you could never slip him a tid-bit. Back in your pack it went. I remember how he paid so dearly for his toast with marmalade smeared on top, or honey if he could find it.

"That reminds me, once Adi found several crates of zwieback that had been forgotten. The sly fox took the packages of it from the *bottom* of each box, so the contents settled down, down...oh Adi was a clever fellow! But he shared with us. I don't like zwieback, but I took it because I was hungry, and more importantly, because Adi *wanted* me to have it. It was one of the few times he could give us food...even if he still didn't consider it 'good enough' to merit accepting food from *us*.

"Funny fellow, our Adi...he was a friend to all, but known by none of us. Except for Fuchsl. 'Little Fox'—a dog who came into our foxhole following a battle with the British. He was a white terrier, a sweet little dog once Adi trained him. Adi once said to me, 'Training

Fuchsl was so *difficult*…he didn't know a word of German!' But Adi, he thrived on difficulty. That dog was the only real joy in his life, aside from soldiering. Taught the animal to climb a ladder, just like a circus dog. If only that dog could've talked, we would have had the key to Adi's heart, his mind…he spoke to that dog like I would speak to you or you. They were true friends, when they sat sharing food, the *Gemütlichkeit* was so strong—"

"The what, Sir?" Mitchell asked as he studiously cross-hatched Court's outline of a woman's man-tailored suit.

"There is no exact word in your language, but it's like an atmosphere of warmth, of fellowship…a *closeness*. It almost hurt me to watch those two, Adi and Fuchsl, for war is not kind to dumb animals or to foot soldiers….

"In August, of 1917, the Regiment was moving to another battle and we were at a railway station…someone wanted to buy Fuchsl, but Adi was against the idea, and swore that he'd *never* sell his dog, not for thousands of marks. As it happened, he didn't sell that dog for anything. Fuchsl was stolen. We had to ship out, Adi couldn't disobey orders to look for him. I felt so sorry for Adi. He was soul-sick. And what made matters worse was the fact that people weren't eating only roof rabbits by then. Poor Adi, he'd never touch dog meat no matter how much his stomach pained him. I couldn't blame him, either.

"You could see in his eyes how much his loss gnawed at him. He was on fire inside, his blue eyes like glittering stars, burning, burning….As if to compensate, he threw himself into battle, as if he could bring Fuchsl back by being the finest, bravest soldier in the Regiment. Odd, how he'd say he was of the 16th Regiment whenever he was asked about his homeland. As if he couldn't admit he was an Austrian, as if that was somehow not good enough.

"And always, in the back of his mind, he brooded about his lost friend. Once, we were in a trench together, and Adi says to me, out of nowhere, 'I'd like to throttle the *Juden* who stole my dog!' This is new information to me. I asked, 'You know that a *Juden* made off with Fuchsl? You know who he is?' 'Not by name or by face, but I know who took my friend.'

"There was a lull in the shooting; I turned and said to Adi, 'So it was a *Juden* who took your dog. One you did not see, one you do not know. But you are certain that it was a *Juden*. How, Adi, *how*? It could have been someone hungry, a German, or an Austrian like yourself. Or a circus owner. You do not know it was a—'

"'It was one of the *Juden*,' he insists. You see, Adi hated Jewish people, more so than many of us did. It was the spirit of the times, a long-standing thing...please, do not look so stricken. You had to have lived there, then, to understand. But...back to Adi.

"'Adi,' I said, 'If ten strangers were to pass you right now, you'd have to make them drop their pants before you'd know for certain which of them were *Juden* and which were not. They're not *all* dark.'

"Adi grumbled something about them 'all being alike' but said no more to me about it. But later, I heard him saying the same thing about the dog-stealing *Juden* to a few of the other soldiers, and so I figured he didn't pay heed to my words. Adi could be stubborn that way. And that dog was such a sore point with him, such a deep wound...to this day, I do not believe Adi has ever gotten over the loss of his friend. His eyes, they still blaze—"

I think Court was thinking the same thing that all of us were thinking when he asked, "Lieutenant-Colonel, what happened to Adi? Is he still a friend of yours?"

Without pausing or letting his hand shake in the slightest, even as his voice came close to breaking, Rolf softly replied in German, "*Nein...Es ist unser Führer.*"

And none of us needed to ask for a translation.

* * * *

Christmas grew near; the Wish Book was close to completion. We even wrote up an index, to be lettered flawlessly by Rolf. None of us ever discussed his tale of Adi and little Fuchsl, there was no need to. Sometimes, the truth needed no amplification. But I often thought about that hungry soldier and the trained dog. I know the other men did, too. It was a classic paradox, the ultimate dichotomy, the man who wanted to ruin the world, to slaughter millions of people, had once loved and been loved by a trusting dog. A stray once owned by his enemies. A hungry mutt who didn't even speak German. It was a small thing, but it stuck in the brain like a burr, refusing to be brushed aside.

Once, when I managed to stall Rolf in his office while the men burrowed deeper into Court's tunnel (I was still an American, no matter what, and my men *were* my men), Rolf told me, "When it was decreed that all the *Juden* had to wear the armbands, I realized that Adi had indeed been listening to me in 1917. And he'd found a way of identifying *all* those people without needing to make the men drop their trousers. I tell myself that it wasn't *my* idea, but still, I wonder...."

"You had no way of knowing—"

"*Ja, Ja*...but it wasn't just that. I often wonder, should we have dragged Adi into our circle when eating the good food from home? Ignored his protests and given him the food anyway? I keep wondering if perhaps Adi was wishing we wouldn't just *listen*, but *act*. You know how it is, you want something so badly you cannot accept an invitation because your *need* would be too close to the surface—yet you *want* it. We should've told him, 'Damn your pride, Adi, we *want* you here with us, and to the devil with repaying us.' And then hoisted him up on our shoulders and carried him over to the food. I know he would have protested, but inside, maybe not....For he had already given us so much. Perhaps, in exchange, we might have begged a little, let down a little of our own guard. But we never went much further than asking once or twice before retreating. Perhaps it was more fun to call him *Vielfrass*, never realizing just how great his hunger was...and not for food, either."

I sat silent, thinking of Court humbling himself to beg for the materials for the Wish Book. I thought of myself, swallowing my pride and going back to see Rolf, even after his words offended me. And I thought of something Rolf had told me, in happier times. He, too, was a lover of food....

* * * *

"But they don't *got* all that stuff in the real Wish Book!"

Court protectively held the sheaf of finished pages in his thick short arms, teeth bared like a mother wolf defending her pups. I walked over to the table, plucked up one of the remaining clean sheets of paper, plus one of the pens, and said, "Then I guess I'll have to draw them myself. And you know what a swell draftsman I am—"

"Berg, you're gonna bollocks the whole thing up! I seen how you draw. Little kids should do it that bad." Court put down the nearly completed Wish Book and pushed me away from the sheet of paper and the pen. Pulling the stopper out of the ink bottle, he sighed and said, 'Ok, now what's all this stuff *look* like? I still think putting it in here is nuts, but your buddy got us the paper—"

"It isn't that...I was just thinking about his friend, Adi—"

"Oh...*him*."

"Yeah," I replied defensively, sitting down across from Court. "*Him*. Not what he is now, but what he was then. A G.I., like us. With nothing from home to share with his buddies. And him not thinking his talent was enough, that his postcards didn't mean shit. How would you have acted in his shoes, Court? Rolf said that Hitler wrote in his book that God told him to do what he did...you remember what they say about people who think God is telling them what to do. They're not well in the head. And in the States, that absolves them of guilt in a court of law—"

"Lissen to the half-Hebe defend—"

Ink sloshed onto the table when I pounded my fist close to the bottle. There wasn't a sound in the barracks save for the whispering crackle of the cook-stove fire as I said, "I don't give a *damn* for the bastard *now*. I'm talking about the foot soldier who *was*. The chump whose dog got stolen. And *his* old friend Rolf is eating his liver out because he thinks he should've done more for Adi back in 1917. That's a lot of years to carry around a load like that."

Court said nothing. Ink dripped through the chinks in the table and plopped like blood on the floor below. I took a deep breath and said, "And once we're out of this hole, and safe in the States, we're all going to think about Rolf, and wonder if maybe we shouldn't have done a little bit more for him. Because he gave to us when he didn't have to. He didn't know a Wish Book from the Good Book, but he went along with it and let his enemies make one, for *their morale*. Hell, the rest of the Krauts give us Axis Sally to cheer us on,. And he *asked* if he could help letter the bottoms of the frigging pages. Asked *us*, in *his* camp. Once we're out of here, you're *all* going to think about this, and don't tell me you won't."

There were a few beats of silence, and then one of the guys, I'm not sure which one, said, "Hell, drawing a few meals on dishes shouldn't be that hard, John."

Court ran the tipoff the pen along the drying ink stain before speaking. "I hope you know how he spells all this shit. I'm not damn good at German."

* * * *

Those last few pages of the Wish Book kept me running that December, while some of the men tunneled, and Court sweated it out over drawings of foodstuffs he'd never seen first-hand, I was pestering Rolf about what sorts of things his family ate at Christmas time when he was a boy. Occasionally, I even coaxed a spelling or two out of him. And once I had enough information, I'd hurry back to Court, so he could caption the finished drawings, and start new ones based on what I'd found out. And then I would run back to Rolf's office, to chew the fat with him and keep him from visiting our barracks as often as he liked to. For once I understood how parents felt when they were trying to keep the children out of the closet where all the holiday gifts are stored!

But the funny part was, it was a good feeling. Even Court began to enjoy his task; the drawings he produced would've made a stone drool. Of *Bunten teller*; a pretty dish loaded with cookies and fresh fruit, which Rolf had spoken of so fondly. A roast *Gans*, surely fit for God to eat. A special tree cake called a *Baumkuchen*, drawn in cut-away fashion to show the concentric rings of batter baked around a tube, much like the rings in a cut tree. The poppy-seed-filled yeast loaf, the *Mohnstritzel* Rolf had bought and eaten before "the other war." Pots filled with the stews Rolf described to me. Oysters. His *Schnitzel a la Holstein*, which consisted of tiny portions of smoked salmon, plus caviar, mushrooms, cooked crayfish and truffles, with a fried egg covering the *Schnitzel* itself, and a topping of anchovies, capers and parsley on top of the egg.

("Looks like a friggin' banquet on a plate," groused Court.)

The *Königenpasteten. Sauerbraten*, swimming in buttermilk and sweet cream and crumbs of honey cake. Marjoram-flecked dumplings.

And to wash it all down, this feast for the eyes, Court drew a page of beautifully-bottled liqueurs and beers, with cross-hatched drops of condensation on the sides of the bottles. I added the items to the index, carefully putting the tiny paired dots over the right letters. I found it ironic that Court chose to put the "Please LEND this Catalogue…" crawl-line on the bottom of every page of food he drew. I'd never dreamed he'd do it without being told to do so…and inside, I rejoiced over his decision.

I was too late to help the poor kid in the trenches, but Court was saved.

* * * *

As Christmas day approached, I was of two minds, though, utterly torn. Not only because of my dual religious heritage, but because of what was to happen on Christmas night…and afterward.

That evening I was to bring the Wish Book to Rolf, to pore over and maybe even cry over, prior to inviting him to our barracks. First for a makeshift "party" of hoarded Red Cross rations, and then… then Rolf would be *our* prisoner. A hostage, the ticket out for my men as they crawled through the now-finished tunnel which stopped just short of the second barbed-wire fence. My objections to the plan were overruled, my men wanted out, no matter how well they were treated here, and no matter what Rolf had done for them.

"Once we're out safe, see, we'll lead our boys to this dump, and set everybody free. Your pal Rolf, he'll be captured, shipped Stateside. Feed him up, do him some good—"

"And after the war? He'll be court-martialed here, or worse. He has to answer to the *Oberkommando des Heerees*—the High Command of his Army. They won't let him off with a slap on the wrist… he might be hanged, or shot. I thought you guys understood, and that that's why you worked on the book for him—"

"He worked on it for us, too. Lissen, if it makes you feel any better, I feel for the guy, too. Kinda. But we gotta get out of here," Court whined, his brown eyes moist. "I can't take it no more, and neither can the rest of us. Even dyin' on that fence is better'n living like this for another year. Or two, or three—"

"I'll do it on one condition…after this all blows over, I don't know *any* of you." I picked up the Wish Book—the cover stiffened with a thin coating of millet-glue over the fat jolly Santa—and tucked it under my arm before stomping out of the barracks, letting the door swing against the side of the building with a rifle-shark *crack*. Behind me, I heard someone close the door, softly…very softly.

When I was a few feet away, I stopped and took a look at the pages of the 944 Stalag 20-C Wish Book, the first and last issue in the printing run. It was a beautiful, loving thing; the one-sided pages almost glowed in the waning winter light. One crawl-line caught my eye, the one about lending the book to one's neighbors. On the other side of the fence, near the latrine, some of the over-worked half-starved Russians were watching me, with a wave I bounded to them, the book held open to the pages of *Gutes Essen*….

* * * *

It took longer than I'd planned, but I finally made it to Rolf's office, Wish Book tucked under my arm. The guards had long ago taken to ignoring me, for a P:.O.W. I came and went freely, but that day, I'd stopped every guard, to show him the book. Their eyes watered, even though the wind wasn't cold or fast enough to make them tear. A few lovingly patted the pages, rough-gloved fingers stopping short of the inked paper. And they rewarded me with smiles, all they had.

As usual, Rolf was seated behind his desk, eyes downcast; his fingers steepled as if in prayer. His mouth worked silently over his crooked bad teeth. Never had I seen a human being looking so dejected…until I saw the pictures from the Death Camps, later on, after the war, all the hollow-fleshed victims—

Rolf didn't look up as I came in and sat down, I held onto the Wish Book, not offering it to him yet.

"Rolf? You ok?"

He looked up at me, and rested his hands, palms down, on the desk. Behind his smudged lenses, his eyes were red-rimmed and bright.

"Oh, it is nothing…I was thinking, that is all. Of how…*perverted* everything has become. I was recalling how Adi used to become so withdrawn every *Wethnachstag*—Christmas day, like today—only perked up after the day had gone. And then, less than ten years later, he sits in that prison in Landsberg and writes in his book that *he* is God's chosen messenger, the savior of the Germans. And people believed him…the last time I went to see the Passion Play, it is ruined for me. Women in the audience shouting '*Es ist unser Hitler!*' when they nailed Christ to the cross…the rest of his cronies, they found places in the play, too.

"It's strange, if he really was God's chosen one, why did he not enjoy the special day His Father set aside for him to give gifts to mankind? I am not sure how you Americans do it, but here, St. Nicholas brings gifts on the sixth day of the month…for on Christ's special day, *das Christkind* brings us gifts. The day of His birth is a happy one, not a day to be sad like Adi was…for me, that alone is proof that Adi is not right in his mission. He cannot be God's chosen savior for the German people, for our country. And it is sad for me, for I want my nation to remain strong.

"I have seen how it can be when it is weakened…but is strength at such a cost real strength?"

I was close to crying myself when I pushed the Wish Book across the desk and into Rolf's sight. Slowly a smile overtook his pale, wrinkled face.

"For *me*?" No, no, it is yours, your work…go on, you and your men should enjoy it. Working on a part of it is thanks enough." Rolf touched the book longingly, before pushing it back toward me.

I saw the want in his eyes, before pride took over and hid it from me. It would have been easy, then, to pick up the book and head back to the barracks—in his condition, Rolf would never willingly accompany me. But then again, the party my men had in mind didn't have to end the way they'd planned it.…For poor Rolf, in telling his tales of Adi and the spurned offers of food from home, had laid himself bare in the process—and not covering that bareness would've been inhumane. Regardless of his country's politics.

"No, *Kommandant*," I said, approaching Rolf's desk. "I'm not leaving without you. And the Wish Book. My men have something special planned for you" (*just as I have something special planned for them*, I remember thinking) "and we want you to be there." Rolf barely had time to protest as I helped him on with his overcoat, and set his heavy hat on his head. And as we walked under the first dusting of stars in the clear, clear sky, I hoped that persuading my men not to escape that night wouldn't be too difficult.

For escape on Christmas night was *wrong*, war or not. *This* Christmas was a time for my men and Rolf to truly rejoice, in the spirit of the Wish Book he and my men had created. The dreams of many men, American and German, had gone into it, had made a dream real. And Rolf's dreams and memories were there, too, because they deserved to be. Nazi or not, he was more like us than we cared to admit, just as we were more like him and his kind than we *dared* admit.

Not caring what the guards thought, I linked arms with Rolf as I steered him toward my home for the past year and a quarter, toward the men who were only prepared for a party of a very different sort. Like it or not, he was going to really share Christmas with us, even if it was only a few hours spent poring over a hand-drawn catalogue.

I knew that all over Europe and the Pacific, soldiers and civilians alike were killing and being killed, in awful ways I wasn't even aware of until much, much later. And I knew that I was arm-in-arm with a Nazi who had shared a foxhole with Adolf Hitler, scourge of my father's people. But it was also Christmas night, the night of miracles, and nothing mattered to me but getting my friend into a circle of my other friends, so that he would be alone with his memories and his guilt.

For if I did to him what his kind was doing to *my* kind, I would have somehow been worse than a Nazi. And that would have been very bad indeed, more evil than the worst evil that walked the earth that day in black uniforms and *swastika* armbands.

It wasn't until Rolf and I got closer to my barracks that Rolf finally spoke "Good thing we're both skinny," he said, and when I looked at him quizzically, he went on, "I doubt you or any of your men would have had the strength to hoist me onto your shoulders and carry me here." Under the shimmer of starlight he smiled at me, his pitiful metal-rimmed teeth twinkling in the faint light. About then was when I noticed that something was wrong; the lights in all the barracks were much too bright, even with the candles and lanterns we'd been issued. Thoughts of cook-stoves overheating, or blowing up, crossed my mind; when my men flung open the door and crowded into the doorway, I saw brilliant light behind them, and my heart was still for a moment—until I saw the…awe on their faces.

"Berg, *Kommandant*, c'mere, quick!" Court was dancing in place like he had to use the latrine and had forgotten how to undo his pants. Rolf and I ran to the door, I let him go in first. All the men were jabbering so much I couldn't make out what they were saying... until Rolf's soft "What in *Himmel?*" made everyone stand silent. I elbowed past my men to stand next to Rolf...and stare in amazement at the table in the center of the room.

Christmas was there, in all its shimmering, glimmering, steaming, sweet-smelling and mouth-watering glory. Everything was there: the *Huntenteller* on a china dish, the roast *Glans* on a silver platter, the tree cake, the spicy stews, *everything*. And not inked illustrations in a hand-made Wish Book, but *real* wishes, the *real thing*.

Food. Not sawdust-gooey bread, or coffee like old dishwater, but all the *gutes Essen* in Germany, spread on that coarse typing paper only a few days before. Even the booze, in moisture-beaded bottles.

Rolf had his hand pressed to his lips; above them, his pale blue eyes were bugged out, staring and wide. Behind me, first one then all the men began to babble, "We was down in the tunnel when we smelled something—" "Like a light, a pure light, then—" "I know goose when I smell it—" "I looked at it and said, 'it was the Wish Book that done it'—"

In the distance, the babble of human voices grew loud, like a roaring beast; I ran to the window and saw that there was a feast in every building, with men standing around, staring and jabbering away, all afraid to actually touch the feast before them. I hurried outside, to the Russian's fence—in the distance, I saw the same glow in *their* barracks....

It was the Wish Book, it *had* to be...but how? It was only paper and ink and a little bit of hope—

Rolf said from where he stood beside me, "It is as I told you; this is the night of *das Christkind*, the child. Not that of my old friend Adi, wherever he has hidden himself on this glorious night. I was right...he is not our Savior. Poor Adi is not blessed.

"Perhaps the Child understands our Wish Book more than he does *Mein Kampf*...."

* * * *

What can I say of that night? No words can do justice to the feast, or to the toasts and *Gemütlichkeit*; it was a feeling beyond words which spread from barbed-wire fence to barbed-wire fence in Stalag 20-C—a feeling that a man once called Adi by his friends sadly could never feel, wherever he was holed up that night.

Songs were sung; bottles were raised high above open mouths. I remember at one point how Rolf took an apple, an almond and a walnut from the *Buntenteller* and said to me and whomever else cared to listen, "*Apfel, Nuss und Mandelkern...Apfel* for the tree of Knowledge, *Nuss und Mandelkern* whose kernels stand for the mysteries of life hidden by a hard shell. It is said that God gives us the nuts, but man must crack them for himself."

And we shared the *Dämmerschoppen*, even though it was long past twilight, and we passed tin mugs of *Göttertrunk*, and come the next morning, the camp was full of *Bierleichen* who snored half on and half off their bunks, or wherever else they had fallen in a drunken stupor. And it came as no surprise that come morning, the empty china plates and silver platters were gone, perhaps Whoever sent them realized that they would only have been sold to further the wrong cause, and to aid the wrong people.

And I was a man who was raised in a dual belief; Christ was both my Messiah and not my Messiah, and come morning I still felt that dichotomy deep in my heart. Christ had shown Himself, but not to my father's people. They were still dying in the camps, in the hell camps. They had had no Christmas feast...but even as the injustice stung me, I realized it made some sense, too. They believed what they chose to believe, what their hearts and consciences told them to believe. And that system of belief did not include our Wish Book, or He who brought our wishes to life that night. It was their choice, made long ago; that in itself was good, for man must have freedom of choice, or he will never be free.

Even if it is painful. Even if it kills him sometimes. For the lack of choice is far, far worse.

* * * *

I wish I could say that things were completely different in the camp after that special night, but the changes were only subtle ones—save for one thing. My men abandoned the tunnel. It was never discussed, never opened again; they knew Rolf knew about it, but likewise, he never spoke of it, nor did he send in the guards to fill it in.

The *cliques* of nationality and rank still remained, but we all exchanged waves more often. Rolf smiled more too, despite his horrible, sad teeth. But no one spoke of that night, not after Rolf went around the camp followed by guards bearing bottles of cheap *schnapps*. "*Katerfrustück*," Rolf said sheepishly, hand held to his aching head, "'Hair of the dog' I think you call it."

And none of us touched the Wish Book again, not until the day when Court picked it up off the chair where it had sat for the past six or so weeks after Christmas, and held it out to me, saying, "Bud, me and some of the others, we got to thinkin'. Suppose some of them Krauts find this, the ones who ain't like Rolf. Suppose they *do* something with it. I mean…."

I nodded, taking the curled Wish Book from his sweating hand. It felt like ordinary paper, but I wasn't so stupid as to believe it. Not for a minute.

"I think Rolf should be here when we do it…it's his book, too. Don't worry, he'll go along with us. I know him," I finished simply, before tossing the catalogue on the table and hurrying across the compound to find Rolf.

* * * *

In Rolf's language, they have an expression, *Der Herrenabend*, an evening for men alone. And late in the day, in the middle of February 1945, seventeen men stood in our barracks in a semi-circle around the opened cook-stove. Fire danced and crackled within, the flames shot up and consumed the 1944 Wish Book in a matter of seconds. The sparks looked like fireworks against the glowing grey interior of the stove. Rolf brushed off his warm hand on his coat; the fire had singed off a few of the fine blond hairs on the back of his hand, his fingers.

We were all silent as the flames licked the cover of the Wish Book. Santa Claus turned brown, then black, then fell in on himself and became fine grey ash. I felt a tear trickle down my cheek; there was so much good in that bound sheaf of typing paper and ink, so much *Gemütlichkeit*….

But Rolf assured me that there was potential for great harm in that book, too; his old friend Adi had been of a mystical bent, even when Rolf knew him. "I think my old comrade Adi would've understood the Wish Book," Rolf had told me in January, "but my enemy Adolf Hitler would *use* it. You see, I got a chance to meet with him, after the rally at Nüremberg in '34. His eyes had not forgotten about Fuchsl, or the supposed *Juden* who stole him. And when he grabbed both my hands in his, and stared at me with those huge intense eyes; telling me how much he'd missed me since the war, all I wanted to do was to pull my hands from his and wipe them on my uniform."

And so when the Wish Book was nothing but a fine smoking ash in our big cook-stove that February evening, Rolf paused to warm his hands over the ashes for a moment, before wordlessly turning around and leaving our barracks. There was nothing which needed saying.

* * * *

As it was, it was a good thing Court and the others abandoned their tunnel; three months after Rolf threw the Wish Book into our blazing stove, the war in Europe was over. Much later I learned that our boys had bombed Berlin on February first; a thousand bombers raiding the city. I'm sure Rolf had known, even out in the middle of nowhere. Just as he knew of other things happening elsewhere. I never asked him, even after the war was long over, but I think he was glad that the beginning of the end had come even as he threw what was perhaps the only hope his side had of winning into the flames. A Wagnerian end to the Nazi cause, if you think about it.

Fitting. Not so much for Rolf, but for the cause he hated and yet obeyed, because it was his way.

* * * *

The Russians and the Americans made it to our camp on the same day, May 10th, 1945. Later I learned that most other Stalag *Kommandants* had marched their prisoners as far away from the rescuing Allied troops as they could...but not Rolf. I walked with Rolf to the main gate, and only when the trucks and tanks were within ten feet of the gate did Rolf sigh, put his pistol on the ground in a show of resignation, and put his hands on top of his head. That pained me;

me, who had come to Germany to throttle the life and breath out of the first Nazi I could lay hands on.

Not knowing what to do, I watched helplessly as the Russians and the Americans—temporarily buddy-buddy in victory—rolled into our camp and herded the Germans into a big truck. But before Rolf was pushed inside, I cupped my hands around my mouth, shouting, "I live in Milwaukee, Wisconsin! Put an ad in *The Milwaukee Journal* when you can! I'll find it, I swear!" I wasn't sure if he'd heard me or not.

Rolf just smiled, and that was the last I saw of him before he disappeared into the green truck. One of the G.I.'s who'd just arrived turned to me, asking incredulously, "Did I just hear you give that Nazi corn-holer your address?"

Shoving my hands into my jacket pockets, I have him a hard stare, replying, "'Course not, Joe. Better clean the earwax out," before climbing into the nearest jeep and riding out of that hole.

There are some things a man must say to survive.

* * * *

Rolf did hear me, and he remembered the name of my hometown paper. Within two years, there it was; two lines in the classifieds, just a last name and a German address. I wrote and posted my letter to him by nightfall.

A month later his letter arrived; during the post-war trials, he'd been cleared of any wrong-doing, unlike many of his fellow camp commandants; most of them had tortured and killed Allied prisoners. Bad rations, beatings, forced work in enemy cities, you name it. But not Rolf.

He was living in München, with a pension, but he was working, too—"to support my 'habit'—we Germans have gone a little 'food crazy'!"

That letter came over forty years ago. Rolf and I still write, sometimes call, and always exchange Christmas cards. Maxine is Gentile, so *that* doesn't bother her, but Rolf himself does. My wife lost a brother in WWII.

In Germany.

She can't understand what Rolf and I shared, and I've never contacted the others from our Stalag. I doubt they'd speak of that night anyhow, or want to think of it. I mean, it *was* a good night, but there was a hint of danger which keeps men's tongues silent even as their hearts and brains quiver in feverish wonderment.

But Rolf and I often allude to the Wish Book; subtle references to it, and to a man named Adi. And to a dog named Fuchsl who didn't understand German. And down at the Post Office where I used to work, I had to stare at the photo of the current President on the wall, whether I'd voted for him or not. He was my President, all politics aside. Just as Adi was elected to be Rolf's *Führer*…like it or not.

And yes, I too often "wish and wonder" what might have happened if Rolf had acted the loyal supporter of the Third Reich and brought our Wish Book to his leader…complete with an extra page, a special page meant to transform a potential weapon into a thing of healing for old, old wounds. Perhaps…if we'd both been more daring, more foreseeing, it might've worked. Court could have come up with a good likeness of Fuchsl if Rolf described the dog. And the power of Adi's old need would've done the rest, I'm sure.

Perhaps, if Rolf and I hadn't been so afraid, so sure things were totally beyond repair or redemption, our Wish Book might have re-united—if even for a few moments, time enough to say a real good-bye, time enough for a hand to give a furry head a final caress—two old, dear friends.

Surely it is not an idle, evil wish; for hate piled on old hate is not the way to create a miracle. Our *Wehnachtstag* feast proved that. For late in the war as it was, such a miracle surely could not have hurt, or made matters any worse…could it?

Always, I will "wish and wonder" about that, whenever I hear the sound of a lone stray dog, barking in the night.

In memory of Fuchsl, who spoke no German

AFTERWORD

I don't think it would be too much of a stretch to say that in one way or another, I'd been gathering (albeit unknowingly) background information on this story most of my life. When I was quite small (and, by today's standards, much too young), my mother used to like to show me a paperback book about the horrors of the WWII Nazi concentration camps called *The Scourge of the Swastika*, which contained many graphic pictures of people who'd been mutilated by the doctors in the camps (one photo, of a tattoo taken from a man's chest and turned into a lamp shade, has never left me), as well as equally vivid written descriptions of the atrocities committed in the camps. Far stronger stuff than, say, Grimm's unexpurgated fairy tales. So I knew from a very, very early age about What the Nazis Did, and more or less Why They Did It.

Fast forward ahead a few years (about five or so), to the time when a co-worker of my mother's mother gave her a hardbound cookbook/social history of Germany, and German cuisine. I still have the book (it is one of the few books which belonged to her which I actually wanted to keep), and from the time I first saw it, I was entranced with the photo and drawing illustrations of the various German foods, complete with the original German names for the meals, plus some social history of the country—including some insight into the food shortages during the two World Wars, and their effect on the German peoples. Not that I've ever cooked any of the recipes in there—I can't stand cooking.

Now really hit the Fast Forward button until I'm college age; as part of one of my History minor courses, I was assigned John Toland's biography of Adolph Hitler, and (unlike many of my classmates) I actually did start to read that massive volume…but when I reached the part about Hitler's experiences in WWI, when he found an abandoned Fox Terrier on the battle field, whom he named Fuchsl, and kept with him as a friend and confidante until the animal was lost at a railway station, I couldn't go on. Now I was perfectly aware of what Hitler had done to countless innocent people (albeit with the aid of willing sycophants), and I also knew that what he'd done was morally inexcusable and reprehensible…but damned if I didn't feel sorry for that young foot soldier who lost his damn dog. Which was exactly what I knew I shouldn't be feeling.

But…years earlier, and thanks in whole to my mother's idiot mother, I'd lost one of my favorite cats, an orange-striped tomcat named Arthur. He'd been ill, and for some reason known only to her, that old toad let him outside…and he ran off. Probably to die; he'd been sick, and never should have been let outside. To this day, I loathe her for that (perhaps more so than for all the other sick, hateful things she did to me throughout my life), so it actually wasn't difficult to get under the skin of that German soldier whose dog was in all probability stolen that day at the train station. So it wasn't hard for me to postulate that Hitler may have mentally blamed the theft of his beloved Fuchsl on a Jew, since he was starting to show traces of anti-Semitism during his stint as a soldier.

However, before I stopped reading Mr. Toland's excellent book, I did get to the part where the *real* origins of anti-Semitism were explained; everything concerning Adi and what Rolf talks about in regard to the whole subject of the Jews and the Germans is taken from the Toland bio. Just as almost all of "Adi"'s experiences and exploits during the war are also factual, save for his conversation with Rolf about the dog.

The next element of this novelette fell into place when I read about a group of British P.O.W.'s whose German captors helped them obtain the materials for what was to become a very special project—a monthly, single-issue "magazine" drawn and lettered by hand by the prisoners, which was then passed form man to man in the camp. The Germans knew what the prisoners were up to, and willingly traded Red Cross materials for the paper and inks—even though the latter items were difficult for the Germans to obtain. I suppose their commandant was just as happy to see the prisoners oc-cupied with something other than an escape tunnel, but I had learned in my history classes that even though the Germans did many awful things during the war, for the most part, they were at least decent, and often humane, when it came to their P.O.W.'s. They honored the Red Cross/Geneva Convention, and some camp leaders allowed the men to do things like hoard their supplies to bake cakes/bread, etc. in their barracks. Others helped the men build boxing rings and exercise equipment (including the infamous Wooden Horse in that one British camp). Granted, the men were cold, and not well-fed, but compared to what happened to the P.O.W.'s unlucky enough to be in Japanese-run camps, the German camp commandants took it upon themselves to treat their prisoners (again, for the most part), in a civil manner; I do know that after the infamous Great Escape, the commandant of the P.O.W. camp was quite shocked to learn that those prisoners who'd been captured were to be shot on Hitler's orders—he had had no intention of killing the men had they been brought back to his camp. Most of these commandants were regular Army, and considered their prisoners to be fellow soldiers.

The last bit of background information came to me by accident; when I was doing the research for my novel *Dark Journey*, I ended up ordering many different reference books (my local library's nonfiction section is a joke), including a Dover Book showing Sears catalogue pages of toys from the 1930's to the 1940's—I'd wanted it for two male characters in the novel, but the majority of the pages shown were of dolls and the like (which eventually made up an extended flashback section late in the novel—if you've read the book, you'll know which scene I'm talking about). However, all the pages shown had these wonderful little tag lines along the bottoms, most of which worked their way into the novelette.

That reference book, coupled with the article I'd read about the British P.O.W. "magazine," solidified the Rolf/Bud storyline for me; I wrote this piece around the time I was working on *Dark Journey*, so it is one of my older works...unfortunately, a lot of editors were either turned off by the Adi/Fuchsl subplot, or didn't think that something like Bud and Rolf's friendship could happen. Too *Hogan's Heroes* for them, I guess. (One editor, whom I would love to name but won't [for my sake, not his!] went so far as to write a two-page, single-spaced rejection letter, where he dissected the work line-by-fricking-line, until he reached page 39 of the ms., at which point he rather proudly wrote "At this point, I stopped reading." What pissed *me* off was that this same editor had quickly gained a reputation as having a glacially-slow turn-around time...and when I saw how he was wasting time on rejections for works he totally hated, and never wanted to see again *anyhow*, I immediately wrote him off as a supreme a-hole jerk. Later on, I heard from other writers how he would mark up rejected mss. with a red pen, plus include a letter saying how much he disliked the thing...eventually, his turn-around time helped cost him his job, but that's another story!) But to get back to the novelette, eventually it did find a good home, up in Canada, in a digest magazine called *Challenging Destiny*. I wish I could reproduce the original illustrations—they were delightful, and quite lovely. All in all, the work was showcased marvelously well...but to this day, when I think of this piece, I eventually start crying. For my cat Arthur, who no doubt died alone and uncared-for. And, as politically incorrect and probably morally damning as it is, for little Fuchsl, who found himself lost and lone twice in his canine life, and even for his owner. The second one, who took him in even though he spoke no German.

While I have no way of knowing just how deep an impact the loss of his dog had on Hitler, I can all-too-easily imagine what he must have felt, there at that train station. And, considering that prior to WWI, he was basically an average person, who—while enduring some personal losses which were no doubt awful for him—seemed able to function normally in society, there's no doubting that the post-war Hitler was a far different person. Was the loss of Fuchsl enough to turn him into a monster? Is there any way to gauge when anyone has reached the point where yet another personal disaster, just *one* more deep disappointment, is enough to forever tilt that person's internal scales of balance off kilter?

I do know that Arthur has been missing over forty-two years now, but that hasn't stopped me from hurting, or from missing him. So, when it came to Fuchsl…who can really say?

AFTER THE AFTERWORD

It's been fourteen years since this novelette was published, and even more years since I actually wrote it back in the mid-1990's, and during that time, a couple of films have come out which feature punishments for Hitler of varying degrees of retribution/sheer perversity/personal satisfaction for the writer/directors, namely: *Little Nicky* from Adam Sandler in the 1990's; and Quentin Tarantino's alternate-history WWII epic, *Inglorious Bastards*. (Ironically, Tarantino is actually *in Little Nicky*, playing a blind street preacher, although Mr. Sandler does not appear in the other film, even though his former SNL cast-mate Mike Meyers has a surprising cameo role.)

As you can surmise, the down-in-Hell punishment doled out on a daily basis to the one-time leader of the Third Reich is suitably whacked out, gross and undoubtedly tasteless, yet understandable in its place in a Jewish comic's fantasy movie. What happened to the Jews (and many other people of different ethnicities and faiths) during Hitler's vile leadership was evil, and if it makes putting the leader of the Nazis into a French maid's costume, then forcing him to have…something (what it is I'll leave unsaid, in case any readers have yet to see the movie, which is actually a lot funnier than even I thought it would be) rammed…somewhere…every day at four in the afternoon, so that albeit comic karmic justice of a cinematic sort is accomplished, I say, Go for it, Sandler. The s.o.b. was asking for it.

And while the version of karmic retribution for Hitler in *Inglorious Bastards* is a wee bit more subtle (Hitler and Joseph Goebbels are killed before they can see the ending of a supposed propaganda film they'd championed and coaxed into being), during the scenes when he's interviewing one of the swastika-marked survivors of the latest "Nazi-killin'" attack by the Bastards, Hitler comes across as unstable, temperamental, and even childish, which is both fitting and more or less true to reality.

Personally, I was quite happy to see Tarantino break from the traditional WWII "sticking-close-to-historical-fact" movie formula; when the events in the French cinema start to build to the climactic scene of destruction and karmic justice, I found myself thinking of my novelette—prior to it being published, many editors had scolded me for not sticking with historical fact, or for creating events which simply made no sense to them.

But as I've watched Tarantino's film again (and again; I'm a huge fan of QT!), I've come to realize that I should have tweaked my ending just a bit, to make the punishment for Hitler more personal… to burn the "Wish Book" was a punishment, a way to make sure that a very sick, cruel man would never be afforded the comfort of his long-lost, beloved pet.

But I missed the bigger, crueler, picture: Burning the "Wish Book" would have made more sense if it had been done *after* Hitler had been made aware of its existence. But I doubt that my German prison-camp detainees, let alone their commandant, would have survived the war if that had been the case.

Now that I think about it, I've come to realize that what I actually wrote almost two decades ago was a fangirl "episode" of *The Twilight Zone*, the one-hour ones, from the fourth season, to be precise. (Mentally, I can even "see" it *as* a one-hour film, peopled with some of the cast from *Inglorious Bastards*, of course…as you can guess, *The Twilight Zone* meant—and still means—a great deal to me….)

But at least I'm more comfortable with what I wrote, now that I've seen what other folks have to offer in regard to How to Punish Hitler....

NORM LITTMAN'S 15 MINUTES

(with John S. Postovit)

"The day will come when everybody will be famous for 15 minutes"

—Andy Warhol

"I don't know what he was about. He was a mystery. But I still miss him."

—James Rosenquist, on Andy Warhol's death in 1987

"Thursday, April 16, 1981…I'm in this period where I think, What is it all about? You do this and what does it mean, and you do that and what does it mean?"

—Andy Warhol
The Andy Warhol Diaries

Click! wurrrr….

The Wanna-Be was back in the gallery. I didn't even need to turn around anymore, like I did on the first couple of days of the exhibition, to know that *he* was back, snapping pictures. But not pictures *of* the pictures, like everyone else was doing. It was kinda hard to tell just *what* the Wanna-Be was aiming his camera at. I mean, he'd have this 35 mm pointing at the stuff *between* the stuff on the walls, or at the line where the carpeting met the white-painted walls. Sorta like a kid who picks up his Dad's Nikon and spends half an hour playing *paparazzo* with imaginary movie stars, until Dad comes home and whupps the stuffing out of the kid's cushions for messing with an expensive camera. And never mind what the old man's gonna say when the pictures get developed.

That's what the Wanna-be reminded me of, even though he was way too old to be playing with a fancy-schmancy camera like film grew on trees and he'd raked himself a big pile.

All it was was **Click! wurrrr….**, move on to the next empty space between things, then pause to drop in some more film when the roll was full. The Wanna-Be had this little plastic shopping bag, the crinkly white kind with the self-handles like they give you in the grocery store (unless they run low and try to sneak one of those old paper bags on you, then grump a lot when you insist on a plastic one anyhow), and I could see the outlines and vague colors of the 35 mm film boxes inside. He had *that* bag slung over his left arm. On the other arm, he had a couple more bags, ones with the college logo on them, from the little gift shop Dean Yarrow's wife and her art-fart crowd run during exhibitions at the college gallery.

The stuff in his grocery store bag never changed, but he had different stuff in his art gallery bags every night. Postcards, sweatshirts with the frat and sorority letters on them, those little pottery gim-cracks the ceramics students turn out by the kilnful—every night there was something new weighing down his right arm.

Tell the truth, I really didn't notice what the Wanna-Be had bought himself on the first night of the exhibition, 'cause there were just too many Wanna-Be's running around who looked more or less like the camera-toting Wanna-Be so that you needed a score card to keep them all straight. There were the girl ones, and the black ones, and the ones who got the glasses or the white wig all wrong, and the ones who couldn't keep their yaps shut and kept spouting, "Hi, I'm Andy Warhol, and for fifteen minutes we'll *all* be famous."

When I walked into the gallery that night, February 20, it was like that picture of the Campbell's soup cans come to life, only instead of can after can of red-and-white labels, it was like face after face of Warhol. All pale wigs and big glasses and black turtlenecks. One of the few folks who did look different was Dean Yarrow's wife, and *she* looked like the soup can picture I was just talking about. It was her dress. A webby papery thing, sorta like a hospital gown but with no sleeves and no slit up the back, and piped with black all around the armholes and neck. Printed all over with soup cans, 'cept for the horizontal gold-and-white stripes on the bottom. It was a Campbell's give-away back, oh, in '67 or '68. Cost two labels and a buck. But on Dean Yarrow's wife, the cans looked like the ones you'd buy at a warehouse outlet, after some kid stocking shelves slipped on a grap and dropped the whole case of soup.

"*Norm*," the Dean's missus gushed, waddle-crinkling over to where I was standing, "You *must* bring in some of those Brillo boxes from that closet of—" She was practically gleeful—gleeful, that's what you call it.. 'Course, why wouldn't she be, here in the boonies of Wisconsin in a fly-speck college on the opening night of an Andy Warhol exhibit that *she'd* arranged. Buku expensive for a college gallery that usually exhibited local-yokel artists or students. But she'd managed to get a giant grant from the state. "Bringing art to the *people*," that's what she'd been gushing all night.

So…it pleased me no end to tell her that I'd tossed out the last box of Brillo, even though I had a whole fresh *case* of them sitting in the cramped room where I store my janitorial supplies. I use it—the Brillo—to rub lime deposits off the restroom faucets. Water's pretty hard up this way in Wisconsin.

Mrs. Yarrow sighed, and I smelled those horrible cheese-nut whahoozies on her breath, the puffy things she bakes up every time there's a new show in the gallery. The ones people take, bite into, and then hide somewhere narrow and dark and out of sight. Now that's a job worse than acting as a "security person" (Mrs. Yarrow's fancy talk) for whatever traveling exhibit is housed in the campus gallery—cheese-nut whahoozie hunting. And the art-farts who come to these exhibits are tip-top whahoozie-hiders. And if you don't find one of them suckers within two days the gallery stinks worse than the football team's locker room.

Just to get even withu Mrs. Yarrow for baking up those smelly puffs—again—I added, "Nope, no Brillo left in this building. Want I should run to the store and buy some?"

Mrs. Yarrow crinkled her fat cheeks and nose until her red-framed glasses rode up above her plucked eyebrows. "Oh, *no*, Norman, not to*night*! This is a very *expensive* collection—Warhol's still *very* hot, you know," she confided, which was about as astounding as saying that the walls around us happened to be painted *white*. That's what I *really* hate about Dean Yarrow's wife—she acts like a person is an intellectual moron if he isn't glued to *Masterpiece Theatre* during supper, or doesn't read *Smithsonian* magazine while taking a crap. Heck, *I* knew who Andy *Warhol* was. I'd seen the reports on the news when they auctioned off his stuff, and I'd bought those *People* magazines with his diary excerpts in them. Actually, the only time I've been kinda confused on all this artsy-schmartzy stuff was the time when I brought along a pen and piece of paper when they had that George Segal exhibit. How was I supposed to know that there's an actor *and* an artist with the same name? (If you can call dummies covered with white gauze bandages or whatever the heck he used on them *art*....)

But art critic or not, I knew me one thing about art—once the artist goes to the big palette in the sky, all those Japanese businessmen start checking over their bank accounts, just panting for when the auction of the painter's stuff will begin.

And *that* night, I didn't even think that the exhibit was anything to start hyperventilating over, even with the guy being five years dead and the room filled with all those Wanna-Be's. I mean, all there was was pictures of *Coke* bottles, and Liz Taylor with way too much make-up And one of a guy wearing a James Dean tee shirt, only instead of one picture being worth, like maybe ten words, there were just four pictures, all alike, and stacked together.

I thought I knew what it was like being a fly, all those multiple images swimming around me as I strolled around the gallery, to make sure no one took anything off the walls and rolled it up in a back pocket. Kind of a stupid job, when you think on it, but it gives me an excuse to wear a sports jacket and tie a few nights a month, not to mention the extra bucks on the paycheck. And it makes Mrs. Yarrow and the rest of the art-tarts happy.

When I couldn't take looking at the pictures anymore, or at the Wanna-Be's (now why can't Madonna paint—I'd go for a room full of girls in those bustier things), there were framed sayings some of the art students had lettered hanging around the gallery—"The whole thing is work. Everything is work" "..a sphinx without a secret" "Great, great, great" "Sex and parties are the two things you still have to actually be there for" and "In the future, everyone will be famous for 15 minutes"

I supposed it was stuff Warhol had said, or that people said about him. From the looks of the hangers-on flitting about the gallery, there were a lot of folks who thought that tonight was when their 15 minutes were coming due. There had been a rumor buzzing around campus that the MTV News crew was following this mini exhibit of Warhol's stuff around, but if they were, someone must've tipped 'em off about the cheese-nut whahoozies, 'cause they never did show up.

The throngs of Wanna-Be's thinned out the night after the big opening. That was when I noticed the old, picture-shooting Wanna-Be. I suppose he was there before, but like I said, it was fly-eye time that first night. And while the old guy wasn't the only wigged and bespectacled person toting a camera, he was the only one who both took pictures *and* kept his lip zipped. The being quiet part didn't bother me none, but the pictures part did. It was kinda weird, how he just bobbed through the gallery, not even looking at "his" artwork, only pausing to take pictures of the nothing between the something. Not a peep out of him, only **Click! wurrrr**....and sometimes he soft crunch of his hand rooting around in that plastic grocery bag.

But to me, the ironic thing was that nobody paid him any mind. Like his get-up made him invisible, even though the twerps on the campus news rag stopped nearly every *other* Wanna-Be for some words of wisdom to print in the next issue. I don't think it was him being really old—easily senior citizen discount age—that made them all shy away from him, because there were a couple of other older men sporting silver-white wigs hanging around the gallery. And him being quiet didn't seem to be the problem—if a Wanna-Be wasn't yakking, one of the little skirts on the paper staff would pester him or her into at least repeating the "15 minutes" bit.

Maybe it was the determined way he took his pictures. No, not determined...*fated*'s more like it. Sorta like he was saying, Don't bug me, I *gotta* be doing this.

Thinking it over, it seems that I really took an interest in the old guy because of his cheekbones. They proved that he was a Slav, like Warhol was (I'd read or heard someplace that his real name was Warhola, which is about as Czech as you can get. Being Czech on Ma's side, I know Slav cheekbones when I see 'em. I don't have Horvokas, Husas, Horacks and Smetanas on my family tree for *nothing*.)

And the Wanna-Be sorta looked like Warhol, only older, which made sense when you figure that if Warhol hadn't of died five years ago, he really would be in his sixties. Anyhow, judging from those pictures in *People*, Warhol looked like something he'd silk-screened—all broad areas of tone, with no definition. (I'm not as blind as Mrs. Yarrow thinks I am—I *do* notice more in life than wrestling and which TV dinner I pop in the oven. I just like to drive her nuts by not bragging about what I know.)

Wasn't easy to follow the Wanna-Be, though. Just when I'd stroll closer for a better look at him (and to sniff out any half-chewed cheese-nut whahoozies), he'd take a left or right and wander past me, off for the opposite end of the gallery. A few seconds later I'd hear him, **Click**ing and **wurrrr**ing behind me—*right* behind me, which made me start and turn around real quick.

But like I said before, after a while I got used to it, and didn't jump in my clothes when he came up behind me. Funny thing, how he always had plenty of stuff from the art gallery shop, but I never noticed *when* he bought it. Like his bags filled by osmosis whenever he passed by the shop itself.

By the third day of the exhibit, the 22nd, I noticed a few new things about the Wanna-Be. He still wore the "uniform" that all the Wanna-Bes wore—black sweater, dark jeans, penny loafers, big glasses, wig, and camera—but there was something odd *under* his dark turtleneck. Big lumps near his collarbones, like giant-size warts or moles, all in a semi-circle. None of the others had had those bumps under their sweaters. And they moved; when he turned his head one time, they all shifted along with his neck.

That's when it dawned on me—he'd swiped something. From the gift-shop, most likely, since all the artwork here was square, flat, and bigger than he was. No wonder he was distant, and did the camera thing. Shoplifter tricks. At last, a chance to do some real security work—"Hey. You. Bud. With the camera." I was trying to sound authoritative, but it came out like Leslie Nielsen playing "bad cop" on *Police Squad*. At least the guy didn't laugh. He turned around, took a picture of something beyond my left shoulder, and asked, "Me?" only it wasn't like a question, exactly. Real flat, expressionless voice. Behind his glasses, his eyes were very brown and kinda flat, like tiny contact lenses held cupped-side out, so all I saw was dark pooled inside, with no reflection of me.

"Uh…I'm the security guard, and I…uh, noticed something under your sweater—" I was talking kinda low, so no one (Mrs. Yarrow in particular) would hear me make an ass of myself in front of a gallery visitor, in case the guy *did* have warts or something. Ones that shifted.

"Oh. You mean this?" Letting the camera swing on its strap, the Wanna-Be patted his collar bones, pulling the knit close to the

lumps. In the even white light, I saw the fuzz-dulled gleam of precious stones. A necklace, with rocks that didn't come from any tacky-
schmacky faculty-run college gift shop.

Feeling like a grade-A prime asshole, hoping that nobody'd noticed what I'd done, I mumbled, "Sorry, Bud…I wasn't sure—"

"I don't like to show them off," the guy droned, his voice barely
rising above the low rumble of conversation around us, "but I like to
just have them with me." He didn't say any more, but didn't move,
either. Like the ball was in my court and it was time to dribble.

"Uh…well, that's okay, Bud. Just my job, y'know. Otherwise
they don't think they get their money's worth."

"I like money too," the Wanna-Be said solemnly. Over his dark-
jacketed shoulder, I saw a picture Warhol'd done. Money. Lots of
dollar bills. It figured; this guy was an *expert* Warhol Wanna-Be.

More silence, the kind that just aches to be filled. It was like the
guy had this vacuum aura around him, so unnatural I just *had* to fill
it up. Like this guy had taken the "…sphinx without a secret" bit to
heart.

Around us, the sporadic groups of visitors ebbed and flowed, and
I think I heard Mrs. Yarrow jabbering around a mouthful of whahoozies, but—and it gets strange here—it was like the Wanna-Be and
I were alone in the gallery. Spooky (I'd read about the real Warhol
having a boyfriend and all), yet sort of reassuring, too. He wasn't
threatening in his silence, like the jocks who've had one too many
and block my way in the halls come night time, so I have to mop
around them. It was like…even as he was there, he wasn't *there*.
Not like other people, when they're complete. I mean, I couldn't see
through him, nothing like *that*, but…well, he just wasn't *complete*.
Least not without a person having to add something to him. Shovel
something into the void.

"Ummm, yeah. Money's good. You've got a point there. Uh,
Bud, you a student here? An artist? I notice you been coming here
every—"

"This is my show." Self-assured, yet not bragging, either. I waited
for the "15 minutes" bit, but he didn't say it. Just stared with those
brown, brown eyes, like he was and wasn't interested in me. Uncom-
fortable, remembering about Warhol kissing all those celebrity guys,
I scratched the back of my neck until I noticed that his bag of film

was mainly full of used film in the little grey-and-black holders, the kind kids here use to store pot in, plus the opened boxes.

"Hey, Bud, you're gonna have some processing bill for all those."

A nod of the silver-wigged head. I saw wisps of greying hair peeping around the bottom edges. Little shadows pooled in the deep pores on his slightly bulbous nose. Only color on his face was the shiny part inside his lips. The guy was unnerving—in one way he looked realer than real, with every pore, whisker and flake of dead skin high-lighted, yet…in another way he wasn't real at all. Like those resin people statues they had here once.

Mrs. Yarrow was laughing at something—Dean Yarrow's lucky that there are no male hyenas in Wisconsin. The Wanna-Be turned to stare at her with all the involvement of a pigeon looking around for something to splatter. Like one thing's as good as the next. Snapped her picture, too. That caught Mrs. Yarrow's attention; she turned around and mouthed, *Get back to work* to me, then turned back to whomever she'd been jabbering at.

The Wanna-Be was gone by the time I turned my head. So I walked around some more, until the gallery closed, and I could do my real job, janitorial work.

After hanging my jacket and good shirt on a bent nail in my office, I got to work, vacuuming the gallery walls and carpet, with that stupid industrial machine that doesn't pick up lint unless I put my back into every inch of nap. (Why the Dean won't spring for an upright is beyond *me*.) The vacuum makes enough noise to make a buffalo deaf at twenty miles, so at first I didn't hear anything as I worked, but when the long hose attachment got all twisted around, I had to shut off the motor—and nearly jumped out of my jeans when I heard that **Click! wurrrr....** from across the room. The old Wanna-Be was standing next to the Liz Taylor picture, his pale face and hands sorta leeching *into* the wall behind him, I hesitated before yelling, I mean it was such a strange illusion. Like the wall was wearing clothes.

Then I came to my senses. "Hey, Bud! What the fuck you *doing*?"

In answer, he snapped a picture of me, grungy tee shirt and all.

"*Hey*! Knock it *off*, Bud! If anyone sees you in here, my ass is burnt brown grass…gallery's closed, Bud. Time to shove off—"

(Funny, he *wasn't* in the gallery when I shut the door—)

"This is where I belong."

"Oh…you mean you came with the show. Like the other guy," I said, thinking of the representative of the collection who was staying with the Yarrows.

"This is my show." Just like he said it before.

Well…the guy wasn't *damaging* the art, and I figured he'd paid to come every night. And wearing a necklace under his clothes wasn't a *crime*—

"Uh…what I'm asking is, do you *belong* here? It's okay with the Dean's wife?"

"Tina?" That clinched it for me; he knew her first name. Few of the students knew Mrs. Yarrow's first name. (The woman doesn't *look* like a "Tina.") So he *had* to be one of her artsy-smartsy cronies, maybe a companion of the guy who travelled with the exhibit. *I* wasn't privy to her "inner circle."

"Then I guess it's all right if you stay. But only until I'm done working, okay? And don't *touch* anything," I pleaded, as I turned on the vacuum. His silvery-wigged head woggled absent-mindedly as he went about taking pictures of whatever it was he saw that I couldn't.

Actually it was kinda nice having someone to keep me company as I worked. I mean, being a janitor suits me fine most of the time, 'cause I'm not much of one for conversation or going out with the guys. I like my wrestling on TBS and USA, and I like my TV dinners extra hot so the steam rises up so thick I don't have to really look at how much of a dump my apartment is. Like the line about the cobbler's kids needing shoes. I'm the janitor with the sloppy house But it's mine, and no one ever comes over, so who's the wiser, right?

I like being alone, but the being lonely part's the killer.

But most folks are twits anyhow, so usually I'm happy alone… yet, for some reason, it was getting to me that night, until I noticed the Wanna-Be in the gallery with me. I guess that's why I got a little panic-filled when I turned around and noticed that he'd left the gallery. "Easy come, easy go," I muttered, and kept on working, until I half-heard something strange, yet familiar, out in the hall beyond the gallery before it branches off into the student lounge. Not the sound of his camera, but the sound of *my* stuff in the "office" being moved around.

The Wanna-Be *was* rooting in my stuff, shoving aside cartons of liquid cleaner and old buckets, mumbling "Great, great," as he pawed over my cleaning supplies. As I watched him from the doorway, he finally found what he'd been after—the boxes of Brillo Mrs. Yarrow had wanted for the exhibit. (I'd seen pictures of those big Brillo boxes Warhol did, after he'd died—and they weren't in this exhibit. I guess Mrs. Yarrow thought nobody'd notice if they were kinda small.)

The old guy quickly pulled the boxes out and stacked them against a corner of the tiny room, then snapped a picture. I waited until he **wurrrred** the film forward before shouting, "You deaf, Bud? I *said* DON'T TOUCH ANYTHING!"

I suppose I shouldn't have done that, blowing up at someone who knew Mrs. Yarrow by her first name, and probably could get me fired, but he was grubbing in *my* space. I mean, I don't have much in life, but it was mine, my little corner of this big, indifferent world, and it's all I'm ever going to have at my age, so him playing with the Brillo boxes was important. Something I couldn't let just go by.

"Oh. This is your stuff. You were cleaning my stuff, so I—"

"You Wanna-Be's are all alike, aren't you Bud? *You*'re nothing, so you latch onto something bigger and better than you just so the *impression* of somebody great rubs off, huh? Wanting to be someone is one thing. Doing it's another. Shit, I wanna be famous, too, but if I am, I want it because of *me*, understand?"

He just stared at me with those flat brown eyes, not agreeing or disagreeing. Empty. Waiting for me to spout off. Which I did:

"Trouble with you is, you kinda do look like this Warhol, and that makes you think you *are* him. Run around snapping pictures of nothing, standing around like a *sphinx*—"

"Truman said that about me. We weren't anything alike, really—"

"Who?" The real Warhol knew half the universe, so I didn't remember which "Truman" he was talking about.

"*Capote*. He said that. About me. I puzzled him—"

"Oh c'mon already. Quit talking about dead guys." It was funny, but I wasn't as mad anymore, even though the Wanna-Be was obviously trying to get to me by *not* seeming to want to get to me.

"Truman dead…know what? I know he is, but I don't believe it because he wasn't around when it *happened*. Like I wasn't." He half-smiled at that, a sad, knowing little smile that looked copied off some advertisement.

"You cop that line from one of Warhol's books?" I leaned against the doorway and patted my pockets for a cigarette. He nodded, but added, "I got it from *me*. It's written in one of my books, if you care to look it up—"

Shaking out my match, I said through a haze of smoke, "Which one, the diary or the one from '88? That party book—" I'd read about that one in a Sunday edition of some newspaper.

"No and no. *The Philosophy of Andy Warhol*. My book," he insisted, and it was then that I noticed that his detachment was chipping away bit by bit. Even his eyes lost some of that flat shine; I could see *in* them a little. And what I saw looked kinda *lonely*. A look I knew from my own mirror.

"Really? So that mean's I'm talking to a stiff, right?"

"Do I look like one?" A real question at last. I noticed that he was sweating; my "office" adjoins the pump room, which heats the gallery.

"Nah," I drawled, as he took off his jacket. Man, was he skinny. He moved stiffly; under his sweater I noticed he had on more than the hidden necklace. A corset or brace of some kind, around his middle. I saw that painting of Warhol they showed on CBS's Sunday news show with Charlie Kuralt, the one showing his scars from when that nutty dame shot him. Whoever this guy *was*, he had *everything* down pat. Patter than pat....But the guy seemed so earnest, so...*driven*, I couldn't bear to be mean anymore.

"Hey, Bud, whatever you want to be called—"

"Some people called me 'Drella whether I liked it or not, but Bud's good—"

"'Drella-Bud, whatever, you up to sharing a 'bach' dinner? I have some sandwiches, nothing fancy, but...and some cookies—"

"Mint ones?" He actually looked eager.

"No...Oreos. But they're double stuff ones—"

"Okay...."

So we sat on cartons and shared my meager bachelor's feast. I know the guy had to have bukus of money, to afford that necklace and all that film, but Hell, he looked *hungry*. And it was my food, not Mrs. Yarrow's putrid cheese-nut whahoozies. I mean, pawing through my stuff or not, he didn't deserve *that* kind of punishment.

As we ate, I talked. About how I could kill the kids when they rammed whole rolls of toilet paper into the johns, and how Mrs. Yarrow's art-fart crowd got on my nerves, and how I wasn't in any rush to come home at night, save for needing a place to sleep. I talked way too much, but the Wanna-Be didn't mind. He just chewed and nodded and listened to me, like I was ten times more powerful than Dean Yarrow or the college president, even. Like I *mattered*. The only time he spoke to me was when I said that I didn't really understand "his" artwork (I was humoring the guy by then, saying this or that was "his" creation, or "his" words.)

"I don't know if anything I did *is* art, even though, on one level, it's *all* art. I mean, people bought my stuff because of who I wa—*am*, and because their friends all bought it…it got to the point where I never could be sure *why* they bought it. But if my art *is* like, *art*, I guess it's because *everything* is art, if you think about it." He picked up his sandwich bag, holding it at my eye level. "I guess this is art, same as my silkscreens in there. You're art, just like Marilyn or Mao. I guess *I'm* art, too," he added with a self-deprecating chuckle.

"No kidding," I mumbled around my bologna on rye.

"Some people claimed I was my own best creation…and I am. Thirty years ago, I didn't know what to do, what to paint…I had no *ideas*. Then I looked at a can of soup and realized it could be art. Art for everyone. You go to the store, and there's art all around you. If it is designed, that's a form of art…but no one had put it out *as* art before. That's why I collected everything. Good, bad, whatever. In its own way, it was art—"

"Auctioned off for a pretty penny, too—"

"Because I saw it as art…no, I know that it sold high because of *me*, period. I may be dead, but I'm not *obtuse*—"

Since he'd brought up the subject, I took a stab at finding out something which had been bothering me. Even if he was a fake.

"Yeah, well, since you're…uh, *dead*, what's it like?"

"Now or when it happened?" I didn't like the look in his brown eyes. For a second I was afraid he might really know the truth—and tell me.

"Uh…whenever."

"I don't remember what it felt like when it *happened*. I was asleep. But now…it's actually an awful lot like it was before. You just *are*, without remembering exactly when you knew it. You go around, but things aren't much better than they were in life. People act nicer when it comes to remembering you, sometimes nicer than they were when you were alive. But not much is different. It's something like going to a party where everyone is so accustomed to seeing you around they don't notice you even if you are there!"

I smiled to myself. Guy's *gotta* be a fake. Spouting platitudes and pop philosophy….Just like the *real* Warhol did, I thought with a little discomfort, like a stifled burp.

"—I was so famous, everybody knew me, so now nobody notices me," he was saying as he gathered up his crinkly bags from where he'd placed them by his feet while he ate.

"You're not *going*?" I asked, too fast.

"'Fraid so…I have other places to be. Other showings of my work. I follow it," he finished simply. I suppose my face betrayed me, or something, for he handed me the grocery bag full of exposed film.

"This is for the food. The cookies were very good. Now I have to go get some tea. I saw a restaurant down the road." With that he was gone; jacket under one arm, gift shop bags under the other, a skinny short silver-wigged old man trotting briskly down the hall.

I started to call after him, but didn't. I'm *not* lonely.

Least not in front of a stranger.

It wasn't until he was gone that I realized there was something odd about the bag of film—it was too heavy. Peering in the white bag, I saw the Wanna-Be's camera nestled among the round rolls of exposed film. I was so busy yakking I didn't see when he slipped it in the bag.

I don't take pictures myself, so I don't know an F-stop from my a-hole. But I knew where I could get those rolls of film developed.

For free.

Being a janitor, I do a lot of walking around the campus at night. Past a lot of rooms which should be locked come day's end but aren't. And sometimes when I clean a classroom I find more than dirty blackboards, if you get my drift. One kid in particular is a real Romeo, carries on like the world's his oyster and there's no such thing as AIDS. After I stumbled on him in six different rooms with as many different girls, the kid got this strange notion he *owed* me something for me keeping my yap shut. Me, I figure it's his life and his business if he wants to be an irresponsible little geek, so I never took him up before on his offer of "anything, any favor you *want*, Norm"—but the punk *is* a photography minor....

And he didn't bat an eye when I dumped the bag of film in the darkroom the next day (I wasn't a *chump*—I took out the camera) and come evening, close to the time when I was getting ready to patrol the exhibit, Mr. Sexy came trotting down to my "office," panting, "Mister *Litt*man, wait'll you see *these*!"

"Don't tell me, they're all blank, right?" I adjusted my jacket collar. Romeo pushed a manila envelope into my hand, saying, "No *way*...why didn't you tell me you were this good? Makes me feel like a piker—"

I ripped open the envelope and pulled out twenty glossy sheets covered with tiny strips of pictures.

"What's this shit? I wanted individual pictures—"

"Contact sheets. I didn't know which ones you'd want enlarged or how big—"

I held the sheets up to the light. Even with the pictures being so tiny, I knew right off what I was looking at—it was like, yet wasn't like, the works I'd been casually guarding in the gallery for the past few days.

Somehow, the Wanna-Be hadn't been photographing blank walls *or* the view over my shoulder...but he wasn't taking pictures of anything which existed in the gallery, either. In fact, I doubt that the things he'd been snapping pictures of could ever look like that in real life.

There must've been over a hundred images, small, but not so small that I couldn't help but see that they were all Andy Warhol's *artwork*. Not bad copies, not even good copies. *His* stuff. I *felt* it.

Except...except...I'd never met the real Andy Warhol, yet there was a picture of *me* among the 1990 model cars, new cereal and dog food boxes, soda bottles and soup cans, *dozens* of other things.

Me, with a lavender face and flat-looking, brightly-colored hair and eyes, colors that clashed in a special way unique to Warhol, just like the ones on the Marilyn and Liz pictures in the gallery.

These were real, *new* Warhol works. Not copies, not something his assistants at that "Factory" studio of his churned out. There was just this *touch* to everything. Not copies, like that pattern on the soup can dress Mrs. Yarrow had. I don't know much about high art, but sometimes knowing isn't the same as *knowing* in the gut. A hundred little things I half-understood told me my hunch was right—the way the colors went together, the simple flat shadings, the odd strings of detail here and there. And the choice of images—like he said in my "office," this *was* art for everyone.

Even a schlump like me. There were pictures of my "office." My mop bucket. My pegboard of tools and electrical tape. My folded lunch bag. And the funny, wonderful thing was, no matter how much he'd doubted himself, this really *was* art. Simple things, stuff I'd considered ugly, even, but when he let me see through his eyes, even my homely belongings were *beautiful.*

I don't know why, but my eyes teared up. Drops of moisture beaded on my eyelashes as the kid said, "Tell me which ones you want copied, 'kay, Norm? gotta get going," but I didn't turn around until after he left. When I moved my head, the light made the tears in my eyes shimmer, in rainbow colors—and I saw the world through different eyes. A *dead* guy's eyes, to be honest.

My can of Comet was breathtaking. My mop glowed. The hallway beyond my door was something out of a fairy tale—the kind I hadn't believed in for years.

I glanced at the sheets again. The pictures were true Warhol... but how he'd painted or silk-screened or what*ever*ed them, let alone snapped pictures of them, was beyond me. Especially in a gallery showing an exhibit of his work five years after his death—

Suddenly I shook the envelope. I heard film stock rattling inside. Mr. Horny-Toad had put in the negatives...but he'd never see them again, that's for sure. Heart doing the rhumba in my chest, I stashed the negatives and contact sheets in my "office," locked it, and hurried to the gallery. Just in *case*—

But he wasn't there. No more **Click! wurrrr....**No Wanna-Be's at all, in fact. Everyone gave up on MTV showing up. Even Mrs. Yarrow was moping in a pink pants suit.

And me? I wandered around the exhibit, intoxicated. It all made so much *sense.* I wanted to hug myself—it's all so clear, so plain, yet so lovely. Everything is art, all around me. Not just the Warhol works, but everything. The biggest damn art gallery in the world *is* the world. And we're all part of the exhibit.

I finally felt important, like *my* 15 minutes had come. And I'd earned them, every last second of them.

But in the middle of all this, I realized that I couldn't just hog all I'd discovered, either. There are a lot of schlumps like me out there, who are just so blind—and the irony was, even the Wanna—even *Warhol*—didn't really realize what he'd *given* to everyone.

The exhibit was closing the next day; more people showed up to help the guy who traveled with the exhibition cart up everything and take it to the next stop on the tour. I showed up early for work, just so I could talk to them, and *show* them. At least that's what I was thinking, that I *had* to share this with the world—both the art and the Warhol-running-around part, but...I suppose I should've known what would happen if I tried to tell it in *order*—

Before I showed them the contact sheets, I explained the part about the Wanna-Be, working up to his payment for our meal, and up to that point the exhibit guys were looking like "Uh, *huh*, *sure*" at each other, but when I mentioned how the camera made the bag heavy—

"Do you have this camera *with* you?" the guy who'd been staying with the Yarrows asked me, his pale eyes glittering. That glitter should've warned me....

Like a dummy, I showed them the camera. And one of the younger guys, who'd actually met Warhol before 1987, began shaking.

"This is one of *his* cameras," he whispered, in this voice that made "*his*" sound like it should've been in capitals, like God or something. "This is the one he bought at Saks in '85, I was with him when he bought it, see, here's the little nick in the casing—I have a *picture*, of him and Jerry Hall, and Andy was carrying this—"

You guessed it. Warhol *did* own that camera. I saw the picture of him, it and Jerry Hall. And the fingerprints were there. *His.* They actually checked, only later on. *That* day, they didn't care about my story about how I got it; they said, "What matters is that it has been *found*!" like they'd stumbled across the Holy Grail in a back alley. Which maybe wasn't all that far from the truth. Least as far as I'm concerned.

The weird thing was, no one was interested in the contact sheets. Oh they looked, with a little magnifying glass set in a round black case, and said, "Nice work," and "Playful anachronisms," and then forgot all about them. There was publicity to arrange, and the auction to organize. I even got a share of the money...after they verified that I really *didn't* steal the camera that no one had actually reported missing in the first place. After all, they keep finding stuff in Warhol's closets and studio anyhow.

And I even got my 15 minutes. On MTV News, all the other news services, too. A nine second segment played umpteen times on umpteen networks. I suppose it all adds up to fifteen minutes. I don't really care about *that* though. It was nice while it lasted, but life goes on, right?

Once all the hoo-haa died down, and Mrs. Yarrow got over her snit over *me* being in the news, and not her in her soup can dress, I took my negatives to the 24-hour photo service down in Eau Claire. The one where they have specials each month, like a free set of second prints, or poster-sized blow-ups of your choice. I picked a month when they gave out free prints, the 4 x 6 ones, too.

When I picked out the ones I liked best, I waited until they had the poster special and had five made up. My Brillo boxes, a 1990 Mercedes Benz, my mop bucket, a white Persian cat, and the one of me. In my grungy tee. Not that I'm *vain*, but there was some scribbling on the bottom of the picture, like Warhol had signed the print plus added a message too. And I wanted to see what those words were.

And when my posters were ready, I didn't unroll them until I got home. I was all soda fizz and antacid tablets in water when I got to the one of me, and read the words written in a sprawling, loose handwriting:

I never said the 15 minutes were consecutive, did I?
Your friend in loneliness and art
Andy Warhol
"Bud"

It made me sad, realizing that I was right, you know. About him being lonely. But at least he's got his art, to follow around, and watch over. Just like I have *my* art now, all around me where I work, and where I live.

So like now, when I watch wrestling, I don't have to have my TV dinners so hot any more. I like the art on my walls, *my* Warhol exhibition—"bringing great art to the people," all right. Sometimes, I wonder how he is, and wonder if he's glommed onto any of his old cameras. If he did, I hope whoever gets the film appreciates it, and is smart enough to keep the camera a secret to himself, or herself.

It's funny, but I miss the guy, even though he left an awful lot of himself here with me. Funny duck, but okay, too. Least he never—you know—came on to me. I think he just enjoyed my company, if what he wrote is true. For a long time, I thought I'd never know for sure if he was just being nice or what, but now I guess I will get to know after all.

I've seen the schedule of exhibits for next year. Mrs. Yarrow wangled another big grant, and got the forty-seven car paintings and drawings he did for the Daimler-Benz people, which he left unfinished when he died. I know that his works are scattered, and shown in a lot of other cities, too, at the same time as Mrs. Yarrow's exhibit, but…you never know, do you?

Just in case, I bought a box of cookies. Mint ones.

And I've been putting tea in my thermos.

'Cause I *like* it.…

AFTERWORD

While Andy Warhol was of mostly Slavic descent, and I'm half Czech, he and I had a lot of personal quirks in common (plus some experts in autism-related disorders suspect Warhol had some form of the disorder, probably Aspergers), including the love of just buying stuff and setting it aside, cats, and popular culture in general, so when he died, it was a deep blow to me emotionally. I cried a lot about it; it didn't seem fair for him to be taken at such a relatively young age, nor was the fact that his death was partly medical misadventure (he received too many fluids while recuperating from surgery, and essentially drowned from within). This story is my way of bringing him back, in ghost form. My friend John Postovit vetted this and added some words of his own in the mix, hence the co-credit. (John is an artist with many gallery showings of his own under his belt, in addition to being a teacher, a former magazine editor, and occasional co-writer with me.) I just love the idea of Warhol wandering around, hiding in plain sight, visiting his own works of art. Ironically, in an issue of *The New Yorker* which came out in August of 2010, a sidebar article sang his praises as an artist, and even dubbed his urine-on-copper works as beautiful. Too bad so few people were willing to acknowledge his genius when he was still around to enjoy the comments. But at least we still have the art, if not the artist....

HE'S HOT, HE'S SEXY, HE'S...

The Miami Herald, June 26, 2000:

LOCAL HISTORIANS TO SETTLE
MORRISON DEATH RUMORS

(Special to the *Herald*)

Ever since his death was reported in early July of 1971, friends and fans of the former Doors lead singer Jim Morrison have expressed doubts about whether or not the poet-musician actually did die in a bathtub in Paris. These doubts are mainly due to the absence of hard evidence supporting the news of his death—including the lack of an autopsy, scant paperwork concerning his death, and, perhaps most tellingly, the numerous supposed "sightings" of the singer in Europe over the past thirty years. Those who claim that the troubled musician did indeed die on July 3, 1971, feel that his remains should be allowed to rest undisturbed. However, other interested parties have been quietly pursuing the possibility of disinterring Morrison's remains, for both historical and as-yet-unspecified legal reasons. According to an unnamed source in the Miami Police Department, these legal reasons may concern a number of still-unresolved paternity suits, as well as the infamous University of Miami "exposure" incident....

* * * *

The Miami Herald, June 27, 2000:

(from the arrests/legal column)

Jean Zidor Desire, aka Papa Zidor, 45 cruelty to animals, disorderly conduct, resisting arrest; paid $596 cash bond, sentencing to be determined.

* * * *

AP wire service, Saturday, July 2000

Noted historian Wallace Davis arrived in Paris today, along with a team of fellow historians and relatives of the late rock-and-roll musician James Morrison, for the official exhumation of the infamous front man for the Rock-and-Roll Hall of Fame (1993) group The Doors. Dr. Davis's only comment about the upcoming exhumation was: "Once we establish that the deceased is, in fact, deceased, it is to be hoped that that determination will forever quell the ongoing and most unfortunate rumors which have surrounded his heretofore uncertain and highly controversial demise, as well as clear up certain unresolved legal matters...."

* * * *

UPI wire service, July 2, 2000
(caption of a photo depicting a portion of the graffiti near the grave of Jim Morrison at Pére La Chaise Cemetery, reading: "Leave Jim Alone!")

FANS OF ROCK STAR PROTEST IMMINENT EXHUMATION

Colonel McClaren, Agent to the Undead: The Life and Extraordinary Times of Papa Zidor, Edward Pike, Pocket, 2006 (excerpt, p. 56)

...Of course, once news of the Morrison "incident" (as it was initially dubbed by an unusually reticent and politically correct press) leaked to the major wire services, nationwide attention was focused on the admittedly eccentric version of Laveauian[1]-style voodoo practiced by *houngan* Papa Zidor and his followers prior to the Paris "incident." While *houngans* (male and female; voodoo is a religion that allows for both priests and priestesses, which further backs practitioners' claims that it is a "true community religion") around the United States and the West Indies immediately decried Zidor's actions, publicly stating that the concepts of zombies

---

1   Marie Laveau, the priestess who started the New Orleans style of voodoo, which utilized elements of black magic in the worship.

and possession for evil purposes are not part of the "true" practice of voodoo, which is itself more of an amalgamation of Roman Catholic beliefs and various African tribal beliefs with an emphasis on benign possession of the faithful by *loas*, or gods, Papa Zidor himself had a very different view of both the Paris "incident" and the eventual outcome resulting from the "incident":

"You make [a] man a god, then that *loa*, he [is] able to possess anyone…even himself. That is [a] natural thing. It is common in voodoo. *Houngan* draw *veves*[2], and *loa* [he or she] come. Faithful play the drums, drink the cane drink laced with sacred herbs, and sing, and dance, until the *loa* come. Go into anyone, ride them like horse, only inside. Way it is in voodoo, way [it] will always be. No need to *make* zombie, no need to give drug to person, let them die, then bring [them] back. [The "incident"] not anything like that. Those who say Papa Zidor do this, [they] are wrong. Him *loa*, it come before that July. It was out there, waiting. I only bring it to original home.

"And I never kill [the] original home. And I never keep it preserved. *Nature* do that, not Papa Zidor. Ask nature why she do that. I just summon *loa*…."

* * * *

MTV, *The Day in Rock*, July 4, 2000:

"…In more unsettling news, according to still 'unofficial' reports, the exhumed remains of legendary Hall of Fame rocker Jim Morrison were said to be missing. Just last Saturday, music historian Dr. Wallace Davis and a team of 'rock' historians arrived in Paris to conduct an official, state-sanctioned exhumation of the late musician, scheduled for July 3, the anniversary of Morrison's death. Details have been sketchy ever since the remarkably intact coffin was removed from Pére La Chaise Cemetery. According to some eyewitness reports, the coffin was actually opened at the gravesite, while other witnesses claim that the unbreached casket was taken by hearse to Dr. Davis's undisclosed headquarters in the city.

2   Symbols of a loa drawn on the ground with cornmeal flour.

Whatever the condition of the casket was on Monday, it has been reported today that the remains somehow 'disappeared' overnight, even though sources claim that the casket itself is still in Dr. Davis's possession, albeit in an 'unoccupied state.' French officials, mindful that Morrison's gravesite is currently Paris's fourth-largest tourist attraction, have the matter under investigation. In more upbeat news, the..."

* * * *

Paris Match editorial, July 5, 2000:

...Must we all fall victim to "historical curiosity"? This unfortunate incident, in which the remains of a beloved and revered cultural figure have been—to quote the historian in charge of this ultimately dubious project—"misplaced temporarily," has only served to bring shame upon the adopted resting place of one of the heroes of popular music.

And is this fair? I do not think it is so; while certain members of the government allowed this to happen, this sad incident in no way reflects the wishes or desires of the people of Paris, or of the world. For the sake of historical inquisitiveness, the mortal remains of this man have been spirited away, for reasons an dpurposes unknown—leaving they mystery of his death thirty years ago all the more unanswerable....

* * * *

Weekly World News, July 17, 2000 (distributed July 10)

WHAT REALLY HAPPENED TO THE LIZARD
KING—AN EXCLUSIVE EYEWITNESS REPORT

(Special to *Weekly World News*)

The Paris police may be keeping quiet about it, and "rock historian" Wallace Davis may be uneager to let Morrison fans know the truth, but according to the bizarre eyewitness description of the events of the night of July 3, 2000, the remains of the legendary rocker were in an almost "lifelike" state of preservation, or so claims Olivier Dupree, one of the gravediggers who helped to exhume the late rocker's coffin.

In an exclusive *World* interview, Dupree firmly maintains that "when Dr. Wallace [Davis] opened the casket, there was no… smell. No hint of decay. I couldn't see the face, but I saw legs, and folded hands no less intact than my own. When he saw that, Dr. [Davis] closed the coffin, and hurried it to the waiting hearse. But I have attended other exhumations, and have seen other bodies buried a far shorter time than [Morrison's], and never have I not smelled the odor of decay and death…."

* * * *

A History of Rock and Roll, Dr. Wallace Davis, Time-Life Books, 2012

(Dr. Davis's notes regarding the
July 2000 Morrison exhumation)

…Whether the remarkable preservation of the deceased was due to some naturally occurring phenomenon, e.g., the known preservative qualities of some modern, preservative-added foodstuffs, or due to some inherent quality of the ground itself, the fact remains that this individual's body was in an almost uncorrupted state, akin to that occasionally found in exhumed members of the Catholic Church prior to sainthood being bestowed on them. The exact cause of this almost perfect preservation will need to be determined by medical examiners more skilled in pathological dissection than are available to me today. Further examination of the remains will be postponed until tomorrow, when a team of U.S. pathologists will arrive….

* * * *

What *Really* Happened to the Lizard King:

…Mr. Dupree's observations in and of themselves are telling evidence of Morrison's lifelike state of being on July 3, but the scene witnessed by a pair of American college students, Peggy Wolk and Clay Mathers, indicates that far more sinister forces were at work that muggy Paris night than simple body-snatchers. Wolk and Mathers were walking past the Hôtel de Lauzun just after eight o'clock when they witnessed a lone male suspect drawing "odd-looking" branching, complex geometric figures on the sidewalk with what looked like yellow sand taken from a burlap-like sack nearby. Mathers used his 35mm camera to snap a picture of the strange "sand-drawing" (see below). Experts on variant religious practices identified the symbol as a *veves*, which is used in voodoo ceremonies to summon pagan gods, or *loas*. According to Wolk, the man was "obviously drunk or stoned; he smelled sort of sweet, like raw sugar, and was singing and muttering to himself while he was working. Clay asked him what he was doing, but the guy just mumbled something in some sorta French-sounding dialect and kept on working with that sand." (Experts identified the "yellow sand" as cornmeal, commonly used to draw *veves*.) Interested, but too wary to stay close to the singing man, Wolk and Mathers crossed the street and then observed the individual. He was reportedly joined "by maybe five, six other people like him, y'know, island types, and one had a drum, and the rest brought bottles of liquor, and they started this weird dance on the sidewalk, but when we saw that they had this live chicken, we figured the heck with it and split," said Mathers. What makes the students' story important to the Morrison incident is the timing; according to Wolk, the "weird dance" began at approximately twenty minutes after eight, the approximate time that Dr. Davis and his team left the disinterred body of Morrison alone in one of the chambers of Davis's as-yet undisclosed Paris headquarters. No one from Davis's team checked on the body (which was still in the casket) until the next morning, when the remains were discovered to be missing. And at approximately eight-thirty that evening, a policeman broke up the "weird dance." The official police record relates that while most of the individuals ran off (including the man drawing the *veves*), the police officer did speak to one woman who claimed to be "summoning" someone, but otherwise refused to comment on the night's events.

While the police still deny any foul play in regard to the whereabouts of the dead rocker's remains, reporters for *Weekly World News* have determined that the man photographed by Clay Mathers is a well-known Miami voodoo priest, or *houngan*, called Papa Zidor (aka Jean Desire), who was recently arrested in Miami for…

* * * *

Excerpt from *Colonel McClaren*, p. 67.

…got out of Paris with his "charge" before the theft of the body was discovered the next morning, using a passport he'd forged prior to leaving Miami on June 29. How Zidor knew that Morrison's body would, indeed, be uncorrupted and intact prior to the actual exhumation is still a mystery; all Zidor would say (either then or now) was that "it is the duty of the *houngan* to protect sacred secrets." It has been speculated by other *houngans* (those not allied with the New Orleans voodoo sanctuaries) that Zidor made spiritual contact with Morrison during a series of ceremonies held in Miami in late May and early June of that year; as several participants from those ceremonies later related (after they'd broken away from Papa Zidor following official public disclosure of the "incident"), they'd seen Zidor create *veves* similar to the one published in several tabloid papers that July…*veves* theretofore unused in any voodoo ceremony performed by Papa Zidor. In fact, those *houngans* (both traditional and those aligned with the Laveauian voodoo) contacted by this author didn't recognize that particular pattern as being associated with any known *loa*.

Furthermore, at least two of the participants in Zidor's ceremonies, one each for May and June, reported being "wildly" possessed by a *loa*, yet once the possession was withdrawn, no one would tell them exactly *which* god had been "riding" their bodies, for Papa Zidor refused to identify that new *loa*, and the actions of the *loa* were not familiar to the other participants. Regardless of whether or not this unknown *loa* was, indeed a spiritual manifestation of the late rock star, Zidor was confident in the knowledge that he could not only summon the spirit of the man in Paris, but that he could also provide a suitable—and, most significant—*permanent* "home" for that particular *loa*.…

* * * *

Rolling Stone headline, 1981

Jim Morrison—He's hot, he's sexy, he's dead

* * * *

Rolling Stone headline, 1991

The Doors: The Making of the Myth

* * * *

Rolling Stone headline, 2001

Jim Morrison—He's hot, he's still sexy…he's undead

* * * *

60 Minutes, "Resurrection of the Lizard King," Sunday, January 14, 2001:

STEVE CROFT: I realize that once a person dies, their soul technically "belongs" to no one except perhaps God, but—

PAPA ZIDOR: There you go, there you go. Inflict *your* belief on *my* faith. For me, for my believers, soul is the soul. *You* are ones who proclaim this man "god," *you* are ones who kept him alive after he die. What happen when I contact his *loa* is act of nature. I hold ceremony, one, two times, he come. Is simple as—

KROFT: But according to my sources, in the religion of voodoo, in order to summon a *loa*, or god, one must perform certain steps asking that *loa* to come, that specific *loa*, who is summoned through music—

ZIDOR; Yes, yes, that is true—

KROFT: —through the use of ceremonial drinks, through…certain animal sacrifices—

ZIDOR: Again! There you go again! I see…I see that wiggle of distaste in your voice, see it in your eyes. Animals are sacrificed to the *loa* so *loa* can bless offering of holy meat, which is to be given to poor at such ceremony—

KROFT: As I *was* about to add, so that the viewers would understand, too. Mr. Desire, we're not here to ridicule your religion, But, as you well know, the result of your ceremony before the

Hôtel de Lauzun last July was the…reanimation of the gentleman sitting next to you. A man who was…*dead* for thirty years, who had only been disinterred that morning—

ZIDOR: Am I the man who did *that* to him? Ask my followers, I do not haunt the graveyards, I do not give the potion which creates the zombies!

KROFT: Mr. Desire, I wasn't accusing you of grave-robbing. I just would like to know why you brought it upon yourself to in essence, give life back to Mr. Morrison here. Or, more to the point, why you felt *you* had the right to do this.

ZIDOR: I am only instrument of the *loa*. I am no god. I give no *life*. (rises from chair)

KROFT: Okay, okay, I didn't say you were. But there's still the question of Mr. Morrison. He's obviously quite…alive, listening to us, watching the whole conversation, yet only six months ago he was…*dead*. Lying in a casket in a cemetery in Paris. Obviously, he didn't reanimate *himself,* If that had been possible, he would have done so sooner—

ZIDOR: In a coffin with no air? With no food? No, no, these things, they happen for reason. I contact *loa*, other man, he do the digging up.

KROFT: Let me put this another way….Ever since July 3, you have been accompanied by Mr. Morrison here, but has he in any way expressed a desire to *maintain* this…unusual existence? Was this whole event *his* doing, *his* idea?

ZIDOR: (smiling) You the question man. Ask *him*.

KROFT: Well, Jim? Can you tell the viewers what really happened to you? How you came to be here?

MORRISON: Uhm? Sorry, I was watching your cameraman over there. He's got this…I dunno, *look* on his face. (smiles at camera) Could you, uhm, repeat that last question?

KROFT: What really happened to you that night? How did you come…*back*?

MORRISON: (closes eyes, shakes head) Steve…if I knew, I'd tell you. It was like…drifting off and waking up. Too fast to contemplate. I…(glances at camera, smiles, and shrugs)

— CUT TO COMMERCIAL —

* * * *

CNN *Headline News*, July 16, 2000:

...We have this breaking news from Miami, Florida: A local *houngan* of the voodoo faith names Jean Zidor Desire has just called a news conference in regard to the disappearance of the recently exhumed body of—just a moment, we're switching to a life feed...

(Zidor is seated behind a bank of microphones in the Miami Hilton conference room)

ZIDOR: I will answer your questions in a minute, as soon as my companion arrives—ah, come here, Jim.

(Cameras pan to left of screen, where a dark-haired man of medium height emerges into camera range; sounds of surprise from unseen audience.)

MORRISON: (walking up to Zidor, then standing behind microphone) Hell...my name's Jim—

(Overlapping voices, cameras moving in for close-up.)

* * * *

Excerpt from *Colonel McClaren*, pp. 80-81:

Zidor's July 16 news conference was a stroke of inspired genius; by publicly showing his "companion" to the assembled members of the press, and furthermore demonstrating that Morrison was acting of his own free will and was able to speak for himself, Zidor circumvented the possible negative reaction of the police and other authorities. Instead of being labeled a mere body-snatcher, Zidor was dubbed a "resurrectionist" by the press. Although the passport he'd used to bring Morrison back into the United States was forged, the fact that he brought his "companion" back to the very city where he was still wanted on indecent exposure charges proved (in the eyes of the world) that Zidor's intentions were not as dishonest as they originally appeared. The fact that Morrison willingly returned to Miami makes it difficult to prove that Zidor was, in fact, holding an unholy "power" over the revived Morrison.

Even after learning that the charges had been dropped[3] in regard to the pending prison sentence, Morrison still chose to remain with Zidor, a fact that eventually brought up the suspicion that Zidor did, indeed, have some sort of hold over Morrison (an extreme example of this was the *60 Minutes* segment devoted to the affair in 2001).

Morrison himself emphatically denied these charges. In a letter to the editor of the *Miami Herald*, he wrote:

> "During my past life this last century, no man, no woman, was my master, a situation which *continues to this day*" (italics Morrison's).

He further stated that the decision not to contact members of his former band, his former associates, and his family was:

> "...based solely on the desire on my part not to further disrupt their current lives any more than they have already been disrupted by disclosure of my current circumstances."[4]

In addition to the *Miami Herald* letter, Morrison wrote similar letters defending Zidor's peculiar actions on his behalf to *Rolling Stone*, the *Wall Street Journal*, *Time*, *Newsweek*, and other magazines and newspapers that had either tacitly or directly criticized Zidor for resurrecting and "maintaining" Morrison in his highly-unusual and "unnatural" state of being; the content of these letters, while specifically addressing the individual claims and/or charges brought by the publication in question, all dealt strongly with his (Morrison's) free

3   Even though the outstanding prison sentence had been under appeal at the time of his death, due to the statute of limitations being seven years for indecent exposure, it was decided that "above and beyond Mr. Morrison's nebulous legal status, i.e., officially dead or officially alive," the 1970 charges would be dropped, with that course of action deemed "most humane," due to "time served."

4   Morrrison did contact the above-mentioned people by viewphone shortly after the July 16 press conference, mainly to prove that he was indeed who he claimed to be and not an imposter; what was actually said during those twenty-six records-substantiated phone conversations (which lasted from five to fifty-six minutes) has remained a mystery. However, no one called during that time later came forward disputing his claim to be James Douglas Morrison, even if each person has steadfastly refused to reveal what was or wasn't said by Morrison at the time of the call.

will in all "decisions and actions undertaken after July 3, 2000, by myself in my behalf."[5]

At no point did Morrison choose to address the improbability of his "current circumstances," however....

* * * *

Rolling Stone #987, 2001:

"View from 'the Other Side': Fame, Rock, Drugs, Death, and Rebirth," Paul Ridgeway reporting

...but in just as many ways, Jim Morrison never *did* leave the scene. Page through almost any issue of this magazine since his death in 1971, and you'll come across his name or that of his group, be it in actual articles, features, reviews, or whatnot, or be it in the classifieds section: Wannabes and would-be hangers-on hawking everything from the relatively benign posters and bootleg concert films to the somewhat tackier eight-by-ten glossies of his grave to the "actual" transcripts of his infamous Miami trial for indecent exposure during a 1968 University of Miami gig.

True, it's difficult for the average "live" person today to fully comprehend what sort of culture shock Morrison may be going through right now—but no one can deny that he has been an inactive participant in almost every phase of the music industry during those years he's been "away."...

* * * *

AP wire service, Monday, March 5, 2001

The last of the ten pending paternity suits against Jim Morrison was dismissed today in a Los Angeles courtroom based on the negative results of DNA tests. The plaintiff's lawyer was quoted as saying, "How does anyone know what being dead for thirty years did to his DNA?" Lawyers for the

---

5   This statement, of course, does not take into account Zidor's possession of the forged passport to which was affixed a thirty-two-year-old photograph of Morrison, nor does it take into account the time prior to July 3, 2000, and after July 3, 1971. At no time was the literal fact of his death in the last century discussed by Morrison, a most curious omission at best, but an ominous one at the worst.

defendant countered with evidence that the defendant's DNA is consistent with that supplied by other living relatives....

* * * *

Excerpt from *Colonel McClaren*, p. 102

Zidor soon found that he needed a great deal of money in order to offset his newly-revived companion's massive legal fees. While Morrison was legally entitled to a share of the publishing rights from both his own books of poetry and the lyrics to the Doors catalogue, his will had been specific about leaving all of his worldly possessions to his former common-law wife, who, when she died in 1974, left all of her inheritance to her parents, who eventually shared the money, property, and other inherited goods with Morrison's family; therefore Morrison in effect had no specific right to those monies and property which had already been legally willed to others.

Zidor, however, discovered that Morrison himself was a valuable commodity; while the former singer now refused to have anything to do with the music industry (a field he had been contemplating leaving prior to his death, possibly in favor of a career in the movie industry), he wasn't averse to giving readings of his prose works, or to lecturing—a fact Papa Zidor took full advantage of at the earliest opportunity....

* * * *

Handbill posted outside the USC Fine Arts Center, week of April 1-7, 2001

FOR ONE WEEK ONLY
April 8-April 14
Live and in Person
Jim Morrison
Reads
selections from
"The Lord" and
"The New Creatures"
7:00 pm nightly
Tickets $25 in advance

$30 at the Door

* * * *

UPI/AP wire services, Monday, May 7, 2001:

In a rare joint statement of policy, the Vatican and the assembled leaders of the U.S.A.'s voodoo sanctuaries (including the New Orleans Laveauian sanctuaries) have issued a decree declaring the practice of reanimation to be a "sin against God, Man and Nature," and further stating that such "animated beings" are not considered, in their view, to be truly "human" beings....

* * * *

MTV, *The Day in Rock*, Monday, May 7, 2001

"...responding to today's unusual 'joint statement of policy,' Morrison had this to say": (switch to taped feed)

"I can't say that this comes as a surprise. I mean, it's not like I'm *not* used to being condemned for things I didn't do...."

* * * *

Excerpt from *Colonel McClaren*, p. 106

...It was around this time that the nickname "Colonel Mc-Claren" was given to Papa Zidor,[6] due to his incessant booking of his erstwhile "client" into concert halls and universities across the United States. While it soon became apparent that Morrison's patience with the increasingly rapturous audience members was growing short (during one gig in Portland, Oregon, during the first week in June of that year, Morrison stopped his reading to ask his listeners, "Assholes, are you really *listening* to me, or just getting off on being in the same room with a guy who was dead long before you were born?"), Zidor continued to book him into whatever venue he could

---

6   From Colonel Tom Parker, Elvis Presley's manager, and Malcolm Mc-Claren, who managed the Sex Pistols and Bow Wow Wow.

find—as long as the advances were good. This soon attracted the attention of the ACLU and other groups....

* * * *

MTV, *The Day in Rock*, Monday, July 2, 2001, also repeated on CBS, CNN, NBC, and ABC evening newscasts

"...and in what was a not-unexpected announcement, legendary rocker and revived poet Jim Morrison announced that he is canceling all further speaking engagements as of this week. While a recording gleaned from the best of his poetry readings and lectures will be available in stores within the next two months, Morrison announced that he has no further plans to 'perform' in public, although he is still open to granting interviews and, quote, 'maintaining contact with my "true" fans and associates,' which is thought to an affirmation of his continuing loyalty to Jean Zidor Desire, also known as 'Papa' Zidor, the man who was responsible for the sudden and unexpected reemergence of Morrison on the..."

* * * *

Rolling Stone, July 2001, interview with Jim Morrison conducted by Brian Preston:

Back when I was younger, perhaps in the early nineties or so, I had this dream about Jim Morrison and his common-law wife, Pamela Courson. In it, neither of them had died during the seventies, but the years hadn't been good to either of them. In my dream, Pamela had become the all-encompassing Mother-figure to Jim, the role she'd begun to play during his last days in Paris, when she was picking out his clothes and trying to help him get his act together, only in this dream she was a little older, a lot grayer, and somewhat fatter—and she was guiding a grayer, chunkier, and *quieter* Jim around like he was senile...or worse.

That's basically all there was to that brief, intense dream—Pamela leading Jim down these stone steps set into a Cliffside, and him just *letting* her lead him. And what freaked me during that dream was how quiet Jim was, how resigned to every little thing he was, as if the farce of a trial in Miami and all the petty legal hassles he'd been enduring for the past few years had finally broken him, left him empty. And then I woke up.

Not long after that, I read about Val Kilmer's dream of Morrison with his brain exposed as he talked to the young actor who was going to play him in Oliver Stone's biopic, and how freaked Val was over seeing this guy's brain-on-drugs... but *my* dream still shook me. That's why I drove slowly to my first meeting with Jim Morrison; I was afraid that I'd find the dream-Jim being led by the arm by his surrogate-companion, Papa Zidor. But once I approached the Miami home of the now world-famous *houngan* from Anse-à-Veau, Haiti, my fears frittered away, for I saw Morrison standing in front of Zidor's screened-in wrap-around front porch steps, "I'm glad you got here before the photographer. I wanted to show you around the place before we got to talking."

While Morrison showed me Zidor's place (aside from a couple of corner shrine-like jumbles of candles, potions from the local botanical, and statue-like dolls which Morrison as-sured me were "nothing like the voodoo dolls used in bad movies. See those pins? They're used to symbolize holy messages for the spirits, not to hurt people," the house was uniformly neat, with a large, well-stocked library dominated by several comfortable reading-style chairs), I studied this again-living legend of my own youth. While he's been on earth (and in it) for almost fifty-eight years, Morrison could pass for roughly thirty or so; his features are a little heavier than those captured in Joel Brodsky's landmark photo ses-sion, and his blue yes (now adorned with barely perceptible contact lenses) are a little more hooded, while his still-longish brown hair is heavily flecked with gray.

But he's still as animated, still as articulate as he was prior to his death in 1971, albeit somewhat more...distant. While exceptionally polite, and open to my casual questions about the house and its voodoo-related contents, I quickly sensed a certain sense of alienation about the man, not a rejection of *me*, or even of his surroundings, but an aura of *apartness* nonetheless.

Once the tour of the house was finished (his manager/ mentor Zidor was nowhere to be seen), we made our way back to the front porch. By that time the photographer had arrived, and while she was busy weaving back and forth with her Nikon, waiting for the right tilt of the head, the right expression to capture for the magazine layout, I turned on my tape recorder and began:

ROLLING STONE: Jim, I hate to ask this first, but it's what the readers want to know. What was it like being—

JIM MORRISON: Dead? Oh, God....I know this sounds like I'm evading the question, but I have *no* idea. It's like, uhm, I was *there*, but can't recall any of it. And that's what's so unbearable... the having been there but not remembering any of it. Realizing that a major chunk of my time on earth was spent...*somewhere* is the most painful thing, especially when there's evidence that I was in a, you know, *active* mode wherever I *was*. Because of what happened with Jean's followers, all that. He *knew*; otherwise, he wouldn't have...although sometimes I wish he hadn't, after all I'd gone through to experience it and all...I just wonder what I was *doing*, what I was thinking....I must've been thinking, been reaching *out*....

RS: Have you ever found out anything about why your...*you* remained as you were before? I think that's the thing that's had people puzzled the most; that you were still uncorrupted—

JM: (laughing) "Uncorrupted"! What a word choice! *That's* ironic.... Getting to your question, though, no, no one knows why. They had to do some DNA testing on me, for legal reasons I can't talk about due to the appeals process and all, but nothing out of the ordinary was found then.

RS: You're aware that what happened to you isn't an isolated occurrence? That certain saints—

JM: Don't bring up *that* mess, okay? I certainly don't think *they'd* (makes sign of the cross) enjoy the comparison!

RS: (laughs) True! Getting away from the circumstances surrounding all of this, how has the readjustment period been for you? Getting used to society, all the changes,.

JM: (with a frown) That's where things start to get to me, finding out how little some stuff has changed, you know, with the racial tensions, and the Middle East mess, and...I don't mean to put down anyone, but it appalls me how little people *think* anymore. I thought some of my audiences were so fucking stupid, but I see the kids now and...God, the people up on the *stage* are even worse than *I* supposedly used to be, and the kids out there just keep egging them on....I get to wondering: If they're what's considered "cutting edge" or whatever you call it now, what the hell were they after *me* for? I never intentionally injured a fan, or did half the things these clods just get away with—

RS: About ten years ago Axl Rose had some major run-ins with—

JM: (waving his hand) Yeah, I read about him. I also read about how insulted he was when that Oliver Stone compared him to me. Actually, I'm insulted that I was compared to *him*.

RS: Speaking of Stone, what did you think....

JM: Well...he meant well. I was glad *he* did the film, and I'm happy to see he made it in Hollywood, but it was such a weird experience...sort of like seeing the tapes of that eighth annual Rock-and-Roll Hall of Fame induction, when that guy, what's his name—

RS: Eddie Vedder.

JM:—okay, him, did "Light My Fire," and I was sitting there thinking, What the fuck would they have done with *me* if I'd been around for that? Ridiculed me for losing my voice, or for having a fat gut? Actually, though, not to sound bitter or anything, I couldn't help but think, The other guys *didn't* need me after all....

RS: Well, under the circumstances, y'know, they had no choice.

JM: Yeah, I realize that, but still, after hearing that Vedder guy, and finding out that the actor who played me did some of the singing himself, I felt so...I dunno, *fungible*...."

* * * *

Excerpt from *Colonel McClaren*, p. 127:

...When asked why he had such an interest in reuniting the *loa* or spirit of Morrison with his disinterred body, Zidor explained with unusual candor, "When I a boy, coming to this country on the big boat from [my] homeland, this rock-and-roll thing, it mean a lot to me. The rhythm, the… power of it, and then there were the words, especially words like from Morrison….He say [a] lot to me, to other[s]. Not words just sung, like other song, but words to *me*. He like god, even when alive…not because he [was] good man always, but [he] wanted to be good *inside*. I felt it in music, felt it in words. That's why I draw *veves* to summon [him?], based on power of words and music. Because of the good in there.

"And when he come walking down [that] Paris street that night, he smile at me, say 'Hello' like I'm old friend. Jim, he like *every*one 'less they cross himl. Always was nonprejudice[d] man, still was when I know him. Maybe that why he leave again, because people prejudice[d] against *him*…."

* * * *

AP/UPI wire services, Monday, December 10, 2001:

James Morrison, former lead singer of the 1960s rock group The Doors, and lately the subject of intense religious and public controversy due to his physically-revived status, was found dead on the eve of his fifty-eighth birthday this past Friday by his mentor and companion Jean Zidor Desire. Morrison had shot himself in the heart with a handgun; according to his written wishes, he was cremated, and his ashes were scattered over the Pacific Ocean. He left a brief note exonerating Zidor, which stated that "a legend has its own life, surpassing that of the being who created said legend— in such circumstances, the presence of said being becomes superfluous. My legend has always lived, may it continue to live unaided and unaugmented." Zidor had only this comment for the press: "Jim never die in the first place, how can he really die again?"

* * * *

Excerpt from *A History of Rock-and-Roll*, p. 325
…I don't know if we really learned anything from the second life and death of Jim Morrison, other than that his *first*

life and death were momentous enough to forever assure him his place in musical and cultural history; perhaps the legacy of his second life and final days is that we *are* incapable of truly listening to and learning from anyone, no matter how much they try, or how intent they are upon their chosen mission in the arts and letters.

* * * *

AP wire service, December 2001:

For the first time in the history of Paris, a non-French landmark has become the number-one tourist attraction. The empty tomb of singer Jim Morrison has surpassed the Louvre, Versailles, and even the Eiffel Tower as the most-visited spot in France. Said one tourist spotted near the empty grave, "It's just the only way to be *close* to him anymore...."

AFTERWORD

The dream mentioned in this story regarding Morrison and his wife actually was a dream I had—I just wrote it down verbatim in the story. Now do I believe that Morrison might still be alive? While I'm 99% certain that he *did* die back in France, there are a few facts which speak for a slight possibility that he faked his death—he did speak Spanish well enough to converse with real Spaniards, in case he fled to that country, and he lost his passport and thus knew how to secure a new one, a vital bit of information should one wish to generate a new, false ID. But no, I do not believe he was lying dormant underground, waiting for a voo-doo resurrection. But one weird bit of lore needs to be mentioned—a few years after this story appeared, there was talk that Morrison would be dug up due to the cemetery not liking all the tourist traffic and graffiti linked to him being interred there, but at the last minute the plans to remove his body were dropped...so we'll never know for sure, will we?

BUDDY HOLLY NIGHT AT THE BONE-GOD'S LAIR

Wisconsin, Winter, 1992…

Six-thirty came and went; when no Bone-God came sliding around the back door, hooded eyes sly, full lips doing the bad-boy twitch, I started setting up the bar myself. Long straws and stir-sticks in their clear compartments on either side of the napkin-holder, fresh pile of funny-sayings napkins in the middle, shot glasses in a line across the folded clean bar towel, almost-clean towel on the metal ring next to the ice tank, five scoops of new ice in the tank itself, put out the bowls of bar chum, turned on the running waterfall beer sign and the neon BUD guitar, gave the pour liquor bottles a perfunctory swipe with the bar rag, and between every motion I kept looking for the goddamn Bone-God to come slithering in, apologies dripping like manna off his lips.

"Don't look like Doug's fixin' t' show." Benny shoved another free pretzel in his mouth, washing it down with a free drink. Not that I'd given it to Benny willingly; a free drink for the first customer was a long-standing tradition at my bar, long before construction-gypsies like Benny Loomis started showing up. I did snatch away the pretzel bowl before Benny could root in it again with his grimy-nailed claws, ostensibly to refill it. *That* could wait until the Bone-God got his fat ass behind the bar, though.

"Maybe Doug's eye ain't healed yet." Benny leaned over the bar, giving the pretzel bowl a longing glance.

"I've seen him banged up worse. Always manages to haul his carcass across the threshold. Time when that professor's wife beaned him a good one with her Bartles and Jayme's bottle, all he needed were a couple of stitches and a half day off."

Benny snorted, until something wet and nebulous showed at his nostrils, head bobbing like a velour car-dog's. "I was there, I was there…ever get the cooler crap off the pour liquor? Splattered like a son-of-a-bitch—*foosh*—"

I had to smile at that, regardless of how disgusting it had been at the time. The Bone-God had been waxing eloquent about some god-damn German philosopher or another, as he was wont to do when the crowd from the university showed up come Friday nights, and this one prof's wife kept butting in, going, "But Dougla*sss*, it was *Hegel* who *saaaid*," only that's as far as she'd get. Don't know what it was that Hegel said, but the lady was sure intent on letting the Bone-God know that *Hegel* had *saaaid* it. Over and over—

Then the Bone-God stopped mixing whatever art-fart blender drink the university boobs were asking for, just flipped off the blender with a majestic sweep of his long-fingered hand, spun on his heels, planted both hands on the counter, and intoned, "Yes it was Hegel who said, 'What is the difference between a veneral disease and a devious midget?' My *dear laaa*dy, Hegel *saaaid* 'One's a cunning runt, and the other—'"

That's when the prof's wife beaned him with the wine cooler bottle, catching him right on the over-hanging brow, and I had to turn the place over to Stu (who is truly a good-for-shit bartender—once he chased some construction gypsy around with a mini-vac because the slob was getting mud on the carpet squares, and Stu honest-to-fuck didn't realize that mud *will* dry and can actually be cleaned up *later*) so I could drive the Bone-God to the emergency room for stitches. And once there, he called the waddle-butt nurse the punch-line of the joke he'd started back in the bar, so the doc who stitched him up did it without the benefit of Novocain after the nurse told him what Doug'd said.

Hiding the pretzel bowl further under the bar, I told Benny, "I doubt a shiner would be enough to keep him flat on his back this long. The Bone-God is indestructible. When the stupid fuck dies, they'll have to write 'You are *dead*' on the lining of his coffin so he stays put—"

Then I saw him, just out of the corner of my eye, peeking around the front door, just one eye, a little forehead and a shock of grey-ing curls showing. The one eye winked. Then a slim finger crooked, beckoning me, as that rumbling rasp of a voice crooned, "Oh Mikey, *c'meeere*."

Jesus I wished he wouldn't go doing that when there were customers in the bar. Even if it was only Benny and his free drink.

Not budging, I folded my arms and leaned against the cooler, shaking my head. "Not tonight, Douglas, whatever it is you want. Big night tonight, remember? People coming to hear a real show for a change? We talked this over yesterday—I don't care *what's* up, or how pressing it is, you are working tonight. Period." I reached over and toyed with the remote; no way no how would the Bone-God set foot behind the bar unless the TV was tuned to either an all-news or all-sports channel. For an ex-college professor, the Bone-God wanted *nothing* remotely cultural on the tube while he was working.

By the time I'd switched the box to ESPN, the Bone-God had pussy-footed across the bar and onto one of the stools. For a guy who could down six-seven-eight vodkas straight, in as short a time as it took to count it down, and had the bloat to prove it, the Bone-God was light on his loafers. Or whatever the fuck he happened to be wearing.

Benny was all set to watch the fireworks, until the Bone-God leaned over him, asking, "Would you like it if I cleaned your glasses for you? They look smeared, Benjamin—mind?"

I'd seen this trick before, but Benny hadn't, so I didn't say diddley while the Bone-God carefully pulled off Benny's specs, handling them delicately by the place where the bows joined the front of the frame, peered at them against the running waterfall light—and then licked them clean before putting them back on Benny's face. With a tight smile and patrician nod of his head.

Benny left, muttering most of the Seven Dirty words routine under his breath, as the Bone-God "heee-heee-heeed" behind his hand. I didn't mind it when the Bone-God pulled that shit on the rowdies, or the kids who were trying to use fake I.D.'s, but you insult one construction gypsy, you insult 'em all—

"Doug."

In a second, the Bone-God was Mr. Studious, hands folded neatly before him, puffy face serious, eyes lowered contritely.

"Mike."

Shit, it bugs me when he does that, 'cause I'm only thirty-three and he's forty-seven (according to his bartender's license, regardless of how shit-headed he acts), and no matter how you slice it, it's a bitch having to bawl out an employee who is almost old enough to be your dad. Especially when he's been acting like the ghost of Eddie Haskell.

"Doug, what does it say on the sign outside the bar? The sign that *you* put up?"

The Bone-God cocked his head of curls to the left, as he delicately probed the blue-indigo edges of the shiner blossoming around is right eye. "It saaays 'Buddy Holly in Concert, One Night Only.' With three exclamation p—"

"Enough, enough. And that night's tonight, right? *Right*? Bone-Head, I'm *talking* to—"

"Oh cut the fucking crap, all *right*?" This was the real Bone-God, the guy I'd hired despite my better instincts, because he'd appealed to my *practical* instincts, Douglas James, PhD., ex-professor, currently the best goddamned bartender I'd ever had the good-bad fortune to hire. A guy born with fake I.D. radar, no matter how old or how smooth the punk using it was; a guy who'd make the shift from snorting, farting, ice-cube-tossing construction workers (speak their lingo, match them cuss for cuss, high-jinx for high-jinx), to regally inebriated querulous snoot-nosed college profs (he'd quote anybody from Adam and Even on down, from every frigging book ever written, and *get it right*) in the space of an eye-blink; a guy just big enough to intimidate would-be bruisers, yet he could melt into the wall long enough to dial the cops without being noticed…a guy who actually kept a running tab of what he drank behind the bar when the spirits called to him, and then *paid* it monthly, off the top of his next paycheck. Didn't waste his time chatting up the talent, yet he never treated the bar-chum-grazing campers like shit, either. And he played cribbage better than anyone I've ever met before.

"All right," I agreed, softly. The Bone-God leaned back on his stool, thumbs hooked in the pockets of his corduroy jacket. A leftover from his university days; leather patches on the elbows, covered buttons rubbed raw on the edges, just John-Keating-*Dead-Poets-Society* perfect. He even wore a knitted wool tie, and a V-neck sweater-vest underneath. Little pale stripes in the cotton shirt, too.

Not his usual Saturday night get-up, billowing shirts cut down past his nipples, so's the sparse hair there could peek out, too-tight jeans or chinos, and always the little carved length of animal bone on a real gold chain one of his former students had given him. I wondered if he wore the necklace under his W.A.S.P. suit.

"Look Doug, you've been so good about working Saturdays *and* Sundays, and always when it's concert night. I *know* I owe you some time off when you ask for it, and I *promise*, next time you ask, when-*ever* you ask, you can have the night—hell, the whole *week* off, but *please*, I-need-you-to-work-*tonight*."

The Bone-God just sat there, shaking his head slightly, eyes hood-ed and narrowed. God, I knew in my heart, my loins, my whatever, that he was going to be a stubborn fuck about this...but I was stuck, too. Stud was studying for some damn chemistry test, and since the kid was planning to graduate come May, I couldn't very well make him put a part-time job over preparation for a life-long career. And besides, Stu was always on scholarship come concert time, ignoring the rest of the customers, alienating whomever showed up for what-ever up-and-coming and almost down-and-out act I'd booked. Ole Joe College incarnate, rolling his eyes when the talk got blue or the beer cans flew at the chicken-wire fence in front of the stage.

Now the Bone-God, he'd play along with the crowd—act the fool, get seriously, sublimely, cool, whatever it took to keep the au-diences happy and not too violent. Not that he actually *liked* con-cert night; always edgy, the Bone-God was absolutely wired come concert Saturdays (and Sundays if the act was really between better gigs). But since I knew him better (slightly) than the crowds who came to fill up the sixty-some chairs ringing the small round tables set up before the sandbox-sized stage, *they* never realized that the Bone-God was being much different from his usual gonzo/gentleman split-up self behind the bar, and I never commented on the Bone-God being wound up tighter than the copper wire on an IUD for fear he'd come *loose*.

But...faculty positions weren't exactly growing on bushes lately, what with all the cut-backs in the University of Wisconsin system (and never mind whatever it was he'd done at the Madison campus that made some of the prof's smirk a little behind his broad back), and I paid the Bone-God better than minimum, *much* better come concert night. And he knew it, but Christ-all-Friday, that man did rub that knowledge right in my puss.

"Doug, I cannot expect someone with whom I've never worked before on a concert night to come in here on less than a hour's notice, especially when my main bartender is sitting right here, right *now*, with no acceptable reason for not being able to work," I said all in a rush, trying to squash any notion he might've had about me asking one of the free-lance bartenders who *very* occasionally subbed for Stu to come in.

"Why not?" pushing out his bottom lip as he said it. I wanted to go over to the cooler, pull out a bottle of wine, and give him a matching scar over the other side of his cave-man brow.

Breathing through my mouth, taking long, painful breaths, I made myself lean far away from him, against the glass shelf containing the for-sale pints.

"Because this place is a fucking *zoo* come concert night, and I wouldn't *expect* a temp to be able to handle it. *I* wouldn't want to handle it. *You* are good at handling it. You *have* handled it. And you are *gonna* handle it. Or you don't work here again. *Ever*," I growled, staring him in the eye, but the Bone-God's eyes are so frigging distant, slightly mocking in their murky blueness, that I wasn't sure if what I'd said had sunk in. I walked over to the far end of the bar, to where the main bar segue-ways over to the hardwood-floored concert/dance party/wet tee shirt contest/muscle man contest area. A twenty-five by fifty foot space where the rowdies who claimed this place come the week-end could stomp and hoot and pound tables without pretense, without need for fancy get-ups or ten-bucks-a-pop programs sold at some geek's concession stand. During the week, the sliding fake wood-grain plastic door hid that part of the establishment, but come Saturday morning, I'd stop by the place to pull aside the divider, and set up the chairs for the night's show. That morning, I'd dragged all the tables off into the liquor room to the rear of the bar, shoving them higgly-piggly between the flats of beer and cases of pour liquor, and pulled out all the folding metal chairs that had been lining the walls in there. There were maybe close to a hundred chairs set up in loose rows fanning away from that small stage. I lost count two rows from the back.

I pointed to the empty chairs. "Gonna be over a hundred people packed in here tonight. Big buzz about this concert already. Not too often one of the real pioneers of rock-and-roll makes a stop in Mad

City, *in my bar*, and I am fixing to make the most of it. And if those fans of his get thirsty, I *don't* want someone who doesn't know his dick from his dispenser hose waiting on them, understand?"

A grunted reply, too guttural to understand, as the Bone-God began grubbing in his pockets for his cigarettes. When he came up empty-handed, and started toward the back of the bar, where the smokes were stacked on the little shelf over the cash register, I blocked his way. "Doug, I feel enough like an ass for having to bawl you out—now please don't make this hard on me, okay? Now pretty soon folks are gonna start coming through that door, so they can watch Buddy Holly, get a good seat. And maybe even sooner than that—" I checked my watch, Holly and his sidemen were due around seven, or so his manager had said "—this evening's entertainment is gonna come marching in here, Fender Stratocaster in hand, thinking that tonight's show is gonna come off without a hitch. And he's getting to be an old guy, and it isn't nice to make someone like him go through any *more* shit than he's already had dished up to him—"

"He's not the only person around here who's old—"

"Oh stuff it, will you? It's your own damn fault you're in the shape you're in. I don't put the booze in the glass, and I don't light up the smokes for you. It's not *my* fault you live on fucking Beer Sticks and maraschino cherries. You're not some no-brains fuck-head walking the girders—"

"I wasn't referring to chronological age, Michael." Spoken like the college professor he was, in fact still was at heart.

"What*ever.* You can talk semantics with me later, but for now, just get behind the fucking bar, okay? If you're a good boy I'll bring Holly over to meet you. Get him to sign a napkin for you. 'Kay?"

"It's not my fault about what happened to him in Iowa. He was offered his chance out of that cornfield…if he couldn't stand the light, couldn't *seize* it, make it *his* slave, it is not my fault. No one can made a man push away fa—"

"*What*?" The Bone-God was off on one of his tangents, mixing philosophy, religion and existential horseshit again. Like he was wont to do when he didn't get his own way. I suddenly pitied all those art-fart professors who came down here come Friday nights, for having had to put up with the Bone-God during the daylight hours, five days a week.

"The man was offered God's mightiest gift, immortality, eternity on silver wings, and—"

"The poor guy had the bad luck to *live* after the charter plane turned to metal confetti in a cornfield, satisfied? I don't call a broken back, a split skull and I don't remember *what* else a fucking 'gift'—"

"No, no, *no, Michael*, he was offered *more*—"

I couldn't believe what I was hearing. "You mean to say that as far as you're concerned, Holly *shouldn't* have lived through that accident? That he *should've* died along with those other two guys? And the pilot? When he had a wife and a baby coming—"

"She lost it—"

"Because she thought the man died. I'm glad, Doug, that you have had a nice sheltered little academic life, and never had to go through what Holly had to live through. Survivor guilt, all that rehabilitation, his divorce...I don't know about you, but as far as *I'm* concerned, Buddy Holly is a *hero*, a living, breathing hero for going through hell and making it out *alive*. And kicking. While Chuck Berry's off videotaping women's toilets and Del Shannon bit the bullet, Holly's been *doing* it. Night after night—"

Off to the back of the bar. I heard a horn beep once, twice, then once again. Holly and his sidemen. And the Bone-God was just standing there, eyes barely open, sucking his puffy cheeks in and out.

Giving him a light nudge toward the bar, I said as evenly, as *nicely*, as humanly possible when one is standing face to face with a five-foot-nine asshole, "Time-and-a-half. I will pay you that much *over* your usual fee. Tonight *only*. Deal?"

The Bone-God was eyeing the stack of Marlboros over the register, and I added, "And you don't have to put anything on your tab tonight. Just fucking behave." As the horn tooted a few more times.

The great god favored me with a solemn nod of his head, and I raced for the back of the bar, without waiting for the verbal confirmation of his promise.

* * * *

Holly and his band were all waiting by the door when I got to the alley-way. Still whip-skinny, face a nest of friendly wrinkles, hair a little sparse but still sorta wavy. Not as long as it used to be, though, in those black-and-white clips they sometimes show on "My

Generation" on VH1. He smiled broadly, but kinda shyly at me; crooked teeth stained yellowish, but still all genuine, save for he few false ones which replaced what he'd had knocked out in Mason City. Timid eyes behind thicker-than-I-remembered plastic glasses, as he held out his free hand to shake mine.

"Michael Davis? I'm Buddy—"

"Oh Mr. Holly, you have no idea how honored I am to have you here," I gushed, meaning every word of it, and not feeling as silly as I must've sounded. I shook his hand, pumping it until the poor guy winced a little through his smile. Shook hands with the other guys in the band, guys younger than Holly, young enough to be the kid Holly's wife had lost when she'd gotten the first premature hit of news on that bleak February 3rd in '59, that her husband of less than a year had bought the farm along with the other three men on that charter flight between play-'till-you're-dead-on-your-dogs concert tour. By the time they discovered that Holly was only injured (*badly* injured) it was too late—Maria had heard the wrong news, and miscarried.

It was amazing, I realized, as Holly and the others walked along the narrow hallway which led from the alley entrance to the swinging door leading to the back of the bar, how good of a job they'd done patching the man's face back together, considering when the accident happened. He looked pretty close to normal, and considering that he was about fifty-four or so, give or take a year, and throwing in maybe twenty years' worth of flying and driving and bussing from date to date on a zig-zag bar-lounge-and-County/state Fair eternal gig, the guy looked *damn* good.

And you could hardly make out the braces under his pants' legs, or the girdle-like thing around his back and mid-torso.

"Y'know, Mr. Davis, this sort of gig brings back a lot of memories for me…when I was just a kid back in Lubbock, I used to pick in little cafés, not much bigger than this. Country crowds, mostly, but I snuck a little variety in, even then." He smiled at me, head bobbing vaguely as he took in the mesh scrim across the stage, then: "Your usuals, they open to more than just one kind of music? I can change the show to suit—"

"What*ever* you want to play, what*ever*," I said as we mounted the broad steps leading up to the stage, then turned right past the place where the chicken-wire barrier stopped and squeezed past it along with Holly and side-men. There was a permanent drum kit out there, plus mikes, per my agreement with Holly's manager. There was no room to squeeze his drummer's personal kit through the barrier anyhow.

As Holly placed his guitar case on the high stool near his mike stand (another thing his manager asked for, since Holly had trouble bending over and all), he said, "I remember when I was on Ed Sullivan's show, and we had these big ole mikes to wear, around our necks, on a cord…reminded me of a baby's pacifier," with shy little jerks of his brown eyes behind those dark-framed lenses.

I just nodded and blinked, choked up just to be standing on the same *stage* as Buddy Holly. I mean, I was only a baby when what happened in Iowa happened, when it seemed like everything but his bare-bones life went down the toilet, and even though his music influenced the bands I grew up listening to (I think Linda Rondstat can retire on what she made from covering his stuff), I hadn't heard too much of *him* until after McLean's *American Pie*, with that line about the "day the music cried," like music was something living, breathing, that could suffer and cry like a person, but once that song came out when I was in junior high, I sought out Holly's stuff, even the stuff he did after the accident, when he was drifting musically, personally, the music he made in the days before things slid down a little further, and he was forced to sell out his catalogue of songs to Paul McCartney.

Because not only was his music good, solid yet adventuresome (regardless of what the teenyboppers of his day thought once he got too sophisticated, too musically varied for their tastes), but because he didn't let what happened to him *burn* him. Didn't become a hophead, even when it would've been fashionable to kill the pain, didn't drink too much. Just divorced his wife quietly when she asked him to, and went on the road when he was able. And stayed there.

I'd read once that he only took off from his gigs back in '85 when his dad died, and in May of '90 when his momma passed on. They'd been supportive of him from the start (no matter what that movie claimed—and they sued about it, too), and the article I'd read in *Rolling Stone* quoted him as saying he owed them a "chunk of time away from my music" to repay them after they were gone. Other than that, though, it was tour, tour, tour.

If you can call one-night stands in bars a tour, which he did, because that's the kind of musician he was; if you are, you do it. All I know is I got him for what I could afford, not at all what he was worth. And looking past the wire-screened stage, I saw the first wave of people start to come in through the door; older folks, mostly, close to Holly's age, with a sprinkling of people my age, or younger. A polite, yet noisy bunch, sneaking peeks our way, but raised during a time when throwing your body across the microphone stand and into the musician's arms was still a no-no.

Back in the Bone-God's day, I told myself, as Holly and his men began a short sound check, and the audience began to settle into whatever seats they could find. I was glad I'd sold tickets in advance (for the seats, the standing room in the concert area proper); one glance at the Bone-God standing behind the bar told me that adding ticket-taking to his list of duties would've been a *baaad* mistake.

He'd taken off his jacket, and his sweater, and the tie. And the shirt was undone to near the navel, which in his case was not at all sexy, at least not at his age, and considering his booze-bloat. I was right about the necklace; he was holding the carved bone at chain's length away from his neck, rubbing the ivory length of animal skeletal remains between his long, surprisingly lean fingers. And he had that son-of-a-bitchin' *look* to his eyes, the same look he'd get before doing something utterly insane, like drawing freehand filthy cartoons on a whole box of plain white cocktail napkins with a felt-tip pen, and then actually giving them to customers, or the time he told a whole bar-full of VFW members from like World Wawr I right on down to Vietnam vets how he avoided the draft by jazzing up his body rhythms with whatever it was he used to take in the '60's, then capped off his pre-induction physical with the boast that he was a faggot. *That* time I'd had to hide the Bone-God from the vets, and after I'd gone through all the trouble of barricading the john door with my body, he thanked me by playing with the cooler the next day and freeze-cracking a whole flat of Diet Pepsi's.

By that time, when I got a look at what the Bone-God had been doing with himself while I was talking to Holly, it was too late to do anything but hope to God Doug wouldn't *do* anything even *he'd* regret come the next morning. The concert area was full, and the non-ticket audience, the folks I'd promised the Bone-God extra money and free booze, smokes and eats to baby-sit, were starting to come in. The paying audience, I could've handled myself, that night at least. They weren't shaping up to be much trouble. The people hugging the bar, they were going to be the problem.

For only the usual late-night cover charge, they were going to see a concert, but since they were in such a shitty place vantage-point-wise, they were going to need a lot of pacifying, jollying-up and ass-licking just to keep them from getting so damn noisy they'd drown out the concert. When it came to the country or blues bands, the Bone-God was so disinterested in what was happening on stage that he could become the customers' slave...but I'd read enough Shakespeare in high school and college (what Lit courses I had to take to satisfy the humanities slots while earning my MBA) to know the "thou dost protest too much" scenario when I saw it.

I knew for a fact how old the Bone-God was. Forty-seven last December 8, about two-and-a-half months ago from that night. Which would've made him fifteen and a couple of months old when Holly and the others were in that plane crash. Same age as the kids *watching* and *listening* to Holly...maybe young Douglas James was hoping to see Holly on that ill-fated tour, at a venue somewhere down the road, in late February, or March, even.

And I *knew* what a spoil-sport the Bone-God could be, if he had to give up something he wanted. Like when I'd kept him from those VFW'ers. *He'd* been raring to go at it with them, take on the whole lot of them, *begging* for them to "just *try* it, you'll see, I'm a match for any of you fuckers, nobod*eeee* fucks with *meee*—" and that's when I all but dragged him into the can and pushed him in there and held the door shut. I lost not only all the soda cans that burst, but had to get a whole new cooler system because he'd fucked up the old one so badly. Because he *claimed* the cooler didn't "sound" right.

I wanted to go up; to him, put a hand on his beefy shoulder, and tell him that I was sorry I hadn't been able to find a way to let him watch the show up close, but that I'd make it all up to him, somehow, but I had to run the light-board (not much more complicated than a dimmer switch on a home fixture, but someone had to start it up) while the show started, and since it was too much trouble to press through the crowd afterward....

When Holly stared the show at eight, with a stiff little bow and nod of his head toward the audience, I forgot about the Bone-God smoldering behind the bar, fingering his bone charm. Started off the show with "That'll Be the Day," only with a bit of a laid-back beat, a little different than the record, but the audience ate it up. Then it was "Peggy Sue," only this time the beat was Latin and words were "Cindy Lou," yet the crowd love it, clapping along to the altered beat, heads nodding. Even though he was a little stiff, Holly threw in a little impersonation of Presley, hiccupping his way through "Bl-blu-blue Suede Shoes." Quirky, but charming, with Holly winking and shifting a little from side-to-side.

Behind me, I heard the usual buzz of the standees by the bar, but after a while, the buzz became more of a loud drone, too loud, and I wanted to go bitch out the Bone-God, but on stage Holly had launched into a slowed-down, swinging rendition of "Every Day," only after a while the words were all mushed up, like bad over-dubbing or—

Only there was no fancy sound-board in the entire stage area. No way for him to even get an echo—if what I was now hearing *had* been a mere echo of what Holly was singing. It was another song, another singer, a plaintive tenor, singing:

"I remember how we cried/when we heard about his frightened bride"

And if *I* could hear it, so could—

Jerking my head around so fast it popped, sending a jab of pain through my shoulder, I looked toward the bar.

At that fucking *idiot* behind the bar, slopping God-knows what pour liquor into his glass, eyes wide and all but floating out of his pasty-pale face, weaving in time to "American Pie" as it wafted from the cassette deck under the wall-mounted TV. And I didn't have any Don MacLean tapes stored under the bar, not a frigging *one*. He'd brought in in *with* him, the jackass. In his Ivy League jacket pocket. And the people before the bar were singing along with the song, MacLean's ode, not Holly's number, slopping beer on each other, shoving, giggling, doing God-knows-*what* else over in the corners where the bar lights don't reach, while the Bone-God presided over all, like some drunken Greek god of dissipation, wallowing in his decadence, free hand waving his lit cigarette like a smoldering baton. The stupid *fuck*—

On stage, Holly quickly finished the son, then, slinging his guitar over his shoulder, said over the "Chevy/levee" din of the bar, "I don't know 'bout you folks, but I'm gonna step off this stage for a minute or two, wet the old whistle...sure be pleased if you'd join me." I wondered if he'd ever had to defuse insane situations before, so I dimmed the stage then hurried over to the rabble near the bar, saying, "Clear out, paying customers coming through, please step outside" in my best "I'm-not-*kidding*-clowns" voice, adding very softly when necessary, "That means *you*, fuck-head!' and finally making my way behind the bar where I pushed the Stop and Eject buttons as quickly as possible, then yanking out the tape and slipping it into my pocket.

The Bone-God glowered at me, flicked his lit cigarette over the bar, and started to take a swing at me, until Holly softly asked, "Bottle of beer, please/"

The Bone-God slumped, no *crumpled*, as Holly nodded and smiled at him, recognition plain on his weathered face.

"Glad to see you again," was all he said, then I handed him a beer plucked at random from the cooler, slid the opener across the bar too, and turned my attention to my deranged bartender as Holly's fans pressed in close to him, jabbering loud enough to cover my whispered, "What the fuck was *that*? *Tribute time*? This negates *everything* I promised you earlier this evening, Doug. Every-fucking-*thing*. I'll *mail* you your last paycheck—"

The Bone-God gave me that little head-tilt and narrowing of the eyes, saying in what I swear sounded like the most sober, rational voice in the universe, "I don't see how embracing one's destiny and chosen fate can be anything but a tribute—"

"Save it for your ex-colleagues, Professor—" I began, until Holly cut in, "Mr. Davis, I'd like to say hello to...Doug, here. We met once, and I'd like to catch up a little, 'fore the second half of the set," just as smooth and natural as if he'd planned a break in his concert all along.

But when he said that, the Bone-God just turned his head in Holly's direction, a big false grin baring his strong, even white teeth for an endless second, before he said very softly, "Evening, Buddy—" and for another second there, it seemed that he was about to add something more, needed to say something else, but instead just sank against the back of the bar, glassy-eyed, slightly weak chin tucked down close to his chest.

Holly took that as some sort of signal to stand up stiffly, and announce loud enough for everyone present to hear him, "Time to hit the stage again, folks…"

As he and his band wormed their way through the crowd, shaking hands, signing bits of paper shoved into their faces, I grabbed the Bone-God by one soft upper arm and pushed him through the swinging back door, down the hallway, and into the liquor room, shoving him bodily into the arm-like up-ended legs of the tables stored there. He landed between two parallel sets of table legs, and, holding onto the upper set, let himself slide down to a sitting position, with his arms suspended limply above him. He looked like a melted Christ.

Before I shut the door behind me, I warned, "Don't puke and gag yourself."

* * * *

What can I say about the rest of the set? Holly was in top form, despite the Bone-God's aural trick; he played most of his catalogue, probably making McCartney a little royalty-richer in the process, and even gave a three-song encore, throwing in "Light My Fire" and "Hey Jude" of all things. The crowd loved it, and *only* they loved it; I'd had to shut the doors when the Bone-God made his unceremonious exit, losing I don't know how much bar trade.

The audience was decent, leaving quietly after snapping some pictures and getting a few more autographs. The last of them cleared out after one o'clock, after Holly and his men "left." Actually, they were waiting in the hallway, leaning in close to the locked liquor room door. Behind it, I heard snoring, moist, snorting sounds. At least the Bone-God hadn't choked on his own vomit. Yet.

Shamed, I turned to Holly, apologies tumbling out of my mouth, until he replied, "No need, Mr. Davis—Mike—I've known your friend for a few years, a long time ago. Before he was your age, even. He really hasn't changed all that much," he added, with more warmth and compassion than was to be expected under the circumstances.

Dimly wondering how Holly's path had crossed (and criss-crossed) with that of the academic Bone-God, I unlocked the liquor room door, letting a wedge of light slide across my bartender's body.

He hadn't changed position; his arms were still raised uncomfortably above his lolling head of dirty-brown-and-salt curls. From the way he was sitting, I could see that he'd wet his trousers. I started to shut the door but Holly poked his head in, asking, "He live close to here? Should get him into bed—"

"You have any pl—ride to catch, someplace to be soon?"

Holly must've been a friend of some sort to the Bone-God; *I'd* have let him sleep there like that until his arms froze upriguht.

With his sidemen helping we got the Bone-God into my car; I figured he could come back later on to pick up his own Ford. It wasn't easy; the Bone-God was a good hundred-and-fifty-plus pounds of dead-to-the-world meat. And half-awake, he'd swing at people. Finally got him into the back of my car, folded over like a soft jack-knife, and after I retrieved his professor get-up from where he'd tossed it on the bar floor, I started up the car, pausing only when Holly began tapping on the window, pointing to the door handle. After I opened the automatic lock, he opened the door, and climbed in gingerly, saying, "I'd just like to see how our friend here is before I leave. Make sure he's okay."

I shrugged; luckily, the Bone-God lived only a few blocks away, in one of those converted crumbling gingerbread and brick houses that now catered to frats and young student couples. And the occasional druggies and whores who float around State Street and beyond. On the second floor, which meant dragging the stuporous bastard up an inside flight of stairs. Holly fished around in that corduroy jacket for the Bone-God's keys, finally extracting the leather-tabbed chain from the inside breast-pocket. Luckily, the Bone-God'd left his lights on, so I was able to drag him straight into the apartment without bumping into anything on the floor.

Holly sort of hung back in the hallway as I hoisted Doug onto an on-the-floor mattress covered with some sort of furry spread, but he did say as I was looking around for a pillow, something, to put under the Bone-God's heavy, lolling head, "Our friend sure does like to read yet," and that was when I took a look around the small apartment, a *real* look. I'd never been inside before, but after working with the Bone-God for the past couple of years, I'd imagined his apartment to be a cave-like thing, lumps of clothing moldering in dropping-like heaps. *Some*thing grotty, primal. That he was a professor was something of an after-thought.

Everywhere I looked, there were books. In milk crates. In piles stacked against the walls, shoved in under chairs, covering the counter of his mini-kitchen, stacked on the small refrigerator, tossed on the microwave, bent spread-eagled on window sills, leaking out of ratty cardboard boxes, stacked on the small coffee table, covering his typewriter stand—

Not just Reader's Digest Condensed Books, or show-off coffee table tomes, but really-*read* books, faded spines of the paperbacks cracked longitudinally white from frequent openings, covers frayed at the top from being pulled off shelves, infrequent dust-covers torn and scuffed. Textbooks for English classes, poetry books, history, philosophy, religion, novels whose titles were unfamiliar to me (no Stephen Kings at all), cartoon collections, and even a stack of white-thumb-print-whorled *MAD* magazines. The smallish stereo system and 13-inch TV looked like commas in that wall of printed words. I'd expected *Playboy* pin-ups, or a rubber doll in the corner, *something* indicative of the Bone-God I knew, but aside from the *MAD* magazines, which really weren't all *that* incongruous for someone bright but demented, I was damned if I could find it in that not-all-*that* untidy room. The place looked lived-in, but I didn't know the man who spent his time there. Whoever he was, he wasn't the Bone-God.

Holly finally entered the room, making his way to the kitchenette. Shyly, he cracked the 'fridge open for a second, peeked inside, then opened it wide enough for me to see. It was empty. *That* was more like my Bone-God; the man lived on fast foods when he remember to eat at all. Holly shrugged, adding, "Was the same when I knew him."

I wanted to ask Holly about the Bone-God; where they'd met, the how and more important, the *why*, but his-godhead stirred on the bed, rising up weakly on one elbow, voice slurred, "Any book...any... one...read me line, I'll...tell ya whose it is. Read 'em all...ev'ry lasss one of 'em...g'*on*, pick a book...puh-*leeese*—"

"Doug, I don't care if you *wrote* all those b—"

"Got one, Doug," Holly was behind me, holding a skinny cloth-bound volume in one hand. An endpaper flapped down; a vaguely familiar-looking bare-chested guy with a thin bead necklace adorned the cover. If I hadn't of been watching Doug, I wouldn't have believed it; when Holly started to read one line, as the Bone-God heard him, he curled into a ball on that spread, pulling it under him in rippling waves. As he covered his puffy face with his oddly supple hands, he moaned, "Oh *fuck* Buddy, not that, not *that*!"

"Must not've read it after all,' I said, but Holly just slipped the book back where he'd found it, saying, "Oh, Doug knows, but he's a little under the weather right now…come morning, he'll tell you who wrote it. You'll see—"

Ignoring Buddy, I gave Sleeping Beauty a kick in the butt, asking, "You planning to fall asleep and then puke? Or are you gonna be okay?"

That mane of wavy graying hair bobbed up and down in assent.

"Fine. Your check'll be in the mail." Leading Holly by the arm, I led him out of there and closed the apartment door behind us. From behind the door, I heard the Bone-God roar, a garble of pain and spite and pissed-off anger that culminated in a grumbled, "Muuutherrr-*fuuucker*!"

On the way down to the car, Holly didn't speak, but on the way back to the bar, he did say, "Don't fire Doug on my 'count, if you're fixin' to do it for what happened tonight. Things ain't been easy for 'im. I've seen 'im do worse, and for no reason a'tall—"

"I've always admired you, Mr. Holly—'kay, Buddy—but I can't say I admire your taste in friends—"

Holly just smiled, showing his crooked teeth. "Not a friend, exactly…let's just say he and I drank from the same well at different times."

Then we were at the bar, and there wasn't much else to say, save for thanks and good-byes. I stayed outside, in the early false warmth of the February night, hands in my pockets, watching the car Holly and his sidemen had arrived in earlier that night, until my fingertips found the tape the Bone-God had brought into the bar. Without looking to see if it was a real tape, or something he'd taped off his stereo, I crushed the tape cassette with my hand then threw the mangled remains (the loose tape slithery-smooth against my fingers, like snakeskin) into the gutter.

* * * *

A few days went by before the Bone-God showed up at the bar. I'd thought over what Holly had said, figured Buddy'd been in touch with Doug during his stint at the university and felt bad enough over the Bone-Head being fired (or whatever it was that had happened to Doug), so I sent the Bone-God a note with his paycheck, telling him that he and I had some serious talking to do, *if* he wanted to come back here.

It was the slow period, from six o'clock to six-thirty or so, when few of the regulars sauntered in. I was restocking the bar, getting the ice tank filled for the late wave of drinkers, when I saw a familiar shape slide past the door, quietly, and dart into the shadows for a moment before deciding to come forward, toward the bar itself. After I realized who it was, I turned my attention to the TV. "My Generation" was on VH-1 (before it became a clone of MTV, later in the '90's); I was bartending, and I was going to watch what the hell *I* wanted to. David Bowie's "Changes" was on, Bowie with shaved eyebrows and cadaverous colorless body encased in spandex. Ziggy Stardust incarnate. I heard the slight *scree* of the barstool as weight settled on it. Then the song ended, and Peter Noone came on with a voice-over, promising a flashback to that old "I'd like to teach the world to sing" Coke commercial, before they switched to a real commercial. Without turning around, I said, "Well?"

A muted cough, then I heard the Bone-God lean forward and squirt something from the dispense hose into his mouth, before he swallowed audibly and said, "Mike, you literally have no *idea*, no conception of how sorry I am about…that night. I—I was just fucked up—"

"That's an understatement—"

"No, really, Mike, it won't happen again. I promise. I wasn't thinking. I-am-so-sorry—"

I turned around to look at him, expecting the Bone-God I knew, but this man was almost a stranger, as strange as the apartment he called his home. Either he'd laid off the booze or he'd been downing water pills; either way, his face wasn't bloated, with the cheeks puffing out like he was blowing up invisible balloons, making his cheekbones and jawbones appear for the first time since I'd know the man. Even his forehead didn't look so craggy, so over-hanging. He had on a brown leather jacket; snowflakes were just beginning to lose their sharp shapes as they melted on his shoulders. At his open neckline, I saw the collar of a darkish shirt, blue or purple. Being slightly damp from the snow, his hair looked a shade darker, resting in limp curls against his brow, his ears, near his fading shiner.

"Doug?" Behind me, the teenagers from all over sang their Coca-Cola-lovin' little hearts out on that hillside in Italy, and then Peter Noone came back on, yammering about something or other, as the Bone-God replied, "I promise, things *will* be different, Mike," his deep-set murky eyes watering a little, and I sighed, turning my head away from him, as Noone said something about colorful black eyes or some cheery shit like that, and The Doors "Touch Me" came on, the live TV show clip where the old guys in the horn section behind Morrison looked so *righteously* out-of-place in their business-men suits, while the Lizard King fumbled with his green maracas and his hand-held microphone as he half-sang-half-shouted *"Touch me"* after the short instrumental bridge, and Manzarek was giving it all—in a subdued fashion—on the organ, and Krieger was sporting a yellowish-green shiner in the background, and there was nothing but silence behind me as the clip ended and Buddy Holly's "Peggy Sue" began abruptly, with that jittery, bouncy beat and Holly shimmying one leg in place as he played, and I said over my shoulder, not taking my eyes from the screen, "You better thank your pal Buddy for me not firing you. He must know you better'n I do, so I took his word for—"

Silence from the Bone-God. A commercial came on, and as I took my eyes from the screen, I happened to turn my head in the direction of the bar mirror behind the pour liquor, the mirror that gets smoke-discolored no matter how much the Bone-God or Stu wash it—

—and saw the ghost for what he really was. Haunted, dreamy-yet-horrified bluish eyes in that pale, pale earth-god face, and those slender hands, fumbling in the air, needing only a microphone and a lone green maraca, and when the ghost turned to look in my direction, all he said was, "You didn't *realize*—"

I turned my head back and forth, from the Bone-God sitting on the opposite side of the bar to the Lizard King reflected in that darkly-smoked glass, and all he kept saying was, "You were watching and you didn't recognize—" over and over, never able to get to the "me" part, eyes widening behind a sheen of moisture that just stayed there, covering his eyes, yet never falling down that strangely-lean and young-old face, and his hands kept clutching, grasping, the microphone that was no longer there, as I rubbed my hand over my mouth and chin, shaking my head No, no *way*—

Closing my eyes for a moment, I remembered what he'd written on his job application, the information on the W-2 forms I made out for him these past two years. "Douglas M. James." DOB 12-8-43—

Forty-seven going on forty-eight back in '92. But in '*seventy-one*, he was twenty-seven, going on—

"Oh fuck," I mumbled from behind my hand, before asking the haunted man sitting before me, "*How*? For Chrissakes, *how*, man?"

He just looked at me, dark-pooled eyes wide, and said softly, carefully, in a low rush of words that *should've* sounded familiar, yet didn't, *couldn't* before.

"It was sort of like what supposedly happened, me in the tub passed out and my wife, she found me. I wasn't dead yet but I should've been, puked all over myself, almost gagged on it, crap in my hair and everything. She shook me awake, banged my head against the rim to get me up and, uhm, I was just so *pissed* because I'd almost *made* it, broke *through*, man, but if I had, either I didn't belong there yet or it just wasn't my fucking *time*, uhm, but...I was so *tired*, felt like an old man, coughing my fucking lungs out, getting drunk, stoned, thinking that had to be the way over, to that 'other side' of mine. But when I came to covered in my own vomit, and *nothing* had changed, then I knew *I* hadda make that change. Cross over any way I could, anywhere I could. Wasn't a new thought with me. I'd half-planned it for years, joked about it, discussed it, hinted...other people were always claiming I *was* dead...and that night in Paris, in the tub, I told myself, 'Time to make that change, man.' My wife...she stayed, had to, to make this thing work for me. I made her say I ...while I, uhm, I just *walked*. Ditched it all. Left Jim dead in that bathtub.

"I stayed in Europe for a while, new name, different clothes, shorter hair, didn't know many languages, though, still too fucked up to learn 'em. Got myself a new passport, made my way back to the States, but I never contacted my wife...too late. Not good for the band to resurface, for everything they'd worked for before I screwed up. Didn't want to face the Miami charges, either. Couldn't. Needed to work, still wanted to *reach* people, all I really had in mind in the first place, actually, before everything else got in the way. I didn't look the same, no one *knew*. So I uhm, decided to backtrack a ways, in an old direction. I had a degree, the educational background...I figured I could do the shaman thing directly, make them *think*, take charge of themselves...I bullshitted my way into a position, faked them out, no one checked. I only wanted people to take *me* seriously, not the fucking Lizard King, not *that* Jim who got away from me, but it didn't work being 'Mr. James' after a time...the old King, he needed to shed that skin once in a while...found out that that skin was Doug James."

He leaned forward across the bar, hands out-flung, nearly fisted, crying through clenched teeth, "You've gotta believe me Mike, I *am* sorry...that night, with Buddy, I was just so damned *scared*. His fans, *rock* fans, they might...might recog—but...but...dammit, they *didn't*. My students, if they did, they never aid, and I was flabby, different-looking by then...maybe they didn't. But Holly's fans, *some* of 'em should've known, shouldn't they have? Or *am* I so...*old*?" He looked up at me then, eyes so bright with moisture they gleamed, naked with pain and fear and hurt and...and a hint of disbelief.

"Jim?" I started to say, but he shook his head before letting it flop down on the bar-top, weary eyes closed. "He's dead. Died in Paris. Didn't you see his tombstone, all the shit written on it?"

Nodding, I remembered; a square stone and graffiti-scarred walls beyond...but I also recalled another memorial, close-by, from a picture circulated soon after the burial. A decorated urn over a thin rectangular sign, reading "Douglas Morrison James" and all those flat shells circling the long oval beyond. A sign with an oddly inverted name...and, resting on an ocean of scruffy grass, far from the killing waters of the sea, an almost dainty scalloped necklace of shells—

—the picture on the book Holly held, young Jim Morrison wearing a thin glass bead necklace on his bare chest—

—*Oh fuck, Buddy, not that, not that*—

Reaching out to place a steadying hand on his leather-jacketed quaking shoulders, as he lay stretched out over that bar-top, I knew that I'd never ask the Bone-God who had once written that book of poetry.

And I never have.

* * * *

AUTHOR'S NOTES

The book of poetry described in this novelette is the original version of The Lords and The New Creatures, *which featured the 1967 Joel Bordsky photograph of James Douglas Morrison on the cover. On February 27, 1992, VH-1 (Video Hits One) broadcast a segment of the show "My Generation" which contains the exact line-up of artists and features mentioned in this work of fiction.*

While this story is fiction, it is based on known facts and personality traits of both Charles "Buddy" Holl(e)y (1936-1959) and James Morrison (1943-1971), incorporating real incidents from their lives and personal histories; it forms this writer's attempt to meld "what if?" with "What would've been likely*" had each man lived beyond 1959 and 1971, respectively. The author makes no claims as to knowing the answer to the still somewhat debated circumstances of Morrison's death; the speculative path taken in regard to his post-1971 life is based on remarks Morrison made before witnesses during the last few years of his life, as reported in Jerry Hopkins and Danny Sugerman's 1980 biography of Morrison* No One Here Gets Out Alive.

By fictionally bringing both men to life, I wanted to show as truthfully and as honestly as possible the likely ramifications of these men surviving past their actual recorded lifespans/time of death; while some of the details might not appear flattering, or within the accepted mythos which has sprung up since their respective deaths, the author has attempted to present these men as fully-rounded human beings—not perfect, not always doing the most logical thing, but intrinsically decent within their own previous standards of public and private behavior.

In particular, due in part to the 1992 film biography of Mr. Morrison, there has been much debate as to who the "real" Jim Morrison was—tragic alcoholic or inspired poet, shaman or sham—and where the true genius of his surviving work rests. My particular "version" of Morrison is based on quotes by and about him, his work itself, on his educational background (which was far more extensive than commonly known), and on the legacy of pain and inspiration he left behind him. While an entire, multifaceted personality cannot be distilled into a short novelette (nor a two and a quarter hour long film), the author has tried to allude to Morrison's chameleon-like ability to relate to many people in many different ways, both adapting and forcing others to adapt to him, by presenting the man through the eyes of a single observer, whose perception of him as partly-fictional character is personal, as well as woefully misinformed in certain regards.

By utilizing the slight *possibility that Morrison went underground in 1971 (a possibility which cannot be 100% discounted, due to a mixture of opportunity, need, and previously-stated desire to do so on Morrison's part), the author has attempted to show the inherent pain and sacrifice of such a decision; while one might leave behind one's past identity, one cannot always leave behind one's inherent personality traits, interests, or memories—a situation bound to cause conflicts in such an individual's "new" life. This novelette is not meant to be, nor should it be construed to be, a slam against either Morrison's life itself, or the possible motivations he may have had for wanting to escape from his life situation in mid-1971; instead, it is intended to be a tribute to what he (as well as Holly) accomplished during his exceptionally brief public (as well as private) lifetime, showing that neither occasional lapses or weaknesses can truly negate positive, creative impulses or the resulting works of art inspired by those impulses.*

AFTERWORD

While the Author's Notes section at the end of the story pretty much says everything I have to say about writing the story and the inspiration for the story *per se*, I do have a few tid-bits to add:

Back in the 1970's through the early 1990's, I used to work at this one combination motel/bar (somewhat of a misnomer, since it was actually more of a hotel in that all the rooms were contained within a two-story self-confined building, rather than spread out in individual cabins or long strips of rooms) which used to be something of a well-known building in my town, before the tornado of September 2, 2002 literally tore it apart, leaving one side of the building open, doll-house style, before it was all torn down later that year—anyhow, I used to clean rooms there, and also clean the bar, do laundry, etc. Several different people owned the place during that time (including one bitch who literally stole the housemaids' tips from the rooms before either me or my mother could clean in there), as well as one family whose eldest son actually ran the place for a while; the kid was one of the dumbest mo-fo's I ever met, and routinely set the temperatures in the cooler so high that he'd freeze-crack open entire cases worth of soda. I just had to add that bit into the story. Plus, a tip for those readers who frequent bars—you do *not* want to drink anything from one of those liquor dispensers; I've cleaned those things, and believe me, you *don't* want to see the gunk that collects in those puppies!!

Regardless of whether or not one believes that Morrison might've faked his own death, there are some facts to consider: 1) Shortly before his death, the singer lost his passport overseas, and obtained a new one—crucial information one would need in order to secure another passport bearing a new identity, and something not all travelers either know or have experienced; 2) The only people who did see his body are dead now, and despite threats on the part of the cemetery to have his remains dug up and moved, he's still there (presumably), with very little documentation proving that he died, and 3) Jim Morrison spoke Spanish well enough to converse with the natives while in Europe; knowing at least one language currently spoken in Europe would've been essential for an escape to another country.

Do *I* think he escaped? It's doubtful, but not 100% impossible, given the information listed above. I think he was in poor physical shape, but then again, some people's health can improve once they're away from situations which cause them stress. At least his memory, and his music, live on....

www.ingramcontent.com/pod-product-compliance
Lightning Source LLC
Chambersburg PA
CBHW050042180626
46810CB00002B/856